LAST CHANCE FOR FIRST

Tom Hazuka

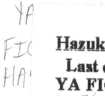

Brown Barn Books
Weston, Connecticut

Brown Barn Books
A division of Pictures of Record, Inc.
119 Kettle Creek Road
Weston, CT 06883, U.S.A.

Last Chance for First
Copyright © 2008, by Tom Hazuka

Original paperback edition

Library of Congress Control Number: 2007938351
ISBN: 978-0-9798824-0-1

Hazuka, Tom

Last Chance for First: a novel by Tom Hazuka

Printed in the United States of America

For the women in my life:
Mom, Christine, Maggie and Olivia

Chapter 1

I T STARTED LAST FALL, at the assembly to kick off the annual magazine drive. The whole school was packed in the auditorium to listen to this jolly old guy, who looked like Santa Claus without the beard and red suit, try to get us psyched up to sell enough magazines to keep the recyclers in business for another year. He said we should show our school spirit and sell a ton of subscriptions so each class would have a pile of money to do whatever it wanted, the yearbook wouldn't go in the red again, etc., etc. Big deal. I was a junior; I'd heard it all before. I'd do my part by selling half a dozen subscriptions to my parents and a few relatives, maybe nice old Mrs. Maruszak down the street.

Right now, though, I was more interested in watching Billy Hagan two rows in front of me as he stretched, then slipped his arm around Sarah Malinowski as casually as if he was at the movies. It was the first time in my life I regretted having 20–15 eyesight. The worst part was that she not only let him, but even snuggled a little closer. Sarah, the girl I dated most of the summer, who had sat with me like that at plenty of movies until she told me out of the blue she wanted to see other people. That was a couple of weeks ago, the Friday before Labor Day.

We were parked down at the beach, not even making out or anything, just listening to the night. It was dead low tide, no wind at all, and the air smelled rank.

"It's not you, Robby," she said. "It's me." When somebody says that, you know it's you.

It was impossible not to watch. When I actually have a pretty girl first like me, then dump me, and I can see no reason why she did either one, it's natural for me to be interested when she's cuddling up to some jerk I can't stand, the slimiest slimeball in the whole school.

My best friend Jim Dolan leaned over to me and whispered, "Guess he's got something you don't have."

That's the thing about a guy's best friend—he doesn't cut you any slack. That's not how we operate. A girl's best friend would have told her what a bitch the girl was who stole her boyfriend, how he wasn't good enough for her anyway. A guy just tells a joke and we pretend it's OK, though of course it's not.

"Yeah," I told him. "A rich old man and a new BMW."

"Don't forget the country club membership, and ski lodge in Vermont."

"If Sarah is that shallow, I don't want her anyway."

Jim shook his head. "You can't lie to save your life. It's sad, really."

"Shh!" Mrs. Joseph the math teacher was in the aisle scowling at us. Maybe she had stock in the magazine company or something. I wanted to yell to her, "Hey! What about Hagan the Degenerate over there molesting my girl friend?"

Suddenly this girl stood up, ten rows away from me across the aisle. I'd never seen her before so she was either a freshman or new here, because in a small school you know everybody, by sight at least. She stood up and raised her hand, and with a grin the pudgy magazine man pointed at her.

"What can I do you for, little lady?"

She hesitated a second. She had short hair so blonde it was almost white, with pale skin to match even after the summertime. Our town is on the beach, Long Island Sound, so it's strange to see a kid with no tan in September.

"Whoa," Jim said. "Is she an albino?"

Whatever she was, she talked too softly for me to catch what she was saying. Mr. Magazine cupped a hand around one ear and said, "You'll have to speak up, missy. These old ears aren't as sharp as they used to be."

Every eye was on this girl as she said, loud enough to reach every corner of the auditorium, "I don't think you care much about this school, or any school. You just want to make money."

For the first time in my life I saw a whole group of people shocked into dead quiet. Even the smart-mouth kids were stunned. The teachers looked as surprised as everyone else—it's not like they could punish her, it's not like she did anything wrong.

Mr. Magazine smiled, but he didn't look happy. "Well, I can't deny that our company needs to make a profit or we go out of business. That's the American way."

"All I'm saying is the kids do almost all the work, and you get most of the money. I don't care if people want to sell magazines. But you don't care about Newfield. You say the same stuff at every school—I heard you last year at Baldwin. All we are is your job. Sorry." She sat down.

Mr. Magazine's smile looked faker and faker. "I understand your concern. But that's the great thing about our system. Everybody wins. Now let's go show the world Newfield High is the best!"

The cheerleaders, who were wearing their uniforms because of the football game that night, jumped up and started waving their pompoms and chanting, "*New-field, New-field!*" Some kids joined in—not everybody by a long shot, but enough to make plenty of noise, enough so if you tried to yell something different it would have been drowned right out. A lot of them weren't doing it for school spirit or anything, but for the chance to yell like lunatics in school and not get in trouble for it.

I just listened. I kept thinking of what the girl had said, and imagining how the Magazine Man went from school to school telling each one it was the best, trying to get the students to scream "*Bald-win!*" or "*North-brook!*" and go out hyped-up to sell subscriptions and make him money. She made me see things I hadn't thought of before, all by having the courage to stand up alone.

I looked over and tried to see what she was doing but couldn't find her. Two rows down, idiot Hagan was pumping a fist in the air with his other arm still attached to Sarah's bouncing shoulders. She turned around, all glowing and excited, then saw me and pretended not to. I waved, but she had already looked away.

"Don't they get it?" I asked. "Don't they understand what she just said?"

Jim shrugged. "People hear what they want to hear." He scanned the auditorium. "Good thing they had the sense to hold this sucker last period of the day."

The final bell rang and we were out of there, heading for the exits in big waves, and the teachers mostly just got out of the way. I wanted to find that girl, but she was on the other side of the auditorium and in the rush I lost her completely. No time to search—I had to catch the bus to our first soccer game of the year.

The game was at Baldwin, the town she came from ten miles down the coast. It's bigger than Newfield (we only have around five thousand people—double that in summer), and richer, and their soccer team had made the state finals three of the last four years. Riding over in the bus I felt nervous, like always, but it was a peaceful nervous, wound tight in one spot in the center of my body, pure power if I used it right.

Jim was an acrobatic animal in goal, making saves like a madman, and I scored twice. We upset them 2–1 in the biggest Newfield soccer win in years. My face was sore the next day from smiling so much.

Chapter 2

I HAD MR. MCLAUGHLIN's creative writing class right after lunch. I slipped in just as the bell was ringing and grabbed a seat in the front row, rather than my usual one by the window. I respect Mr. Mac a lot and didn't want to disturb his class. He gave me this look that I think was appreciation, and started calling the roll because he wasn't sure of all our names yet.

"Petunia Armstrong," he said.

What? I thought I knew everybody. I spun around and there she was, solemnly sitting at my favorite desk in the back. The white-blonde girl from Baldwin.

"Please call me Pet," she said.

Mr. Mac nodded. "Pet it is. Welcome to creative writing, where words are royalty."

"Thank you," she told him, as solemn as ever. "I'll try to be a good peasant."

Kathleen Meier, who thinks she's hilarious but is almost always wrong, piped right up. "Pet? Does that mean you're like, really tame or something?"

Pet didn't miss a beat. "It means Petunia is a ridiculous name, and Pet is a lot better than Tunia."

"Tuna!" Jack Marshall laughed.

"See what I mean?" Pet said.

"Exactly," Mr. Mac said just stern enough, staring at Jack, then Kathleen. "So now that we've got this name thing under control, let's move on." He picked up *The Catcher in the Rye* and looked around the room, stopping at me.

"Robby, what sticks in your head from the first few chapters?"

"Old Mr. Spencer's chest in his bathrobe, and Ackley's green teeth."

"Good! And why do you remember them?"

"I don't know. Because they're gross, I guess."

"Did you laugh?" he asked.

"At Ackley I did."

Mr. Mac stepped back in fake horror. "So you find green teeth *humorous?*"

I didn't feel on the spot, because Mr. Mac isn't that kind of teacher. But it was a good question. What was so funny about green teeth? I wouldn't laugh at a real person with teeth that bad. I was trying to come up with an answer when I heard Pet's voice behind me.

"It's not the green teeth that's funny, it's the way Holden tells about them."

This was her first day in our class, so she must have read the book before. Mr. Mac looked real glad that she was there, which made me a little jealous. I was used to being the kid who said most of the smart things.

"Exactly," he said. "Like when your parents give you grief and tell you it's not *what* you say, it's how you *say* it. In fiction it's not so much your story that matters, it's how you *tell* that story."

That got me thinking about the story I was trying to write, about a kid whose older brother was valedictorian and a sports hero at his school, and how unfair the kid feels it is that everybody expects him to do the same. Which, if you want to know, is the way things are with me. My brother Paul played football for four years at Notre Dame and goes to law school at the University of Michigan. I gave up football for soccer a long time ago, which disappointed Paul and my dad—they congratulated me on making All-League last season as a sophomore, but wish I had done it in football instead. And though I get mostly A's I have no prayer of being valedictorian with Lori Peplowski around.

I raised my hand. "How do you find the right voice when you're writing about what really happened? What choice do you have when you're not making it up?"

"Any thoughts on that?" said Mr. McLaughlin. "Anyone?"

I glanced back at Pet. She had a little piece of a smile on her face, and her eyes on me. I sort of smiled back. Her eyes were bright—and for the first time I noticed the thin, gleaming gold ring in her nose. Body piercing at Newfield High is pretty rare, and it weirded me out for a second. But then I thought, Hey, it's kind of cool, actually. I guess.

"Well," Mr. Mac said. "The answer is that we *do* make it up—because our perceptions determine what we experience, and another person's perceptions of that experience could be totally different. For instance, I might think this is the most interesting class in the world, while some of you—and I know this is hard to believe—are bored out of your skulls."

"Whoa," Frank Fortunato said. "That's deep."

"You got it," Mr. Mac said. "Most things worth thinking about are. Keep that in mind as you search for the right voice for your stories."

We got into discussing *The Catcher in the Rye*, and whether we'd like Holden Caulfield if we met him in real life instead of in a book, and the class went by as fast as always. I hadn't looked at the clock once when the bell rang, and notebooks closed and a school's worth of kids poured into the hall.

I pretended to write something, but really I was timing it so I'd stand up right as Pet got to my desk. Not to bump into her or anything—I'm not a total geek—but just to naturally strike up a little conversation.

I did bump into her. Not intentionally, but because I jumped up at the perfect moment to meet her, didn't check behind me and got plowed into by Skunk Darwin, center on the football team. Like a domino I fell right into Pet.

"Sorry," I said.

"Jeez, Robby," Skunk said. "Why don't you look where you're goin'?"

Mr. McLaughlin shook his head. "Citizens, is it too much to ask that you walk out of a room without assaulting one another?"

"Please excuse them," Pet said. "They probably aren't sure where the football field ends and the rest of life begins." And she kept going, out into the hall.

"Nice nose ring, cannibal," Skunk said, because he's a mental midget and has trouble with girls who are smarter than him, which is virtually all of them. After all, he got his name when he was eight years old and tried to pet a skunk that came into his back yard. He was only taking this class because he stupidly thought it would be easy.

"Skunk," Mr. Mac said as I hurried after Pet, "doesn't Coach Malfetone give you guys any lessons in being gentlemen?"

She wasn't tough to find, being just twenty feet down the hall and the only one in sight with bright white hair. I jogged up to her, and matched her stride. "Hey," I said. "It was an accident. I apologize. And I don't play football."

She stopped at her locker, and looked at me like I was contagious. "*I'm* sorry. I don't like jocks."

That got me so steamed I forgot to be nervous. I can't stand it when people assume athletes are dumb. In cases like Skunk's it happens to be true, but the percentages are no different from anybody else. But then it hit me that she hadn't said anything about intelligence. It was a straight case of dislike for no reason, pure prejudice. What kind of crap was that?

"Well, maybe I don't like snobs who put down people for no reason."

"And maybe I couldn't care less what you don't like."

Taped to the inside of her locker door was a photo of a ballerina with a male ballet dancer, whatever they're called. The ballerina was on her toes, her arms crossed gracefully over her head. The guy wasn't doing much of anything.

"I'm not a jock," I said. "I'm a person who happens to play sports. How would you like to get stuck in some lame category?"

She closed the door and clicked shut her lock. "I already am," she said softly, without looking at me.

That floored me. There I was, completely in the right, yet I felt guilty. "Then you should know better," I wanted to tell her, but instead I said, "I'll see you, I guess. In class or something."

She tried to smile but her lips were trembling. Silently she walked away.

I watched her turn the corner, my stomach tight like right before I take a penalty kick in a soccer game. Then the bell rang and I ran to my next class, the words "I already am" whispering over and over in my head.

Chapter 3

WE WON OUR NEXT TWO GAMES, 3–0 and 4–1, and I scored four of the goals. I was stoked about the way we were playing, and how I was doing, and my co-captain Jim was a kamikaze wizard minding the net. Throwing his body around he made some tremendous saves, including two shots that looked like sure goals, and even a penalty kick. Keep this up and we had a real chance to win the league and do great in the state tournament.

The magazine drive was almost over. The thermometer on the big cardboard sign outside the gym was colored in red magic marker nearly to the top, showing that the school had passed its sales goal but still had room to climb if we weren't slouches. I did the usual, hitting up my parents and grandparents for a couple subscriptions, but I felt funny doing it this year. I kept thinking of Pet as I filled out the forms and collected the money.

"*Y la señora* Maruszak?" my mother asked me at the dinner table. She thinks learning Spanish might help her business, so she's always throwing in Spanish words to practice.

"She doesn't want any," I said. That was almost the truth; the fact was she didn't want any *more*, because some kid got to her first. Still, she looked sorry for me and might have sprung for *Good Housekeeping* or *Modern Maturity* if I'd pushed the issue, but I didn't. She was probably living on Social Security and didn't need my overpriced magazines anyway.

Mom gave me her skeptical look, the one I dislike even more when she's right than when I'm under suspicion for nothing. "That's strange," she said. "She always bought subscriptions from Paul."

See what I mean about getting compared all the time? It's so second nature to my parents I doubt they even realize they do it. They're not bad to me—they're nice, they're good. But sometimes I just want to scream, "Yes, but I'm not Paul! I'm me!"

Dad saved me by changing the subject, though I doubt that was his intention. "So," he said, "are you going to the football game tonight?"

I shrugged. "I don't know. I suppose. Unless there's something more interesting on Home Shopping Network."

When Paul was on the team and made all-state, Dad went to every game, and even now he rarely misses a home game. But he almost never sees my soccer games, because we play in the afternoon while he's at work. He's a machinist, and makes precision parts for all kinds of stuff, including NASA rockets. Mom used to go a lot, until she got her real estate agent's license when I was a freshman and started selling houses full-time.

"You should support your team," Dad said.

"It's not my team. My team is undefeated." The football team was 0–2.

Dad pursed his lips. "All the Newfield teams are your team. That's what school spirit's all about."

"Of course it is," Mom said. "I don't know why you've become so contrary all of a sudden."

"I'm not contrary," I said, realizing how ridiculous that sounded.

"Maybe you're not going to the game or anywhere else, because maybe you're grounded." Dad's voice was like a hacksaw on metal.

"I'm sorry," I said. "I was just trying to be funny."

"Apology *aceptado*," Mom said. "Now let's celebrate that *casa* I sold today on *Playa* Walker." She wanted to defuse this argument before it escalated into something worse. It's scary how easy you can get on a path that leads to trouble. My parents raised their glasses (Mom chablis, Dad Schlitz) and I held up my milk, and we clinked them together. "To good luck," Dad said and I was smiling inside, because I knew that tonight I'd be drinking something stronger than milk.

"Be careful," Mom called as I jogged out to Jim's beat-up Dodge. I waved to her without turning around. Jim's parents had bought the car for him last summer after he was on the honor roll three straight marking periods. I've been on the honor roll *every* marking period since seventh grade and didn't get a car, but I'm not complaining. My parents let me use one of theirs most of the time, and it's not like my brother had a car in high school either.

"What's up?" Jim said. He had a wicked bruise on his cheek, all purple and yellow.

"Yo, did you go twelve rounds with Mike Tyson, or what?"

He shrugged and began backing out of the driveway. "I got kicked diving for a ball today. The sucker swelled up on me."

That's a goalie for you, the most macho characters around. "I couldn't play keeper in a million years. I'm not insane enough."

Jim grinned. "Insanity definitely helps. So does not being a pussy."

"Meow," I said, laughing.

"So what's our plan for tonight?" Jim asked. "There's a party at Tricia Langhammer's, but not till after the game."

"Want to go?"

"To the game or the party?"

"Both, I guess."

"What the hey. Let's see how big a cheer we get when they announce that we won again. Maybe Lisa Birnbaum will finally realize I'm the man of her dreams."

"Yeah, right," I said. "And maybe they'll have a keg at the game, with free beer for students."

Jim obviously didn't feel like laughing about Lisa. I could never understand why he liked her. She was one of the hottest girls in the school but had a vacuum between her ears, was stuck-up and only dated football players. To give you some idea, she was Billy Hagan's girlfriend all last year. It doesn't get much worse than that. They even got their photo in the *Newfield News* after one of the football team's few wins, Billy the quarterback lifting Lisa the cheerleader in the air, both of them grinning like they just won the lottery. Jim was depressed for days after he saw that, though he liked her picture so much he cut it out (leaving Hagan behind in the paper except for his hairy arms around her) and taped it to his bedroom wall. I busted his balls the first time I saw it and I thought for a second he was going to deck me.

"Speaking of beer," I said to break the silence, "I could use a cold one right now."

Jim nodded toward my lap. "You're sitting on 'em."

"So," I asked, "where'd you get them this time?"

It was a running joke of ours. Jim had someone, who would buy him beer—no hard stuff, just beer—but he wouldn't tell me who it was. The person made him promise not to, and Jim kept his promises.

"The beer fairy," Jim said. "He put it under my pillow. And by the way, you owe me five bucks. The fairy's price went up."

I felt under the seat, and found two cans slipped into foam rubber huggies to keep them cold—and to keep them camouflaged, because to anyone who saw us they could just as easily have been sodas. Though we were driving the back roads, where no one was likely to see us. Away from downtown and the beach, Newfield is mostly woods, with two-acre zoning so there aren't that many houses. I popped both cans, kept the Notre Dame huggie and gave the UConn Huskies one to Jim. As always, the first sip was bitter, but the best part wasn't the taste or even the buzz—it was the excitement of doing something you weren't supposed to.

Jim took the seldom-used road to Pine Lake, the one that curves around the far side then turns to dirt and peters out after the last houses. The lake is real shallow at that end, so choked with weeds by the Fourth of July you can hardly fish there. My best friend and I sat on the hood, sipping beer and watching the sun set over the trees. Our team was undefeated, we were playing great, the whole world felt good.

I held my can upside-down, draining the last couple drops of warm swill onto the dirt. "I just might put on a buzz tonight," I said. "Let's celebrate."

Jim leaned back on the hood, looking up at the darkening sky. The stars were appearing, thick out here away from any light. "I already am," he said.

That floored me. Of course he meant something completely different than Pet did, but hearing "I already am" made me think of her. My stomach felt full of slick butterflies. I almost told Jim what Pet had said and how I'd been thinking about her, but I chickened out. Instead of opening up to what was important to me, I opened up another beer.

I had drunk three by the time we got to the game. It was already the second quarter, I saw on the scoreboard as we pulled in, and we had to park in the far corner of the lot. It burned me how we could win games, play excellent soccer and draw one-tenth the crowd that the hopeless football team did. Maybe it would be different if we played on Friday nights—a cheap date and all that, and the buildup of waiting all week for it. Or maybe people just prefer a sport where the athletes smash into each other on every play.

I dumped some Tic-Tacs into my palm, and passed the pack to Jim. We couldn't show up with beer on our breath. A whistle blew and the crowd groaned. The scoreboard changed from VISITOR 10, NEWFIELD 0 to VISITOR 16, NEWFIELD 0.

"The doormats are getting their butts kicked again," Jim said. It's not that we root against the football team, but we never forgave Coach Malfetone for what he did the summer after our freshman year. He knew Jim and I were good enough to start for his team, and behind Coach Reynolds's back he tried to convince us to quit soccer and play football. "Play a man's game," he told us, "not some pansy European sport." He was so mad we turned him down that he gave us B's in gym that fall, though the football players got A's even if they were injured and didn't go to class. It was my lowest grade and Dad couldn't believe it. The last straw was this season, when Malfetone asked Jim and me to kick—just kick, not play from scrimmage—for the football team. Once in practice I nailed a 44-yard field goal, and Jim could punt the ball a mile, but after the crap Malfetone had pulled on us we told him to forget it. Dad was really disgusted with me for that. He would have understood if I'd told him my

18

reason, but I didn't rat on Malfetone. Not because I didn't want to, but because I'm no rat.

As we crossed the parking lot, the VISITOR score changed to 17; obviously Baldwin, unlike Newfield, had someone who could kick extra points. After their rare touchdowns Newfield usually went for a two-point conversion, which they made about as often as Billy Hagan took a test without cheating.

"Do you feel bad for not playing?" I asked. I did, a little anyway.

Jim looked at me like I'd suggested running naked onto the field. "I've had four beers tonight—I don't feel bad about anything." He seemed to slur his words, but after three beers myself I figured the problem could have been my ears, not his mouth. Even so, I was glad we'd be sitting in the stands for awhile instead of driving around. The gory car wreck video they showed in driver's ed was not something I could forget. Seriously, I almost threw up. It was *bad*.

We got inside in time to see Newfield fumble the kickoff return. A Baldwin guy scooped up the ball and ran in for another touchdown. "Brutal," Jim said. We surveyed the stands for a place to sit. I knew Jim would pick a spot close to the cheerleaders and Lisa Birnbaum, and since I didn't care one way or the other I just followed him, trying not to do any moron thing to show I'd been drinking.

Newfield actually put together a nice drive for a touchdown. Painful as it is to admit, Billy Hagan made some sweet passes and a long run, though he got buried on a roll-out for the two-point conversion. So the half ended 24–6. Jim got up and looked around the stands. He waved at someone or other, then headed the other direction down the steps. "Be right back," he said.

"Where are you going?" I asked, to bust his chops. I knew perfectly well he was going to try and meet up with Lisa.

"To stretch my legs," he said. "And shut up unless you want to walk home, chump."

"Tell her Robby sends a big wet kiss."

"Were you born a douche bag or did you have to practice?"

We always kidded around that way. We didn't mean it, it was just best friend guy stuff. I watched him head down the steps, walking extra carefully because of the beer. Nobody else would have even noticed it, but we're not best friends for nothing. I felt like going to the car to sneak another brew myself, but they don't let you back in if you leave—they know the parking lot would turn into a party. The beer was going through me and I thought about hitting the bathroom, but the line is always long at halftime and I didn't need that. The Baldwin band was playing and they weren't half bad. I was actually tapping my foot to the music when someone from behind sat next to me. Please, I thought, don't let it be Sarah with her "We can still be friends" crapola. She only does that to rub it in that she dumped me.

"Hey, Mr. Goal Scorer." It was Pet, speaking in the happiest voice I'd heard from her yet. The nose ring was gone, replaced by a single stud like a shiny brass nail. She was wearing jeans and a sweatshirt, same as me, except mine was plain gray and hers was black with AMNESTY INTERNATIONAL in white letters on the chest, which gave me an excuse to look there.

"Hi," I said, happy all of a sudden. I smiled and told her the truth, "I never thought I'd see *you* here."

She smiled back. "Old habits die hard."

"What old habits?"

"I can't even say. It's too embarrassing."

"I won't tell," I said. "Cross my heart."

Pet hesitated, but her eyes were shining. "You promise not to barf?"

20

I nodded, and she leaned closer like she was going to whisper a secret. Our shoulders touched. "I used to be a Baldwin cheerleader."

"No way!" I remembered what she said in the hall about jocks. "I mean, that's unbelievable. You like football."

Her eyes darkened. "I hate football! I was only a cheerleader because I was so insecure then I did what *they* wanted, not what *I* wanted."

"Who's 'they'?"

"Almost everybody! Jocks. Barbie Doll girls who think being popular is the most important thing in the world. Cretins who think the jocks and Barbie Dolls are cool." She looked away, down at the players warming up for the second half, the cheerleaders jumping around and mostly being ignored by the crowd. "And my parents, of course. Not to mention my big sister the prom queen who said to let guys beat me in tennis or they wouldn't like me."

She plays tennis well enough to beat guys and hates jocks? What's up with this girl?

"Pet, then…what are you doing here?"

"I don't know. I thought I might see some friends from Baldwin."

"Did you?

She shook her head. "No, just from Newfield."

"Really? Who?" I was curious to know who she was hanging out with already.

She looked up at the sky, then at me. "You?" she said.

My heart started thumping like when I call up a girl for a date. The pressure was on; I had to say something.

"So, um, does it hurt to get your nose pierced?"

You *idiot*! I screamed in my head. I can't believe you said that!

Pet threw back her head and laughed like I'd told the best joke ever, laughed so hard she started crying. As she wiped away tears with the back of one hand, she put the other on my knee. Not for long, but she put it there. And then it was gone, as if it had never happened. But we both knew it had.

Six Baldwin guys crunched the Newfield kickoff returner. "It doesn't hurt as much as that," she said. She pointed toward the sideline. "Your friend's been hanging around that bubble-headed chickie all halftime." Lisa was waving pompoms and hopping like a berserk pogo stick, while Jim reluctantly left her to climb back up the bleachers.

I took a chance. "Pet, why is your hair white?"

"Why not? I've already tried black and pink and green. I just felt like going white for awhile. OK, and I didn't have the nerve to show up at a new school with green hair. People would *really* have hated me then."

"What are you talking about? Nobody hates you."

Before she could answer, Jim was there. He nodded at Pet. "Hey," he said, kind of gruff.

I didn't want Pet to take that the wrong way. Jim wasn't mad at her, just in a sour mood from getting nowhere with a girl who wasn't worth his time in the first place.

"Pet Armstrong," I said. "Jim Dolan."

"Oh yeah," Jim said. "The magazine girl."

"I'm more the *anti*-magazine girl."

"Whatever. That was pretty cool, what you said in front of everybody."

"Thanks." Pet touched her nose ornament. I doubt she even realized she did it, but Jim sure noticed.

"Does that thing itch?" he said. "What about when you blow your nose? It must get gunky as hell."

Pet gave him a cold smile, and turned away to watch the game.

"Come on, I'm kidding. Don't you have any sense of humor?"

"Don't you have any sense of taste?"

"Oh, excuse me. Sorry I'm not cool because I don't wash my hair with Clorox."

"Yo, Jim," I said. "Let's chill, OK?" I knew it was the beer and the disappointment over Lisa making him talk this way. It wasn't *him*.

"I'd better go," Pet said. She put her hand on my shoulder as she stood up.

Jim saluted. "Take it sleazy, Whitey." He was trying to be funny, to cover up the tension, but it just came out more obnoxious. Pet hesitated, like she was thinking of saying something back. Then she headed down the bleachers.

Jim scrunched up his face. "What's her problem, anyway?"

"Her problem was that you were a complete douche."

"Whoa, listen to Loverboy. Got the hots for Miss Bleach Head or what?"

Pet hit the bottom step and walked toward the exit without even a glance at the game. I stood up.

"Man," I said. "You are rag city tonight. I'll see you later." And before I had time to think about what I was doing, I started after her.

"It's your funeral," was the last thing I heard him say, but I didn't turn around.

Chapter 4

WHAT ARE YOU DOING? I thought as I hurried down the steps. What do you think you're doing? I began wondering who else was asking that question. What's Robby doing leaving his friend, leaving the game, running after some bizarro chick with dyed hair who has a cow over selling a few magazines? And later, at Tricia Langhammer's party, or at school on Monday: Did you hear what Fielder did at the football game? Can you believe it?

I had no clue whether any of that was really happening, or would happen, but Newfield is small and gossip travels fast. And though I'm ashamed to admit I cared what people would think and say, the truth is I did care, at least a little. Enough not to make eye contact with anyone, and take the long route to the exit so I wouldn't pass in front of where my parents always sit. I heard my name called out once, but pretended not to and kept going.

"No returns," Mr. Barnett the science teacher told me at the gate. He looked like he could have played football himself thirty or forty pounds ago. "If you leave you'll miss the greatest comeback in Newfield High School history."

"I'll chance it," I said, already scanning the parking lot. Maybe Pet was gone, and I was stuck like Captain Bozo lurking around till the game let out.

Then headlights went on, back near Jim's junkmobile. I sprinted like a fiend, not caring if Mr. Barnett noticed or not, and weaved in and out of long rows of cars. No way I was going to let her get away. I cut across a stretch of grass by the entrance and barely beat the car to the stop sign. I ran up to the driver's window.

Instead of Pet, there were four ugly bruisers I'd never seen before.

They had to be from Baldwin, with no greater ambition than to beat the snot out of a Newfield kid in an unfair fight. My heart flip-flopped and I got set to run again. But they didn't rush out to beat me up four-on-one. Instead they locked their doors and peeled out, burning rubber into the street.

That's when I realized no one wants to mess with a crazy person—which is what I must have looked like from inside that car.

Tires screeched as their taillights disappeared around a bend. Those are the kind of guys you read about in the paper, I thought, kids who lose it after a few beers and end up wrapped around a telephone pole. They don't know how to handle it like I do. I wished I had the key to Jim's trunk, to get a beer to pass the time. How did Pet get away so quickly? Why did I hang back of her, even a little? Who cares what people think?

You do, I told myself. Unfortunately.

"Who? Who?"

What's that? An owl? A mourning dove? I stood still to listen. The crowd roared at the game, and I had to wait for quiet. It wasn't really quiet—I heard crickets, a car shifting gears down the road, a referee's whistle—but you know what I mean.

The owl changed its call. "Who? You? Who? You?" Trying to follow the sound, I walked backward on damp grass that needed mowing, turning in a slow circle. Overhead a huge full moon looked almost close enough to touch.

Then the tall maple tree on the side lawn started laughing. "OK," I said, "I've made a total fool of myself. You happy?"

The laughter stopped. "Relax," Pet said from somewhere in the branches. "You only made a partial fool of yourself at most. And I was impressed how you scared off those Baldwin creeps. Hey, come on up."

"I don't want to climb a stupid tree."

"Why not? Not sophisticated enough? Afraid someone will see and think you're weird? Good! The world needs more weird—everyone's so normal it's like they're asleep all day!"

I couldn't remember the last time I'd climbed a tree. But when she put it that way, like a challenge, I didn't have much choice. Still, when another car left the parking lot I slipped behind the tree and waited for the headlights to pass before I swung myself onto the lowest limb, and started playing monkey man up the trunk.

The maple bark was fairly smooth—not paper smooth like birch, but a far cry from rough-grooved oak—and it felt good to climb a tree. Though to be honest I was glad it was night and no one was likely to see us. I couldn't see Pet. She was a voice in the dark behind the leaves, and maybe she was right. Maybe weird was what the world, or at least Newfield, needed. I was so normal it was ridiculous.

I was so normal it was weird.

Pet was perched on a fat branch fifteen feet up. She gave me her hand and I sat next to her. I felt invisible and ready for something new to happen, like I was in a secret clubhouse or some magic place in a kids' book. Through a gap in the leaves I saw the stop sign, and imagined watching myself run up to that car and nearly getting my butt kicked. But nearly doesn't count. Those guys ran from me—and Pet saw it.

"You're grinning," she said. "I'm up here with the Cheshire cat."

"You must like *Alice in Wonderland.*"

"I *love Alice in Wonderland.*"

"Give me a break," I said. "If you love something you like it too."

Pet looked out through the break in the leaves. "I wish you were right."

I wondered what it would be like to kiss a girl fifteen feet up in a tree, in the dark, with the romantic sounds of a bad football game in the background. Pet touched my shoulder, and I hoped I'd soon be finding out.

"For example," she said, "I love my father, but I don't like him at all. I don't think anyone does."

"Come on. What about your mother?"

"She doesn't love him *or* like him. They got divorced last year."

"Is that why you moved to Newfield?"

Pet's knee grazed against mine. "No spit, Sherlock."

She kissed me quick on the lips, so quick it was over before I knew it happened.

"'Spit' doesn't mean 'spit,'" she said. "But I don't swear. Swearing means you don't have enough creativity to say it your own way."

"Or it means you're pissed off."

Pet ignored that one. "The next time somebody cuts you off in traffic, yell 'Duck stew!' at him."

"Or her."

"Right. Or 'you bucking brasspole.' I try to think of a different one every time. By the time I do, I usually calm down."

"Pet, I'm sorry but that's pretty lame."

"That's the point. People get all bothered by lame stuff and forget about what matters."

"So what matters?" I asked.

Pet smiled. "I don't know. Climbing trees at night with your friend. Getting to know somebody. What do you think?"

I looked over at her, feeling real warm inside. "I think you're right," I said.

We sat there on the thick limb, close as can be, and didn't talk for a minute or more. If you've ever been out on a first date, and I bet you have—not that this was a first date or anything—you know how long a minute of silence is. It feels like an hour. You're trying to think of something to say, but it can't be stupid because then you'll look like some dork who's trying to think of something to say. But the thing is, this wasn't uncomfortable. There was just the two of us in a tree with the night all around us, all the way to the stars.

Pet finally spoke. "Wouldn't it be strange to be a tree? You'd grow and grow and grow without knowing it until one day you'd die, without ever traveling even one inch."

"It's a good thing they don't have brains," I said, "or they'd be brutal bored."

Pet grinned. "And scared zitless when somebody comes with a chainsaw."

We sat close together up in that big maple, swinging our legs and talking and feeling great that the other one was there, and nothing else in the world mattered. We didn't even realize the game was over until cars started piling out of the lot, Baldwin fans honking their horns like they'd won the Super

Bowl instead of one lousy slaughter of the weakest team in the league.

Pet nudged my shoulder. "Isn't that your friend?"

She pointed. Jim was in the line of cars, inching along, with Lisa Birnbaum in the passenger seat. They were both hiding cans of beer in their laps. Lisa bent over to take a secret sip, and I saw a wide smile on Jim's bruised face before they passed beneath us and out onto the road. I'd love to have broken his stones with a phone call, but Jim's parents hate cell phones so he doesn't have one. I didn't either, unfortunately. Over the summer I'd lost mine, and my parents wouldn't let me replace it till Thanksgiving, when maybe I'd "be thankful enough to take care of it."

"You dog, Jimbo," I said.

"Jealous?"

"No way. I'd rather be in a tree with you any day."

"Or night?"

"Especially night."

Pet looked me in the eye. "Me too," she said.

"Though I wouldn't have minded getting a couple of those beers before he left. I paid for half of them."

Pet didn't answer. But the quiet that followed wasn't peaceful like our silence a few minutes ago. This quiet was tense and nervous. The world was different, just like that, and I wanted it back the way it was.

"Is something the matter?" I asked after a while.

"No."

Why do people always say no, when everyone knows the truth is yes? Maybe for the same reason people ask if something is the matter, when they already know the answer.

"Are you sure?"

Pet shook her head. "Robby, have you ever hugged a tree?"

Hug a tree? "No, not that I can remember."

"You should do it. My cousin Donny, he was in the Peace Corps in Thailand and he told me about it. He said it's like the tree hugs you back, without any arms, just by being there for you."

"Did Donny do lots of drugs in Thailand?"

"Please don't think it's stupid. Please don't."

"I don't think it's stupid." But I was lying. I thought it was totally stupid.

"Let's hug this one," she said.

What the hey, I figured, it's not as if anyone will see me except her. "You got it." I slid over and wrapped my arms around the maple. You know what? I didn't feel stupid. I can't say I felt like the tree was hugging me back, but I didn't feel stupid.

"You don't understand," Pet said. "It has to be down there, on the ground. Doing it up here isn't a hug, it's only shaking hands."

She started climbing down. I watched her for a while without moving. She looked up at me. "You don't want to?"

I couldn't tell if Pet was testing me, or just really wanted to do this and didn't care what anybody thought. Either way, hugging that tree in full view of cars leaving the parking lot was a hundred times worse than being seen leaving a football game. This was social suicide. Nobody would remember me as a soccer player or a student. Instead I'd be the nerd who hugged trees with a wacko albino chick.

The expression on Pet's face was almost pain. One look at her and I hurt too. Tomorrow was tomorrow, tomorrow could wait. I had to erase that expression now.

"Sure I want to," I said, and this time it was only half a lie. I felt with my foot for the next lowest branch, and followed her down.

Way more cars had left than were still in line, but one was enough if it was the wrong one. I tried to stay on the back side of the tree, away from the traffic and all those eyes, but the placement of the branches didn't much cooperate. I hung down and dropped the last few feet to the grass. In the end I didn't hesitate about hugging the tree—I figured I could hide behind it. It did feel good, in a way, holding onto that big solid maple, my cheek pegged against the bark to stay out of view. It reminded me of kissing my dad good night when I was little, the sandpaper of his beard against my face smooth as a girl's. It had been a long time since I'd kissed him. Pet's arms came from the other side and she was hugging partly the tree, partly me. I hugged back. Pet peeked around the curve of the trunk. Her smile was like sunshine in the night, and I couldn't have cared less about anything else.

Until, over her shoulder, I saw my father.

He stared out the window with his mouth open. It was too late to pretend I hadn't seen him. I made a little wave, which meant I had to take one arm off the tree. Pet noticed right away.

"Who is it?" she said.

Dad waved back, but the look of disbelief on his face was stronger than ever.

"My father," I said into the bark, wondering how any of this had happened.

"Cool! Can I meet him?" Pet whirled around.

People started honking their horns; in front of Dad's Honda was empty space all the way to the stop sign. He took off in a hurry without looking back. I could only begin to imagine the interrogation I was going to get from him and Mom later.

Not to mention the comments in school on Monday, because right behind him was a car full of cheerleaders, then Sarah Malinowski in her father's gleaming Cadillac. I knew. I'd been

32

in it before. It had a killer back seat, and the thought of Sarah using it with Billy Hagan instead of me tasted like dirt. All those girls were smirking as they slowly rolled by. Sarah dialed a number and was blabbing on her phone by the time she reached the stop sign.

"You know something?" Pet said. "I can barely stand the sight of a cheerleader's uniform. I could lose lunch right now. I mean it."

"Come on, they're not that bad."

"You're right. They're worse."

"Freak!" yelled a voice in the traffic. "Yo, Pet, you as easy with the Newfield football players as you were at Baldwin?"

I couldn't tell who said it. Faces in cars stared at us as they passed, mostly kids I didn't know, and some of them were laughing. A blond idiot stuck his head out an Acura sunroof.

"Hey Pet, Newfield lost 46–12. You gonna do your best to make those poor slobs feel better?"

The other guy and the two girls in the car nearly wet their pants laughing. I wanted to help but what could I do, go over and get pounded two on one? I could try what I did to that other car, run at them like a lunatic, but that wouldn't work here. No way those guys would take off with the girls watching.

Pet tugged on my sleeve. "Come on, Robby. Let's go."

"That jerk can't say that to you!" I took a step toward them.

Pet grabbed my arm. She whispered fiercely in my ear.

"Why not?" she said, fighting not to cry. "It's true."

Chapter 5

"WHAT'S TRUE?" I ASKED. "What are you talking about?"

"Please, Robby. Please let's go." With a death grip on my arm Pet led me past the last exiting cars, back toward the parking lot. I didn't know what to think, what to believe. The lights on the football field went out, and suddenly it was easier to see the stars. But I didn't feel much like looking up.

One car sat all alone in the middle of the dark lot. Pet steered us closer. It was a new silver BMW convertible, with the top down. Even in the starlight it gleamed. MY PET, read the front license plate.

Feeling crummy or not, I was impressed. "Nice wheels. Where did you get this?"

"It's embarrassing," Pet said in a tiny voice.

"What do you mean, embarrassing?"

If anything, her voice got smaller. "My father bought it for my sixteenth birthday."

"So what are you complaining about? This is great!"

"I'm not complaining. I'm just embarrassed. I didn't do anything to deserve this. Babies are starving in Africa, while I have a new car because my sad dad wants me to still love him."

"How do you know that's why he did it?"

"Because he gave me the keys and said, 'I want you to still love me no matter what your mother says.'"

Man, I thought, talk about pathetic. "Does he have a lot of money?"

Pet stared up at the sky. "Tons. And he works like a slave for it. He always left before I got up for school, and didn't get home till eight or nine. I hardly ever saw him. "

She kept looking up, far away from me. We were both quiet again, but it was nothing like the peaceful quiet together in the tree. This time something big was getting in the way. I saw a shooting star and thought how some people would make a wish on it. My neck was getting sore. I looked down at the blacktop. A beer bottle was smashed nearby.

"Pet," I said. "*What's* true?"

She finally took her head out of the sky, and joined me staring at the asphalt. "Robby, I really want you to be my friend."

"I *am* your friend."

"I want you to stay that way."

"What are you talking about?" I put my hand on her cheek, and gently turned her face toward me. Believe it or not, doing that was pretty daring for me.

Slowly she raised her eyes. "I want to believe you. It's just...it's just that's not the first time a boy told me that."

"Well, I'm not 'a boy'. I'm me, Pet. Me. Robby."

She took my hand. "Is there someplace we could go to talk?"

"This *is* someplace." Why wouldn't she just say what she had to?

"Someplace not a parking lot with broken glass that smells like beer?"

"Whatever," I said.

36

Pet handed me the keys. "Take us there, OK?"

Now that was a sweet surprise. "Twist my arm," I said, and got in the driver's seat. I headed toward town on the back roads, warm wind whipping our hair. Driving that cool machine definitely improved my mood. Still it was Friday night after all, and I could really have gone for one of those brewskis in Jim's cooler. That nice buzz we put on at Pine Lake was ancient history, and I wouldn't have minded getting it back. Instead, Jim was generously feeding my beers to Lisa the cheerleader. What a gentleman. What a guy. Especially since I was sure she wouldn't give him the time of day in return.

Pet called into the breeze, "Where are we going?" You have to talk louder in a cruising convertible, or the words fly away before you can hear them.

"Trust me," I said. That wasn't the world's best advice by a long shot, but it seemed better than the truth—that I wasn't sure where we were going. I drove to the center of town pretty much on autopilot, not really thinking of anything. Or maybe I had too much to think about, and none of it would come clear. I stopped at a red light across from the town hall and the firehouse. To the left, up on a hill, stood the white wood Congregational church that every town has around here since Puritan days, though most of them have burned down a few times since then. On the right behind a stone wall was Newfield's oldest cemetery. Pet pointed over that way, into the dark.

"There's a tombstone in there from 1694," she said. "And a couple others before 1700."

"How do you know?"

"I checked it out the day after we moved here, so I'd feel at home. I like going to graveyards. They're peaceful."

"I guess," I said.

"It's like the past is all lined up in these neat rows. No confusion."

The light turned green. I had to make a decision. But all I could think of was how I was with a girl who had stood up in front of her new school to say its magazine drive was a scam, and made herself at home in town by visiting cemeteries. And climbed trees at night outside football games. And had a sweet new car that embarrassed her. And promised to tell me a truth that made her sad, but hadn't done it yet.

And I liked it. No matter what, I liked being with her. That was *my* truth. I glanced in the rearview, pulled a tight U-turn and gunned it up the hill to the little church parking lot.

A couple seconds went by, and a couple cars. "Robby, um, what are we doing here?"

I grinned in the yellow light of the streetlamp. "Going to the glowing tombstone," I said, low and spooky like Dracula. "It's anybody's guess if we make it back."

"Cool." Pet opened her door. "Where is it?"

I was kind of disappointed that she wasn't a girl about it, pretending to be scared even if she wasn't, until I remembered that was a main reason I liked her in the first place.

"Follow me. If you're brave enough."

Pet rolled her eyes. "Puh-*lease*."

We ran down the hill and across the road, laughing the whole way. There's a break in the stone wall and some steps down by the stop light, but we weren't interested in steps—it's a short wall and we just climbed straight over. I offered Pet my hand to help but I should have known better. She beat me to the other side all on her own. Nose ring or no nose ring, that girl was an athlete.

"My favorite one's back here," she said, heading off through the stones.

"Do you have them all memorized, or what?"

"Not really." Her voice drifted away from me in the dark. "Just the good ones."

I followed her. Being alone at night is not one of my favorite things, especially in a cemetery. Unlike Pet, I spent as little time as possible in boneyards. "Peaceful" was not the first word they made me think of. "Dead" was.

"This is it! Robby!"

Cutting through rows of stones to get to her, I tripped over a pot of plastic flowers and sent it flying. I put it back on the right grave, I hoped. Pet was out back, over the crest of the hill, where the slope runs down to the trees and the stones peter out. She had her hand on one of the old markers, the gray slate ones.

"Check it out," she said.

"I can't read a thing. It's night."

Her hand found mine in the dark. "Touch," she said. "Like Braille."

I did. It freaked me out, though. It felt like trespassing, like climbing on someone's house to rub their roof. Weirdest of all I didn't feel any letters, just Pet's fingers between mine sliding along cool, flat stone.

"It's smooth," I said. "I don't feel anything."

"Sure you do. Smooth is something. Smooth is a lot." Pet's hand stopped, and mine stopped with it. "It's smooth," she said, "because the outside layer of stone cracked right off. Like somebody peeled it. And the words are all gone."

"You're kidding me, right? Your favorite stone is the one you can't read?"

"Sure. Because then I can make it say whatever I want."

This girl was the strangest agent I'd ever met. "Like what?"

"Like 'Here Lies Petunia, Freed Slave And Revolutionary War Hero. Died In The Year Of Our Lord 1791.' Or 'In Loving Memory Of Pet Armstrong, Murdered By Savages 1694, In The Sixteenth Year Of Her Age.' I look at all the other graves and wonder what those people were like, but with this one I try to imagine *me*, if I'd lived in another time. Have you ever thought about that, how you wouldn't be the same even though you were the same, because everything else would be different? Like a hundred years ago there wouldn't have been any football game tonight, and no cars. So we probably wouldn't be here."

I didn't want to imagine that. Instead I thought how quiet the night would be without cars, how black it would be without electricity. How different it would be, standing here with this girl who would definitely not have had a nose ornament in those days, or her hair dyed white. You're not just you, I told myself. You're you *now*, in this place. And that's where I wanted to be.

"Maybe the name was still on this stone then," I said.

Pet still held my hand. She squeezed it a little and gestured down the hill toward the woods, only ten yards away. "Probably the stones in there were still straight, not all crooked and knocked over by tree roots."

A breeze picked up, and I smelled the salty muck of the river at low tide. It reminded me of the question that wouldn't go away.

"Pet, what's the thing that's true? What do you have to tell me?"

"Lots of the tiny stones have no name on them, or just 'Baby.' I guess they didn't even have a chance to give them a name. Sometimes the mother died at the same time."

"Why won't you tell me?" I grabbed her by the shoulders. "Hey! Look at me! Why won't you?"

"Because I want you to like me."

"I like you! I'm not going to *stop* liking you—unless you keep playing this stupid game!"

She looked deep into my eyes, like she was trying to find something there.

"Really?" she finally asked.

"Really," I said. "Really and truly."

So that's when she told me, there in the town's oldest cemetery with the stink of low tide in the air. The Congregational church bell rang the hour. If this was a story I'd make it better, and spookier, by having the clock strike midnight, but the truth is it was only ten. We waited, listening until the last ring died away. Pet put one hand on the gravestone that had no words any more.

"What's true is that I used to be a Baldwin cheerleader, and I used to be a freshman, and I used to be so naive I thought losers like that guy who yelled at us were cool, and I was so insecure that I'd do anything to hang out with them."

"No way."

"I wish I could say the same thing." Pet gripped the stone with her other hand too, like she was standing in a church pew. "One night after a football game I went to a keg party at a kid's house whose parents were out of town. Everybody cool was there, and I felt lucky to be invited. So when a senior halfback paid attention to me I got excited, and when he said let's join in the drinking games, I said yes. I didn't want anyone to know I'd hardly had a drink in my life. We started playing quarters and there were more games after that, but I don't remember because it seemed all I did was lose and chug beer."

It sounded like plenty of parties I'd been to. What's the big deal? I thought. Kids do that stuff all the time. Pet stared at the ground. There was a catch in her voice, like she had a sore throat and it hurt to talk.

"That's all I remember till I woke up on a couch by myself. I had a vicious headache and felt like I was going to puke any second. I didn't know where I was or how I got there. Then I saw my cheerleader skirt crumpled on the floor and it hit me I was cold. I looked down and almost screamed. All I had on was my Baldwin sweater."

Pet sounded like she was going to cry. "I found my panties hanging from a football trophy on a shelf."

An awful, phlegmy taste rose up in my throat. "I'm sorry," I said. "I'm really sorry."

"So now you don't like the slut, right? Go ahead, admit it."

"Don't say that. I still like you. Besides, it wasn't your fault."

"Of course it was my fault! Drink like a fool and awful things happen. Which is why I don't drink any more."

I saw what she was saying, but there was a lot more to it than that. "That doesn't let those dirtbags off the hook," I said.

Pet ran her fingers over the smooth stone. "Exactly." Her voice was ice. "You're absolutely right. Which is why I told you before I can't stand jocks."

I wasn't sure where that left me, and didn't like the feeling. But then I thought of something more important.

"Hey!" I said. "You were passed out, you don't know. Maybe nothing even happened."

I figured that would make her feel better, but instead she started crying for real. I put my hands on top of hers, on the gravestone.

"What's the matter? Pet, come on, please, what's wrong?"

She turned away from me. But her hands stayed with mine on the stone.

"That's what you mean by 'nothing happened'? Some slea-zeballs take a passed-out girl's clothes off and leave her on a couch? How about if one of them takes a photo and puts it on the Internet? Is that still nothing?"

"I'm really sorry. I didn't mean *nothing* nothing. I meant at least, maybe, you know..."

"I wouldn't get pregnant? Or a disease?"

"Yeah, I guess."

"Well, I didn't get pregnant. Or sick."

"That's something," I said.

"Yeah." Pet managed to smile, sort of. "Not nothing at all."

"No."

"You don't hate me?"

"Cut it out, will you? Repeat after me: 'Robby doesn't hate me.' Ready? 'Robby'..."

"Come on, Robby."

"Good—there's the first word. Now say 'doesn't'..."

Pet's smile wasn't fake any more. "Doesn't."

"Hate..."

"Hate."

"Me..."

"Me."

"Now boys and girls, can you say it all together?"

Pet laughed out loud. "Robby doesn't hate me."

"Very good! I knew you could do it!"

The words were hardly out of my mouth before Pet was kissing me, really kissing me, like a girlfriend. And I kissed her back like she was. We hugged each other, though from the waist down we got no closer than the eroded gravestone standing between us.

"In fact," I said. "Robby thinks she's great."

A police car screamed by on the Boston Post Road, siren wailing, strobe lights flashing. Seconds later an ambulance followed, barely slowing down as it ran through the red light by the firehouse. We held each other tighter.

"I always wonder who's in trouble," she said. "Whether it's someone I know."

"Me too."

"It's ugly, isn't it, how you hope it's not? That's like wishing the bad news on somebody else."

A second police car zoomed by, same direction as the first one. My stomach felt squishy and floppy. I don't like to be reminded of all the awful stuff that can happen. I'd rather pretend that everything's all right, and is going to stay that way forever.

Pet's arms loosened around me. She pulled away and I let her go.

"I'm so scared I'm shaking," she said. "What a wimp."

"Wimp? You were brave enough to stand up in front of a whole school and say what you thought."

"That wasn't courage. I was just so angry I didn't have any choice."

"I call that courage."

"Well, you're wrong but thanks anyway."

We were smiling again. I had an idea. "Want to go to Tricia Langhammer's party?"

"About as much as I'd like a beer tap between my eyes."

"It was just a thought."

"I'll drop you off there if you want."

"You won't come in?"

"Robby, I haven't been to a drinking party since...the one I told you about. If you want to go that's fine. No problem."

Of course I knew it *was* a problem. Pet wouldn't like it. But what right did she have to tell me how to live my life? Not that she had or anything. She had even offered to take me to the party. But it wasn't what she said—it was the way she said it.

My pride wouldn't let her think that she could control me, just like that. So I heard myself saying, "OK, I'll take a ride to the party," though all I really wanted to do was stay with her.

"No problem," Pet said again. "I should get home anyway."

She didn't seem angry, or disappointed—she didn't seem anything. Which kind of ticked me off. Didn't she care that I was leaving? I knew I wasn't being fair, being a jerk as a matter of fact, but that only made me angrier and more disappointed, mostly in myself. Pet took hold of my hand and started walking. Since I was attached to the hand, I did too.

"Hey," I said, "we didn't see the glowing tombstone."

"Let's not look for it tonight. Let's pretend we're back in the old days when this cemetery was new, and they didn't have streetlights."

How did she know a streetlight caused the glowing tombstone? Had she been there at night, by herself?

"Is that OK?" she asked.

"Why not? Let's pretend."

Compared to our sprint into the graveyard, our exit was almost slow motion, as if we didn't want our time together that night to end. We zigzagged through the rows of headstones in a crazy pattern, instead of the direct route. We took the stone stairs in the far corner of the lot, instead of climbing straight over the wall. We looked both ways before dawdling across the empty street. Again and again I wondered what she was thinking, but I just held her hand and kept going, all the way up the little hill to her car.

Which is when I noticed something wrong back by the trunk.

"What's that?"

After we took a few steps closer I wished I hadn't. Scrawled in what looked like pink lipstick next to the MY PET license plate, were the letters HORE.

"The spelling champion of Baldwin High," Pet said.

"What scum," I said.

"Ignore the ignorant." Pet was trying not to let it get to her, but it was.

She had some tissues in the glove compartment, and we wiped off the illiterate graffiti. But the sadness in her face showed it was easier to erase the word than it was to ignore it.

"Forget the party," I said. "I don't feel like going."

"I'll take you. It's no big deal."

"I don't want to go. I'd rather be with you."

I'd never said anything like that to a girl before, and I half couldn't believe I'd done it. Her face brightened up just like that, like the sun peeking out from behind a cloud.

"Really?"

"You calling me a liar?"

She kissed me on the cheek. "I'm calling you sweet. But I do have to go home soon. Eleven o'clock curfew."

"Mine's midnight on weekends."

"Mine's twelve on Saturday. Anyway, what I'm saying is unless I take you to the party, I guess you're going home."

I wondered what Jim was doing. I wondered if the party was hopping, and figured it was. I wanted to be there. I wanted a cold beer. It's not as if I was going to be able to hang out with Pet anyway. Yet with all that, what did I hear myself telling her?

"Sure, I'll take a ride home."

I didn't ask to drive, though it would have been easier because now I had to give Pet directions. I kind of wanted to see her behind the wheel anyway. This may sound sexist and crazy, and lots of guys can't do it either, but I'm always surprised when a girl knows how to drive a stick shift. Don't get me wrong—I'm *pleasantly* surprised. I even think it's sexy, watching her push those pedals and shift gears, running the machine.

We took the back roads because they're more fun, but also the quickest. My parents bought a house out in the semi-sticks before prices went crazy, and now they could sell it for like four times what they paid, but they won't. They're not going anywhere. They like Newfield.

"So," Pet said. "What are you going to do?"

"This weekend?"

"After next year. Can you believe it? We're almost seniors already."

"Go to college, I hope on a soccer scholarship."

"Where?"

"I don't know. My brother Paul wants me to go to Notre Dame, where he went. But I've had enough of following in his footsteps in high school. I don't need four more years of it in college." Which was true, but there was something else too, something I barely admitted to myself. What if I didn't get a scholarship to Notre Dame, or worse, didn't even get accepted?

"So many schools, so many choices," Pet said. "Sometimes I think we might as well just flip a coin. Right or left?"

"Left."

Our house was less than a mile up that road, and soon Pet was pulling into the driveway. The porch light was on, like always, but so were lights in the living room and my parents' bedroom. Sure I was coming home early, but they never stayed up till eleven unless they went out, which wasn't often and certainly hadn't happened tonight, because Dad went to the game. Then I remembered, and my stomach went sour like when that ambulance passed by: Dad saw me hugging that tree with Pet.

They were waiting up to grill me about it. I saw both my parents standing at the picture window. This was not going to be fun.

"Almost eleven," Pet said. "I better get moving."

I opened the door and got out, then leaned back in. "Thanks for the ride. It was fun."

"Yeah," Pet said. "It was."

"See you later."

"Bye." That was it, a scrap of small talk after all we'd done that night. I closed the door and she backed out of the driveway.

I thanked God I hadn't gone to the party, and that after my time with Pet the beers I drank earlier had completely worn off. At least I wouldn't have to explain with any alcohol jumbling my tongue. On the way to the front door I sucked on some more Tic Tacs, just in case, dreading what was waiting for me, debating how I should answer their questions.

But there were no questions. Instead, I was barely inside the house when my mother grabbed me in a bear hug so tight I could hardly breathe. She was shivering like she was outside in a T-shirt in December.

"You're OK!" she said. "It's a miracle you weren't with him!"

"What are you talking about?"

My mother looked at my father. He looked at me. I'll never forget his face right then, his eyes wide and wet and his mouth all crooked because he was chewing on his lip.

"Roger Powell just called." Dad was trying to stay normal but his voice cracked real bad. "Jim totaled his car tonight over on Beeching Road. Jim, he's...Robby, I don't know. It doesn't look good."

Chapter 6

WHAT COMES NOW IS THE best part or the worst, depending on how you feel about a lot of things. For me it started out the best, sort of, anyway, because when Dad called the hospital we found out Jim's car looked way worse than he did. He'd been wearing his seatbelt—we always do, we're not insane—and the blood all over the place that scared everybody came from one cut on his head that only took eight stitches to fix. I begged to borrow a car and drive to the hospital, but my parents said no, Jim needed rest and besides, visiting hours were over. I hated to admit they were right, but they were.

I never did go to the hospital. After a horrible night's sleep I called Jim's house early the next day, and his stepdad said he'd be coming home later that morning so I should just visit him there.

"Odd," he told me. "You guys not together for once. You dodged a bullet, big guy." He was acting kind of tough and joking now that Jim was all right, but I bet last night was a different story.

Suddenly there was this strange silence I didn't expect. It was probably only six or eight seconds, but that can seem like forever on the telephone. It felt weird and I wanted to hang up, but that's not an option with your best friend's parent. Mr. Powell cleared his throat.

"Robby, was Jim drinking last night?"

"No." I figured that wasn't a total lie because we were drinking early, yesterday evening, not last *night*. But they were weasel words and I knew it.

"Is that so?" he asked, in a tone that sounded like, "I don't believe a word you're saying, kid, and I'm very disappointed in you."

"I'll see you this afternoon," he said. "We can talk more then." And he hung up.

Which meant that though I was psyched to see my friend, I also dreaded it. Jim and I had to get our stories straight, so as not to get trapped in a lie. Not to mention I felt like scum for ditching Jim at the game. No matter how big a jerk he was being, or how glad I was to spend time with Pet, the fact was that if I had been with him maybe nothing would have happened.

My Mom almost never makes a hot breakfast—we usually have cereal and fruit. And she certainly doesn't do it on Saturday, which is a huge day in the real estate business, with lots of people off work and ready to look at houses. But that day, as I hung out in my room reading and doing homework, avoiding her and Dad until I could leave for Jim's, suddenly the smell of fresh waffles drifted into the air. I tried to ignore it, but after a minute I put down my pencil and closed the Trig book. Waffles are my favorite. Mom knew that. She was trying to cheer me up.

It's strange how sometimes you actually want to dislike your parents, because it's easier that way. But then they do stuff like hug you instead of getting on your case when you come home, and make you waffles without asking, and even if the last thing you feel like doing is talking to them, you really have no choice because you know they love you. Still, I didn't go to the kitchen until she knocked softly on my door, and told me what I already knew.

"Robby?" I heard the knob turn and the door creak open a crack. "I made waffles this morning."

"Yeah, Mom. Thanks."

"Are you hungry?"

She knows I'm almost always hungry. "I'll be there in a minute."

"They're ready when you are."

"OK." I waited, chin in my hand, drawing crazy patterns on my paper shopping bag book cover. "If you can't do the time, don't do the crime," my Uncle Brian says. But he's talking about real criminals, not kids just screwing around. Then I thought of that photo of Pet getting put on the Internet. I thought of my best friend smashing his car into a tree. Good times can go bad. Real bad.

I headed downstairs to breakfast. Suddenly I didn't feel like being alone anymore.

Dad was drowning a stack of waffles in maple syrup. He pushed the bottle over by my plate and looked at me, his fork an inch over his food, ready to cut through.

"Robby, that girl you were with last night. Does she have health problems?"

"Dad, she dyes her hair. That's all."

Mom poured more batter on the sizzling waffle iron, and put down the lid. She sighed. "I can't understand why people refuse to be satisfied with the way God made them."

I almost blurted out, "How about refusing to be satisfied with the way God made your kid? And expecting him to be perfect and play football and be valedictorian?" But I kept my mouth shut. What was the point? They'd just say they loved me no matter what (which was true) and didn't really care about that other stuff (which wasn't true at all).

"You can't be too careful these days," Dad said.

"Why are you making such a big deal of this?"

"I'm not making a big deal of anything. I just don't want you to do anything you'll regret later."

"I don't know what you're talking about."

Chunks of waffle speared on his fork stopped halfway to his mouth. "I'm talking about AIDS," he said.

"AIDS? Dad, come on!"

"Here you go," Mom said, sliding steaming waffles onto my plate. "Nice hot ones."

"AIDS!" I said. "Give me a break."

Dad pushed me the butter. "The disease won't give you a break. Not you or anyone else."

"We're not accusing you, Robby," Mom said. "We're just reminding you to be careful."

"She doesn't have AIDS, OK? And it's not like we did anything anyway."

"What were you doing with that tree?"

"What tree?" Mom had a clueless look on her face like when I talk about new music. Once when Jim and I were listening to Rabid Plastic she told us, "Now I know how my parents felt about the Rolling Stones."

"Climbing it," I said.

"What's this about a tree? No one told me anything about a tree."

Dad finished the last bite. "In the middle of a football game? Jim didn't leave."

"Well, look what happened to him," I said.

"You said he left the game, Alex. You didn't say anything about a tree."

"Will you cool it about the tree? Robby and the girl climbed a tree. OK?"

"Why did you climb a tree?" I remembered Mr. Mac telling us the line Edmund Hillary gave about why he climbed Mount Everest.

"Because it was there," I said.

Dad squinted at me, and I knew it was time to get out of there before a real fight started. "Nobody likes a smart aleck," he said.

"Sorry."

"You have so much potential, Robby," Mom said as she licked waffle batter off her finger. "It would be tragic to waste it."

"Potential" is a word I hear a lot around our house. What it means is, you could be as perfect as your brother if you'd just try harder. Right then was the closest I ever came to telling them about the times I covered up for Paul when he'd been out partying. I'm not saying it happened often, but it did happen. Like the time I found Paul's keys in the front door and Dad's car parked with two wheels off the driveway. I took the keys, put the car in the garage and said nothing, not even to him. Mom or Dad never knew.

"These waffles are great," I said. "Thanks for making them."

We all knew I was trying to change the subject, but that was OK because no one really wanted to talk about it in the first place. Though I know Dad was thinking that if I had been down there on the field playing football—where I belonged, as far as he's concerned—then none of that tree nonsense would have happened. He would have been cheering for me instead of worrying about my life.

"You're welcome," Mom said. Dad remarked that the lawn was getting high and I volunteered to mow it. The last thing I needed was to be on their shit list, especially since I wasn't sure what was waiting for me at Jim's. I powered down two more waffles and headed out.

"Give Jim our best," Mom said as I took Dad's keys off the hook by the front door.

Dad's voice made my stomach sink. "Ask him if he's ever heard of a designated driver," he said, and I wondered if we were in worse trouble than I'd thought.

Jim lives halfway across town, on Beaver Brook Lane, though there aren't any beavers, and if there was ever a brook it must be buried by the road or something because it's gone now. Some people still call it Timothy's Hill, for the freed slave who supposedly lived there after the Civil War and whose grave they say is out in the woods. Jim and I looked for that grave when we were little, with no luck. I guess I don't believe the story any more than I do the legend of Leatherman's Island out in Keller's Pond, or that the glowing tombstone belongs to an old man poisoned by his young wife so she could marry her lover. Unless the legend has been around longer than Newfield has had streetlights—then I'd start wondering.

For now I had other stuff to worry about, like what I was going to say to Jim's parents. After a ten-minute drive I pulled in and saw the garage doors were open with two cars inside. So they were both home, Mrs. Dolan and Mr. Powell. It's funny—Jim's mom kept his dad's last name, even after they got divorced. Maybe she just got used to it, or kept it to make Jim's grandmother happy. I don't know, could be she just likes it better. Jim's dad lives out west now, in Utah. As I walked toward the house I wondered if they had called to tell him about the accident. Squirrels were going nuts up in an oak tree, and as I passed under it, hunks of chewed acorn fell on my hair and shoulders like dandruff. When I got out of range I stopped to shake them off.

"Those varmints don't have great manners," Mrs. Dolan said from the garden off to my right. I hadn't noticed her in the tall, bushy tomato plants. She has short brown hair and is the prettiest of all my friends' moms—it hardly seems possible that she could have a kid my age.

"Hi," I said. "Is Jim inside?"

No, Jim's outside running a marathon the day after he spent the night in the hospital. What a butt-brain question.

She picked a fat tomato and put it in her basket. "He's waiting for you. I think he's watching some fishing program with Roger."

"Thanks." That's what I was afraid of, that we wouldn't get a chance to be alone and make sure our stories matched. I turned away, not feeling too fine about any of this.

"Robby?"

Something in her voice made me freeze. Suddenly the same nervousness hit me that I get before taking a penalty kick in a soccer game. I *want* to kick it, I know it's almost a sure goal (I'd only missed one, ever, and that was in junior high), but still there's this nasty little voice in my head saying, "If you choke and blow this you let the whole team down." If I don't ignore that voice I'm dead, the shot will go wide, or high over the top of the crossbar. So in a game what I do is, I block everything out but the thought of the ball in the goal. Before I even kick it, I see the ball blasting into the back of the net, the goalie all sprawled out and hopeless, not able to even get a finger on it. Then I copy what I've already done in my head, and Newfield scores again.

I looked at Jim's mother. There was a cute smudge of dirt on her cheek that made me think Mr. Powell was a lucky man, and Jim's dad must have been nuts to move away.

"We were really scared last night," she said. "*Please* be careful. Promise me you guys will be careful."

"I promise."

"Cross your heart?" she said, leaving out the "and hope to die" part.

"Absolutely."

As I walked to the house I felt her eyes following me, but probably I was just being paranoid. Through the picture window I saw Jim and Mr. Powell watching TV in the living room. Some guy wearing hip boots and sunglasses was playing a fish on a fly rod, standing in a fast-moving stream surrounded by mountains. I opened the screen door and knocked, with my knuckles, not using the heavy brass ring. It felt strange because normally I'd go straight in without making anyone get up for me. You do that at your best friend's house where you've been a hundred times before, and you feel comfortable. But today I didn't feel so comfortable.

Mr. Powell opened the door. "We were wondering when you'd show up."

On the couch Jim looked up from the TV. A thick white bandage was taped to his forehead. "Hey," he said.

"Hey. How you doing?"

He pointed at the bandage. "It only hurts when I laugh."

"I'll try not to tell any jokes."

"Want something to drink, Robby?" Mr. Powell asked. He checked my face to see my reaction. A couple seconds went by before he added, "Coke? Orange juice?"

"No thanks."

"I could use some more vitamin C myself," he said. "Jimbo?"

Jim held up his half-full glass of OJ. "I'm OK."

"And very, very lucky to be," Mr. Powell said as he left the room.

Jim pretended not to hear that. At least, he made no sign that he did. He sipped orange juice with his eyes on the screen.

I joined him on the couch. "When can you play again? Will you miss any games?"

Jim raised the volume with the remote control. "They found the beer cans in the car," he whispered quickly. "And the huggy Paul gave you. Deny everything. I told them I only drank at the party, not with you."

"But—"

"Just lie! Do it! Don't let the team down!" It was a fierce whisper, and the wild look on Jim's face matched it. I shut up.

"I'll be healed in a week," Jim said in a normal voice. "Good as new."

Don't let the team down? What was Jim talking about? Before I could say anything Mr. Powell came back.

"Sure you don't want anything, Robby?"

Yes, I thought. I want to be alone with my friend. I want last night never to have happened. Then I remembered Pet and changed that to: I want Jim's accident never to have happened.

"No thanks," I said again.

It's a strange, sweaty experience to sit in a room with your best friend and his stepfather, watching men you don't know catch fish on the boob tube, waiting for the ax to fall over something that's bad enough by itself without having punishment dumped on top of it.

A commercial came on for a very expensive, very stupid-looking fishing lure. "You couldn't catch a cold with that thing," Mr. Powell said, getting up out of the recliner. He left the room.

"What do you mean, do it for the team?" I whispered. But before Jim could answer, Mr. Powell was standing in the doorway, his lips pressed tight together. I saw what he held in his hand and my stomach went queasy, full of fluttering butterflies.

It was the Notre Dame huggy Paul gave me.

"I believe this is yours." He tossed me the huggy and I dropped it. That was not only embarrassing, it showed I was nervous. I knew that's what Mr. Powell was thinking, standing behind the recliner with both hands gripping the chair back, his eyes shifting from me to Jim on the couch, then back to me again.

Jim stared at the TV screen. "Roger," he said, his voice shaky. "Please don't do this."

All these years and it still sounds funny, Jim calling Mr. Powell by his first name. When we were little he called him Uncle Roger, but he stopped that a long time ago. Mr. Powell isn't his uncle, after all, though he isn't his dad either. I guess there's always this problem if your parent marries somebody new.

"Don't do what, Jim?" Mr. Powell's voice was full of sarcasm.

"I told you, Robby wasn't with me drinking after the game."

Right away I noticed the truth that was practically a lie, the kind of stuff I had told my own parents. Yes, it was true—I'd only been drinking with him *before* the game.

Mr. Powell stared me down. "Robby?"

"It's true," I said.

I tried to keep eye contact with him, to show I was confident, but soon I looked away. On the TV a bass was jumping at the end of the line.

"After what happened to his granddad we expected Jim to have more sense," Jim's mom said. I hadn't seen or heard her come in. She walked over to Mr. Powell, and the two of them stood there like a scowling team against us.

"Do you remember Grandpa Dolan's accident, Robby?" Her voice was tough and hard, nothing like it was out in the garden.

I nodded. Jim's grandfather got hit by a car while he was running at night. It was hit and run, and the driver never got caught.

"Then you remember how terrible it was." She put her arm around Mr. Powell's waist and her voice got small all of a sudden. "Last night we thought it happened again."

She started to cry. Mr. Powell wiped his cheek with the back of his hand. I looked away, feeling sick. This man who had fought in the Vietnam War and seen people killed was crying because of us. Jim was staring at the floor. I wanted to make things right for his parents, just erase last night's mistakes. But since that was impossible I wanted to do the next best thing—get the hell out of there.

Suddenly Mr. Powell was yelling at us. "Drinking and driving is the stupidest thing a person can do! The stupidest! It's saying, 'I don't care about myself or anybody else!'"

His face turned so red it was scary, almost purple. His fists were clenched tight on the chair. "One mistake can change everything!"

Even Jim's mom seemed blown away by his reaction. We were all dead quiet, nobody looking at anybody else. There was nothing in the room but tension, and a guy with a southern accent on TV explaining how to catch bass with plastic worms.

"Robby," Mr. Powell said, "I think it's time you got going."

I stood up. Jim stayed on the couch. "See you Monday in school," I said. "When can you play again?"

Jim shrugged. He wouldn't even look at me. I could've smacked him for being such a weenie, but I figured I'd be in a pissy mood too, in his place. So I just told his parents goodbye and headed for the door.

"Robby!" Mr. Powell said.

Oh no, what now? With my hand on the doorknob I turned around. He was holding the Notre Dame huggy by his ear, like a quarterback with a football. He let it fly, and this time I caught it with one hand.

"Thanks," I said, though thankful was about the last thing I was feeling. If you want to know the truth, what I really felt like doing was going somewhere and drinking some beers.

I'm not saying that's intelligent. It's totally moronic. I'm just trying to be honest—it's what I felt like doing. I *didn't* do it, but I felt like it. For what that's worth, and as low-life as that sounds, I felt like it.

Chapter 7

I WAITED A LONG TIME at the stop sign at the end of Jim's road, unsure where to go, thinking of Pet and wishing I knew where she lived. I don't know what I'd have done if I *had* known—probably just driven by and hoped for a miracle that she'd be in the yard and I'd have an excuse to stop, say hi, tell her what happened. I remembered last night's kisses, the quick one in the tree and the long, slow one with a gravestone digging into my thigh. I closed my eyes and lived them again, almost as real as the first time, until a car horn blasted behind me and I had to move.

I drove around aimlessly, full of thoughts but no answers, until I happened to pass the high school. I pulled into the lot by the soccer field. The school was closed so I couldn't get my stuff in the locker room, and there was no way I was going home for my ball and old soccer shoes, or I'd have gone out and practiced by myself. I love everything about soccer, even just standing on the springy turf and feeling the earth under my cleats. I can spend hours doing drills, like trying to keep the ball off the ground without using my hands. Later I dribble the ball around, making quick cuts, then boot it hard and sprint after it over the grass and nail a shot on goal with all I've got, keeping my head down so the ball doesn't sail over the top like a field goal in football. Sometimes the ball smacks a post or the crossbar with a noise that says this guy has a vicious shot, he's a real player. It's like a baseball pitcher with a mean fastball that explodes into the catcher's mitt. I love to hear it in practice, because it tells me I'm good. I hate it in games because it means the keeper just got lucky, and I missed a goal by inches.

I walked to the field. I needed to talk it over, talk it out. But a conversation with myself right then was like the sound of one hand clapping. I'd learned that phrase from Mr. McLaughlin, when we were talking in class about being paranoid to show other people what you've written, for fear they'll think it sucks.

"Well guess what?" he said. "Keep it to yourself and you'll never hear anyone say it's good, either. If you don't take some chances in life, why bother?"

Standing on the edge of the field, lining up an imaginary ball for a corner kick, I knew he wasn't talking about taking chances like drinking a ton of beer and getting behind the wheel. Not at all. He was talking about the opposite of doing something stupid. Suddenly I decided to take a chance. I was going to visit Mr. Mac, just like that, out of the blue, and see what he thought. I kicked the ball that wasn't there, putting a little sidespin on it so it curved in toward the goal, then jogged to the car and took off before I could change my mind.

He only lives about a mile from the school, in a two-story yellow house he told us was built before the Civil War. That's only medium-old for a New England town like Newfield; one house in the center of town has a sign on it, "Built 1696." Mr. Mac told us there's a hidden room in his basement that supposedly was used to hide runaway slaves for the Underground Railroad, on their way to freedom in Canada.

"There's no proof of that," he said. "But it's too good a story not to believe it."

I parked by Mr. Mac's blue Toyota at the end of the driveway, near a saggy-roofed little barn that was probably built last century. I got out and walked toward the house where the terrified fugitive slaves used to hide on their way to freedom. Mr. Mac was right—there was no sense not believing that story.

Leaves crunched under my feet, just a few because it was only mid-September, but in a month Mr. McLaughlin would be knee-deep in them if he didn't keep up with the raking. There were big maples and a tall oak back here, not counting the woods beyond the stone wall that bordered his lawn, and more trees in the front yard. The maple nearest the house had great branches for climbing. You, or a girl—or both of you—could hide up there and no one would know unless you wanted them to.

Until November I thought as I knocked at the back door. Then these trees will be as bare as skeletons until spring, and you couldn't hide at all.

I waited, hands in my pockets, my heart beating faster all the time. I was pretty nervous about showing up at a teacher's house, even my favorite teacher's. But that shows how messed up I was by what had happened, that I wanted somebody to talk to that bad. I knocked again, louder. Nothing. Half depressed and half relieved, I left. Doesn't matter, I told myself. You shouldn't bother him anyway, especially on a weekend. Deal with it, you wuss.

I was halfway to the car when I heard the door open behind me.

"Yes?" Mr. McLaughlin asked, kind of defensive. Maybe he figured I was some kind of salesman or something.

I turned around. "Hi."

He smiled big. "Robby! What brings you to see me on a day when you don't have to?"

"I don't know. I was just driving around so I thought I'd stop by."

You could tell he didn't really believe me. I doubt a kid had ever knocked on his door uninvited like this, except for Halloween but that doesn't count. He waved me over. As I got close I saw he was wearing an Amnesty International sweatshirt, and of course that made me think of Pet, and last night.

"Come on in. Sorry I was late getting to the door, but I was in the middle of tying a nail knot."

"A what?"

"It's the knot you use to connect your fly line to the leader. I don't care how many times you do it, it's a tricky one to tie right."

"I didn't know you were a fly fisherman."

Mr. Mac grinned. "There's always a lot we don't know about people." The grin twisted into this fake sour look. "Don't you know that by now from creative writing class? Haven't you listened to a word I've said?" Mr. Mac clapped me on the shoulder and guided me through the door into the kitchen.

"I should take off. I don't want to hold you up if you're going fishing."

"Relax, I'm not leaving till four. They usually bite best at sunset."

We stood looking at each other on the kitchen linoleum. Suddenly it felt awkward. I'd never felt that way with Mr. McLaughlin before. But I'd never talked to him outside of school before. I knew I shouldn't have come. I wasn't even sure why I had.

"So. To what do I owe the honor of this visit?"

"Well, like I said, I happened to be in the neighborhood so—"

Mr. Mac held up his hand like a traffic cop. He looked me in the eye.

"Robby, what's wrong?"

I hesitated. Getting the words out was harder than I expected.

"Hey," Mr. Mac said softly. "Come on in and sit down. Apple juice?"

"Thanks." He filled two mugs from a pitcher in the refrigerator. He gave me one then walked down a hardwood-floor hall that creaked under our feet to the living room. We sat at opposite ends of a dark blue couch. He flipped a pair of coasters on the lid of the wicker trunk that he used for a coffee table. EEN HEERLIJK BIER, mine said.

"What does that mean?" I asked.

Mr. Mac leaned closer. "A um, something beer. I don't speak Flemish. I pocketed it in a Belgian pub, probably in Bruges."

We looked at his coaster. CARDINAL, it said. "That's a Swiss beer," he told me. "Brewed in a little city called Fribourg. I studied there during my junior year abroad in college."

He spent a whole year in Europe! I've never been anywhere. Unless you count once to Disney World, but I was so little I couldn't even go on the good rides. Paul had most of the fun.

Mr. Mac gazed straight ahead, like he was lost in his memories. He smiled, at what I could only guess.

"Cheers." Mr. Mac held out his drink to me, and we clinked glasses. I felt kind of grown-up somehow. We drank together. Then he sat back and crossed one ankle over his knee.

"So, buddy, what's on your mind?"

I told him everything. Well, not everything. I left out most of Pet and me up in the maple tree, and at the graveyard. And

I kept my mouth shut about that scummy photo and all the garbage at Baldwin High.

Mr. Mac didn't say much, just listened. I admitted about the drinking and how guilty I felt about Jim, especially since he was being such a great friend and taking all the blame. I told him how tough it was being younger brother to a guy the whole world thought was perfect, how everyone figured I was next in line, I'd just march right behind him, get my name on the same trophies, get the same college scholarships and go on to be President or something without hardly trying. Well I did try, but it didn't always put me number one. And number one was what people expected.

I must have gone on for ten minutes. I never talk about myself that much.

"I'll stop whining now. Forget it, it's no big deal."

Mr. McLaughlin shook his head. "It's a very big deal. Living up to other people's expectations can eat you alive. I know."

"What do you mean?"

He pointed over my head. I turned around and saw a framed photo on the wall, of Mr. Mac in a tuxedo, and a beautiful long-haired blonde woman in a wedding gown. Mr. Mac's hair was long too, almost to his shoulders, nothing like the close cut he has now. They were standing outside a white wooden church on a sunny day, holding hands and smiling.

"My parents freaked when I married Judy, because we were barely out of college then went to live on a commune in Vermont to grow organic vegetables. They expected me to join the family business like my brothers, or at least to do something they considered normal. And now we were going off to be what my mother called 'hippies' and my father called 'bums.'"

Mr. Mac picked up his mug, then set it back down without drinking.

"But I'd spent most of my life doing what other people wanted, and I'd finally had enough. So what did I do? This time I did what *Judy* wanted, and spent a year farming, which I didn't much like, until the farm went belly-up because the commune treasurer had been ripping us off the whole time. Let that be a lesson to you—never trust a 300-pound vegetarian with bad teeth whose name is Neil but calls himself Moonglow."

"Thanks for the advice. I'll try to remember that."

"Moonglow was a hypocrite, too. Once I borrowed his truck and saw a greasy Burger King wrapper on the floor. Some vegetarian. Turns out he was Joe Cholesterol Carnivore on the sly."

Mr. Mac went to the kitchen and came back with the juice pitcher. He refilled my glass. "So Judy and I go to work for my father, figuring we'll save some bucks, then quit and go traveling. But she liked making money so much that she wouldn't quit. And she wanted me to stay too. So that was that. I went to South America and India, then to graduate school. Judy's still with the company, a vice president now like my brothers."

He reached over and slapped me on the knee. "Hey, you came over here to talk about *you*, not your English teacher's divorce. Tell me about your expectations, Robby."

"My expectations?"

"Exactly. Your great expectations."

"I guess I expect to go undefeated in the league then do well in the tournament, maybe be state champs."

"Do you *expect* to be state champions?"

"I can't speak for the other guys—"

"I don't want you to speak for them. What do *you* expect?"

It felt uncomfortable, too personal to be sharing my dreams. But he's not asking for your dreams, moron. He's asking what you expect.

"No," I said. "That's too much to expect. But I *hope* it happens. And I'm going to try real hard to make it happen."

"Do you expect to be valedictorian?"

"Not unless Lori Peplowski moves away. Or gets a bad case of senioritis."

"Do you *want* to be valedictorian?"

"I don't know. I guess. If it happens, it happens."

"So you're going to try harder to win the soccer championship than to be number one in school?"

I was starting to feel like a witness in court being cross-examined. That wasn't why I came here.

I tried to explain. "I always do my best, but in soccer you win or lose on the field, and it's easy to see why. Everyone knows the score. But in school a teacher could give you an A– instead of an A for who knows what reason. I got killed by a B in gym once because Coach Malfetone was mad that Jim Dolan and I wouldn't play football."

Mr. Mac had this light in his eyes that he gets all the time in class, whenever a good discussion starts. "Playing Socrates," he calls it, and I knew for sure he was going to say something to make me think. It's what he always does. Which is why kids love his classes, except for a few clueless losers you have to feel sorry for.

"Sports aren't subjective? What about if a ref blows a call that costs you a game? Or *gives* you a game? Everyone knows the score, as you say, but they might argue all night about how it happened."

He was right, I saw that in two seconds. I wanted to say something halfway intelligent, not because I have a big ego but because I wanted Mr. McLaughlin to be proud of me and not think I was—to use his phrase—a "mental slug."

"I guess what I mean is I'm just going to do my best in soccer and school, and that's all I can do. Spending all your time worrying about being number one, that's crazy. What fun is that?"

"Bravo! Couldn't have put it better myself. You get an A on the pop quiz."

When Mr. Mac said that to me I got all electric inside, the best I'd felt since I heard about Jim's accident. I had to fight not to cry. But I didn't want him to see that. And he didn't. All he saw was the bashful grin I wanted him to see. To deflect attention, I nodded toward the guitar leaning in a corner.

"You play guitar?"

"Not as much as I used to. Do you?"

I shook my head. "I tried for a while, but I got frustrated and gave up." Actually, I never got past the stage where the strings tear up your fingers. Supposedly you develop calluses, but I didn't stick with it long enough.

Mr. McLaughlin picked up the guitar. "It's like anything else. You have to struggle through the beginner's stage before it becomes much fun." He sat down and strummed a chord. Suddenly his fingers started flying over the strings, and then he sang this cool song. I don't recall all of it, but this part stuck with me:

> I've been doin' some hard travelin', I thought you knowed
> I've been doing some hard travelin', way on down the road
> Heavy load and a worried mind, lookin' for a woman that's
>   hard to find
> I've been doin' some hard travelin', Lord.

He had a good voice. Not a *pretty* voice, but I don't like that kind anyway. "That was great," I said.

Mr. Mac grinned. "It's a Woody Guthrie tune. You know, Arlo Guthrie's father."

"Oh really?"

I had never heard of either of those guys, but I was afraid of looking like a dumb-ass so I just nodded like I knew what was going on. There's no such thing as a stupid question, he tells us all the time in class, but still I was chicken.

Mr. Mac set the guitar on the couch. "Not that playing *Hard Travelin'* was a hint or anything, but a fishing buddy expects me to pick him up soon, and I've still got some knots to tie."

I stood right up. "Sorry. Thanks a lot for helping me out."

Mr. Mac put a hand on my shoulder. "No problem. I wish I'd had the sense when I was your age to talk to somebody. And listen—you might not want to hear this, but I wish now that at least occasionally, that somebody had been my parents. It's a mistake to shut them out. I hope you don't."

"Mostly they're the ones who shut *me* out."

He lifted his hand to cut me off. "Just give it some thought, OK?"

I shrugged my shoulders.

"That's the spirit," he said, and we were both smiling wide as he closed the door behind me. Halfway across the yard I glanced behind. He gave me a wave through the glass. I waved back, feeling warm and good, but also confused with a lot of stuff I hadn't figured out yet.

Chapter 8

MONDAY MORNING WAS WEIRD in school, with all sorts of people asking me how Jim was. Not just kids, either; a few teachers cornered me too, and even Wally the wheezing custodian. Everyone just assumed that if it concerned Jim, I'd know about it. And they were right, even though for once we hadn't been together.

One good thing about the accident was that I didn't catch much grief about Pet and the strange scene at the tree. Sarah Malinowski was the only one. She passed by my locker and said in this fake, sugary-sweet voice with a smile to match, "Wow, Robby, I figured you might be desperate after I broke up with you, but not *that* desperate." That was it—not another comment from anyone, at least to my face. It was almost like it never happened. But I didn't fool myself. Stuff doesn't just go away, and it's amazing how cruel people can be. Like when they yelled at Pet Friday night.

Pet. If you're wondering what she did the rest of the weekend, well, that was on my mind too. Even as I drove away from Mr. McLaughlin's on Saturday I was thinking what to do that night. My best friend, the guy I'd normally go out looking for fun with, was home with a stitched-up head, and I had no other plans. I drove around for an hour and ended up down at the nearly deserted town beach. There were only two other cars in the lot. I walked over to the cinder block building that holds the snack bar and changing rooms, now closed for the season. There was a pay phone there, and a phone book, but no listing for Armstrong. I expected that; she had just moved here, after all. When I called Information, though, there was no Armstrong in Newfield.

Which is why I amazed my parents and first mowed the lawn, then actually stayed home on a Saturday night. I spent the night catching up on schoolwork, and started a new story for Mr. Mac's class. It was about a kid who feels guilty when his best friend dies in a car crash, because he didn't do all he could to make sure the friend didn't drive drunk.

You know how school can be, really hectic with just that couple minutes between classes, so on Monday even though I was looking for her I didn't see Pet until lunch. She was way ahead of me in the line. I thought about going up and trying to take cuts, but I hate it when slimeballs do that. Once I saw a fight break out over it, and Mike Mulvey got shoved butt first into a garbage can. So I waited. I hoped to meet her eye but she didn't turn around, just moved silently through the line with no one talking to her. I was just getting inside the door where the trays are stacked when Pet left the other door by the cash register. She headed to an empty table on the other side of the room. A few girls watched her, whispering and giggling behind their hands. Sarah Malinowski lifted her carton of milk toward Pet's back like she was making a toast, and said something that made Billy Hagan spew half-chewed sloppy joe out over the table. Hagan yucked it up like it was the cleverest thing he had ever done. Considering what a baboon he is, he was probably right.

I slid my tray along the rails. Everyone bitches about the cafeteria food, but it's really not too bad. We all make barf jokes, but check out how many plates have anything still on them after lunch. Almost none, except for girls who are always on a diet, fat or not, and hardly take a bite no matter how good it is.

I pocketed my change and left for that daily little piece of weirdness, walking into the lunch room and picking a seat. Every day this odd game, these quick decisions. You're friends with some people here, a few over there, and there, and there too—so where do you go? Maybe there's an empty chair next to a girl you'd like to know better, but everyone else at that table is a butthead, or maybe by the time you get your courage up to actually sit there someone else does it first. Now this time, far across the room so going to her couldn't be more obvious, was a new girl with bleached white hair, the outcast who won't sell magazines, the only person in the whole place reading a book. And if I went to her, unless I took a circle route that would totally call attention to itself I had to pass right by a table of my soccer buddies.

I noticed Sarah watching, and Hagan the smirking cretin, and my decision got real easy. No way I was going to let those two influence what I did. I acted more from pride than from any noble desire to do the right thing, but the fact is I acted—though looking straight ahead to avoid as much eye contact as possible. "Yo, Fielder, what's up with Jim?" asked Nick Rossi, our center fullback, but I pretended not to hear him and kept walking fake casual through the rows to Pet's table. Call me paranoid, but I felt like a roomful of eyeballs was staring at my back. Which is why I was a semi-coward and slipped into the second chair from the end of the table, instead of directly across from her where I wanted to be.

"Hey," I said.

Pet didn't look up from *Catch-22*. I started to worry, even started to get a little ticked off. Then she stuck in a concert ticket at her page and closed the book, smiling up a storm.

"Sorry to be rude. I just had a couple sentences to finish the chapter."

I've been meaning to read *Catch-22* since Mr. Mac recommended it, but haven't got around to it yet.

"I was going to call you on Saturday." I hoped I didn't look too disgusting, talking with my mouth full. I chewed fast and swallowed in a hurry.

"Why didn't you?"

"Because you're not in the phone book or information."

Pet giggled, a nervous giggle like any other girl. I hadn't heard that before. "Sorry, Robby, I forgot. You probably looked under Armstrong."

"That would be a good assumption."

"It's under my mother's and stepfather's name. Nassaney." Pet wrote her name and number on her bookmark, as if there was any chance I'd forget whose phone it was. She slid the ticket across the table.

"Lyle Lovett?" I said.

"He's totally cool. Fantastic concert."

"Is this your cell number?"

"I don't have a cell phone. I think they give you brain cancer."

A gooey hunk of gingerbread smacked her in the face. It bounced off and landed on her book. It was one of those times when something happens so fast, and so out of nowhere, that it doesn't seem real for a second.

"Don't turn around," Pet said.

"But—"

"Please don't start anything."

"*Start* something? Whoever threw that's the one who started it!"

I turned around. I don't know what I was planning to do, but I looked. And of course that meant Hagan.

But Hagan seemed too busy sucking on Sarah's neck to have just chucked a dessert. I knew he was too big a glutton to have thrown his own, but one of the girls might have donated hers. If Hagan did it, though, he should sign up for drama club, because for a low grade moron he sure was a good actor.

I quickly scanned the room, and wished I hadn't. The only ones who looked suspicious were my teammates. Not because they were laughing, but because they were fighting so hard *not* to laugh. They always screwed around at lunch, keeping things lively and stupid—I should know, I sat there and was part of it often enough. But now that table was dead quiet, a bunch of guys staring down at their trays. Nick Rossi's shoulders were shaking, and his weren't the only ones.

What should I do? Go over there and try to be tough? We had a big game tomorrow, which would be hard enough minus Jim without having players pissed off at each other. I was a co-captain, along with Jim and Nick, and the last thing I wanted was to hurt our chances of winning. We had worked too hard for that.

"Robby, if you do anything I won't forgive you." Pet's teeth were clenched together, her lips barely moving.

"I guess," I said. My reluctance was an act, though. The truth was I was big-time grateful to her for giving me an easy way out.

Pet cleaned the cover of *Catch-22* with her napkin. "See? All gone. It *is* gone, isn't it?"

She lifted her chin so I could check out her face. I was supposed to be looking for pieces of gingerbread but it was hard to get past her lips, remembering them on mine in the dark.

"Is it gone, or what?"

"It's gone." I felt somehow that part of me was gone too.

She smiled shyly. "I have a confession to make. When I was pretending to read the book, I was really watching you, to see where you'd sit."

"Really?"

"No, dummy, I made it all up. Of course really."

"Are you sorry I bothered you?"

Her smile wasn't so shy this time. "I can live with it."

The bell rang. Pet and I walked together in the crowd, our shoulders sometimes touching, not caring who saw us. Creative Writing didn't meet that day, so we split to go to different classes. Twenty minutes into Spanish, with Mrs. Sugg courageously but boringly trying to teach us the subjunctive tense, something hit me like dessert in the face.

Was Pet not wearing her nose ring, or was I was already so used to it that I didn't notice?

Chapter 9

I TRIED TO PAY ATTENTION the rest of that day, but I kept thinking of Pet, and her getting bombarded in the lunchroom. I wondered why Rossi did it (*if* he did it), and what I should do about it, and most of all how we were going to beat Pearson tomorrow with Tommy Francis in goal. Maybe he'd rise to the occasion and play great, but I wasn't counting on it. Pearson was tough, with only one loss, and that was to Baldwin, 3–2. Luckily our game on Friday was against pitiful Northbrook, turkeys who hadn't won a single game. So if we pulled it out against Pearson, we'd still be undefeated when Jim came back next week.

It was up to me to come through. I had to put the ball in the net, probably more than once, or chances were that we'd get our asses handed to us on a platter.

Soccer practice was at 2:30, which gave us twenty minutes from the time school ended to get out on the field. Not that it's hard to do—change your clothes, lace up your cleats and jog out there. Notice I said jog, not walk. Coach Reynolds's Rule Number One is you never walk to or from the field, and that includes games, not just practice. Away games, too. We step off the bus and run a quick lap of the field, clapping our hands in this loud rhythm, then circle up for calisthenics, yelling each repetition—"ONE, two, three, FOUR!"—in the deepest, baddest voice we can manage. It's supposed to psych out the other team, but mostly it gets *you* psyched up to get out there. I guess it's like what the army does with soldiers, which might make it a little sick—a game's not a war, right?—but I don't care. It feels cool when you do it.

Last period Monday I had my other English class, with ancient Mrs. Rieth, and as usual it was torture. When the bell rang we bolted out of there. The only thing crazier than a high school hallway between classes is the same hallway when school lets out. Rush hour traffic, with an attitude. I donkeyed around at my locker, hoping to see Pet again, but when she didn't show after a couple minutes I had to hustle to practice. Coach made you run a lap for every minute you were late, and I mean *run*. Dog it and he didn't say a word until you were finished, then he yelled at you to do it all again. Show up ten minutes late, try to slack off on the punishment laps and have to run double, and you were one suffering puppy by the time you ever kicked a ball. I've seen guys quit the team right there, just walk away and never come back. But I haven't seen many be late more than once. Coach said, "You know the rule, so deal with it. If not, go work at McDonald's or somewhere you belong, because you're not a Newfield soccer player."

I hurried into the locker room. Through the plate glass window of the coaches' office I saw Reynolds talking on the phone. He was chewing a pen, shaking his head with a sour look on his face. He glanced up and gave me this strange scowl I couldn't begin to understand. I kept moving to my locker.

At Newfield every kid gets a combination lock and a little square locker to keep your smelly gym stuff in, then when you change you use one of the tall lockers to hang your good clothes. But if you play a varsity sport you get your own tall locker back in the Team Room, at least until the next season starts and someone on that team takes your place. That rarely happens, though, because almost every good athlete at Newfield in other sports also plays either soccer or football, and they just keep the locker all year. (For instance, I'm the left fielder for the baseball team. Which leads to many pitiful jokes about my name, like Out of Left Fielder.) And if you're not a good athlete, it's kind of just understood that you don't try to kick someone out of the Team Room and take their big locker.

The Team Room was packed with soccer and football guys getting dressed for practice, so it was not exactly the most civilized spot on the planet. Usually I like the goofing around. It's fun to unwind after class. But today was different. Today someone had nailed Pet in the face, and I had a damn good idea who it was: the senior co-captain who basically hated my guts, and who had to have a good game tomorrow at fullback to keep the heat off our chump backup goalie. I wanted to confront Nick real bad, to see if he was man enough to admit what he did. But even more, I wanted to win tomorrow.

Rossi's locker was one row beyond mine, closer to the far door we used on our way to the field. So I couldn't see him, but I heard his voice loud and clear as I was twirling the combination on my lock.

"Some captain! Fielder puts a bitch in front of the team!"

I heard Billy Hagan's hyena laugh. But there was silence from the guys who dress in Rossi's row. They knew I was right there on the other side of the lockers. I lost track and spun my lock face too many times and had to start over. Kids in my row like Barry Leeds and Gil Gigliotti, both seniors, and especially freshman Richie Bonnaccorso, were tying their soccer cleats

79

and adjusting their socks just right, being so careful as they pretended not to be paying attention that it was totally obvious that they were. I had to decide, and fast. Confront Rossi, or let it slide? It's not like Jim wouldn't be back by next week. We just had to make it through the next two games.

I had to hustle or be late for practice. The other guys in my row were dressed and ready, but only Richie Bonnaccorso got out of there as soon as he could. Barry rearranged stuff in his locker. Gil did hamstring stretches inside, instead of on the field. Suddenly, as if the silence became too much, Barry broke it.

"Is it true, Robby?" he asked, real soft so his voice wouldn't carry to the other side. "Jim can't play?"

"Of course he can't, he was just in an accident."

"No, his *parents* said he can't play. For a month."

The words were like ice water down my back. "No way!"

"Way, dude. Why do you think Coach is going batshit on the phone?"

A metal locker door slammed on the other side. "A bitch!" Rossi said, making the word sound like he was spitting on the floor. "Ain't it a *bitch*?"

Gil and Barry stared at me a second then left. Their plastic cleats joined dozens of other football and soccer shoes clicking on the concrete as they headed out. I put on my own cleats, wrapped the long laces around the soles for support and tied them tight. Most all of the soccer guys were gone and I knew I was on the edge of being late. I couldn't be sure, though. The hands of the locker room clock in its protective wire cage have been stuck on 8:47 since probably before Paul was a freshman. Only the clock in the coaches' office works, though you have to go in there to see it. I picked up my lock from the bench and got ready to run, then noticed a strange flash of color.

My stomach felt like it was full of mud. A pink Post-it note stuck crookedly to the back of my shirt. TAKE PET TO THE VET, it read. I peeled it off. Who knew how long it had been there, and who had seen it without telling me. I seemed to remember people slapping me on the back in the hall, but I couldn't be sure.

"You gonna stand there reading love notes or get to practice?"

Coach Reynolds was a stride away, right arm stretched out against the last locker like a barricade. He's gone soft around the gut, where the whistle hangs down from his neck, but less soft than most men over fifty, and his bald head makes him look tough, not old. I tossed the note in the locker and quickly closed the door.

"I'm not late, am I Coach?" I snapped shut my lock.

He shook his head. "Not yet." He leaned closer. "Robby, we might have a problem."

I nearly fell over. Reynolds had never called me or any other player by first name, ever, as far as I could remember. Right away it reminded me of when Coach Malfetone tried to sweet-talk Jim and me into kicking for the football team. Some guy who's the boss and wants to stay that way, yet isn't above kissing some butt if he thinks it'll get him where he wants to go.

Do you get the idea I didn't like my coach? Well I didn't, not his personality anyway, though if winning is what you care about, he knows how. Which makes me a hypocrite, because what I did with Nick wasn't much different. I wanted to win. If getting in Nick's face meant more of a chance we'd lose, well, maybe I start puckering up my lips instead.

"Problem?" I said, trying not to give myself away. But my heart was hammering.

"Listen, Robby." He hesitated as Malfetone waddled by with his crewcut and his clipboard, in his red coach's shorts a size too small. Malfetone gave a brief, surly nod to Reynolds, but ignored me like I was a lint ball in the corner. He'll never forgive me for bailing on football.

Reynolds gripped my biceps, hard. "Come in the office a minute." His friendly voice didn't fit with how his fingers were digging into my arm, and he hung on all the way to the office.

"Park yourself," he said.

My two choices were the cracked, green vinyl desk chair or a stool by the dented Army helmet hanging on the wall, which Coach said had been used in Vietnam. He never said *he* had been in Vietnam, though that's probably what he wanted people to think. I took the stool. It was missing a cap on one leg and wobbled when I sat down.

Reynolds leaned on the edge of the metal desk and folded his arms, whistle hanging an inch below like it was growing out of them. Chewing his lip, he stared down at the grubby gray carpet. Then he raised his head and looked me in the eye.

"So, co-captain, how do we get Jim back on the team?"

I was rubbing my arm where Reynolds had held it. "Back on the team?"

Coach flashed a painful smile. "You want to win, don't you?"

"Yeah."

He leaned close. I smelled onions on his breath. "Well, how many games do you think we'll win with Francis in goal? Do you want to lose our chance at a championship because Dolan's parents want to teach him a damn *lesson*?"

I breathed through my mouth to avoid the raunchy aroma. "I guess not."

"Damn straight." Reynolds moved a welcome step back. The smile I didn't trust returned to his face. "That's why you're one of my captains."

"What about Rossi? How come you didn't talk to him?"

Coach's smile grew bigger, and twice as fake. "Everyone knows you're Jim's best buddy. His parents like you. If anyone can talk them into changing their minds, you can."

"Talk to his parents? I'm just a kid!"

Reynolds nodded like he had this wired. "It's about pride, Robby, and honor. The honor of Newfield High is on the line. We win and the whole school wins. Everybody's proud. Everybody's proud of *us*." He pointed a thick finger at my face. "Proud of *you*."

He sounded like those TV commercials for the Marine Corps. But I sure didn't feel like one of the few and the proud.

"Coach, I can't do it. It wouldn't work anyway. Jim's parents, they're not like that."

Reynolds's lips turned from a smile into a thin, grim line.

"I'm not going to *beg* you to help this team, Fielder." He almost spat the words. "Get out to practice. I don't feel like looking at you right now."

I didn't want to look at him either. I jogged out to the field. Instead of joining the team for calisthenics, though, I just kept going and started doing laps. I yelled to our assistant coach, Preston Bass, and pointed to my wrist where a watch would be. "Two thirty-six," he called back. So although I was late through no fault of my own, I ran six laps, and ran them fast. I wasn't about to show up six minutes late and try to pretend that was normal. I was a captain. I owed it to the team to set an example, no matter what.

I was into my third lap when Preston broke the team into groups to do drills. That's another one of Reynolds's rules:

no scrimmaging on Mondays, just drills and conditioning. According to him we spent all weekend playing, so Mondays we had to learn to get back down to business. I thought it was pretty idiotic. So did Preston. He was only twenty-two, right out of college and looking for a full-time teaching job, and he had been a starting halfback at UConn for three years so you know he's good. Early in the season Preston was working with us on corner kicks, practicing putting spin on the ball to arc it in or away from the goal. For awhile it was just him and me in the corner, and Reynolds was out at midfield yelling about something or other. I asked Preston about not scrimmaging on Mondays.

He pulled back the ponytail that Reynolds detested. But when Stuart Barnett, our former assistant coach, got accepted off the waiting list at the last minute and left for grad school in California, Coach had to find a replacement fast and couldn't sweat stuff he usually would—like a ponytail, for instance. As a result, we gained a great coach.

"My philosophy is we're here to have fun," Preston said. "I'll leave it at that. Now keep your head down and watch the ball. There's plenty of time to see where it goes later."

Reynolds didn't make it out to the field until my fifth lap. I wondered if he was surprised to see me running. After all, I was only late because of him. It hit me that despite how fast I was moving, Reynolds might decide to be a bastard and a half and make me run double for dogging it. I picked up my pace as he got closer, and felt fire in my lungs as I suddenly realized something.

Jim's fierce whisper at his house that he should take all the blame—it was because he already knew his parents' decision. That's why he told me not to let the team down, because telling the truth might get me the same punishment, and where would the team be without both of us? He didn't want to be the reason our team crashed and burned, and he did what a captain should do. He put the team first.

I was dragging after those laps, but I pushed myself hard all practice. It's not like I was in dog-meat shape, not with all the working out I do, and Reynolds was a slavedriver to get us in condition. He liked to say that if a team has more skill than us, we'd outwork and outhustle them and win anyway. Corny, but also sometimes true. The best team doesn't necessarily have the best players. And vice versa.

I kept worrying about how to deal with Rossi. Near the end of practice I tried to say something. Nick and I were taking penalty kicks with Tommy Francis in goal. There was tension and plenty of it, and when I thought about Pet getting nailed by that gingerbread it only got worse. But with Preston there watching us and giving advice to Tommy, it stayed beneath the surface.

Much to Nick's annoyance, I shot the penalties in games, but if I was ever on the bench when one got called (which hadn't happened yet, and I hoped never would), it would be his job. Tommy sure needed the practice. We were used to Jim's incredible anticipation, where half the time he seems to know where the ball's going before the kicker does, so Tommy's slow reactions were a letdown. Not terrible, but brutal in comparison to Jim. The key to winning tomorrow was to protect Tommy, test him as little as possible, and the key to that was Rossi at center fullback. So I'm there simmering, ticked off at Nick but holding it in for the good of the team. It helped knowing that was what Pet would want—if not for the good of the team, then just to avoid fighting.

Thinking about Nick distracted me, and my next shot flew over the crossbar. I sprinted after it. It was another one of Reynolds's rules—miss a shot and you immediately chase the ball. Running, not walking, or as Coach put it, "strolling in the goddamn park." No exceptions, from the best player to the lowliest freshman—you miss it, you chase it. Reynolds liked to say, "That'll either teach you to put the shot on net, or get your sorry asses in shape from all the running."

So my sorry ass was running after this ball when I heard a loud "Damn!" behind me. Nick's ball sailed over the goal too. I made my decision in less than a second. It was more instinct than anything, if you can call instinct wanting to win a big game tomorrow and knowing I needed Nick on my side to do it. I veered off the path to my ball and intercepted Nick's. I'd do him a favor and the ice between us might start to thaw. I trapped the ball and booted it back to him by the time he reached the end line by the goal. Without waiting for his reaction, I got my ball and dribbled back at top speed, pretending I was on a breakaway and streaking down the field to score.

When I looked up Reynolds was standing with his arms folded, barking something to Preston out of the corner of his mouth but staring straight at me.

"Fielder, what does a guy on this team do when he misses a shot?"

"He chases the ball."

Reynolds nodded. "Very good. My captain's not as dumb as he seems. Now, do you know why Rossi here has to run a lap?"

Nick glared at me like I'd just keyed his car's paint job.

"I guess because he didn't do that," I said.

Reynolds pushed it. "And why didn't he, if I might ask?"

"Because I kicked the ball back to him." I heard the disgust in my voice, and they must have too. Preston walked away without a word and began sending penalty shots in on Tommy, continuing the practice the kid badly needed and which now had been interrupted.

"So you knew the rule, and you broke it. Is this the example a captain should set?"

"I thought it was stupid for us both to be chasing balls, and Tommy standing there doing nothing."

Reynolds jerked his thumb over at Preston and Tommy, like a baseball umpire calling a runner out. "Tell you what, next time you're gonna do some thinking, give me fair warning."

"Look," I said. "It's my fault. I'll run Nick's lap."

"Oh, don't worry, you've got one of your own."

"I'll do his too."

Reynolds smiled, but happiness had nothing to do with it. "Is that any way to teach the team concept? We're in this together, and nobody's bigger than the team. Now get moving." He turned his back on us. "Are you clowns practicing to beat Pearson tomorrow," he screamed, "or just playing with yourselves? C'mon, work! Or do you need a few killers to get motivated?"

A killer is Reynolds's sadistic invention: a full-field wind sprint, end line to end line, then back again. A half-killer is to the midfield line and back, and that's torture enough. I don't care what kind of shape you're in, those things hurt. Everybody hates them. As soon as they heard the threat, all the guys started looking really busy, really fast.

"A *bitch*," Rossi said, and took off.

I ran after him. This was my chance to talk to Nick, to make things if not right, at least OK. But when I caught up to him and said "Hey," instead of answering he picked up his pace. I did the same to stay with him. "Nick," I started again, and he ran even harder. Me too. Within fifteen seconds it somehow changed from a punishment lap to a footrace. He wasn't going to let me talk, and I wasn't going to let him show me up in front of the team. I saw a white-capper zit on the back of his neck, and that became my goal as the pain built up—stay even with him no matter how much it hurt, don't fall behind and have to see that gagger of a zit again. My chest was on fire and a stitch dug in my side like an arrow, but no way I was going to give in. My right hamstring felt tight as a guitar string, but physical pain I could handle. Losing to Nick at that moment was a different story.

We crossed the starting point in a dead heat and collapsed in the grass. I was panting like a sheepdog on a hundred-degree day. Wussies, you might be thinking. Well, try running full-speed around a soccer field after a two-hour practice and see how *you* feel.

I was so wiped out it took me a while to notice the clapping and the whistles. The team was going wild. Even Reynolds was grinning, for real this time.

"*That,*" he yelled, "is what's known as *effort*! If the rest of you ladies worked as hard as your captains, this team would get somewhere. And you'd hand Pearson their candy asses on a platter! That's it for today. Get a good night's sleep and show up tomorrow ready to kick heinie! Warrior pride!"

Preston trotted over to us. "I hope you lunatics have something left for tomorrow," he said, not smiling, then joined Reynolds and followed the team in. Nick and I sat up, elbows on our bent knees, still huffing and puffing. We gave *everything* on that run. Competition or not, we had done it together. I thought of dead-tired boxers leaning on each other as they hug after the fight. Yes, I thought, it brings you closer. Rossi was hard to stomach sometimes, but he acted that way out of insecurity, which got worse after his parents' divorce last year.

"Nice run," I said. "You're one fast mother."

"Go play with your pet," he said, and beat or not he got up and began walking to the locker room. Then, as if afraid Reynolds might see and want more laps out of him, he picked it up to a slow jog.

I watched his back, too stunned to even be pissed. I sat on the grass until Rossi was in the building. My heartbeat had nearly returned to normal when I ran in myself. Then as I reached the door it started thumping again, because I realized what I was going to do.

I went straight to the coaches' office. Reynolds was pumping up soccer balls, carefully checking the pressure. You'd think that would be the manager's job, but he never let anyone else do it.

"Coach, about what you said earlier. You know, Jim's parents...."

Reynolds licked the needle and pushed it into a ball. "So?"

"I'll do it. I'll talk to them."

He tried to stay cool, but he couldn't stifle a big fat grin. "I knew I could count on you, Robby."

First name basis again. Right. I quoted one of the hokey signs on the locker room wall, those corny sayings that just also happen to be true. "There's no 'I' in 'team,' Coach," I said, and turned and walked out.

Chapter 10

I GOT A RIDE HOME, as usual, from Chris Bolger, in the green Taurus he inherited from his grandfather. It's funny, I wouldn't call Chris my friend, because we never did anything together outside of soccer practice and driving home during the season. After that I'd hardly see him. Sometimes I'd try to kick in a couple bucks for gas, but he never would take it. "It's right on my way, Studly," he'd say, though it wasn't really. He called everybody Studly. Well, not girls of course. Girls he barely talked to at all, because he was shy and had no confidence. He had bad acne, and you could tell it bothered him. Once I picked up a silver tube by his gearshift and Chris grabbed it out of my hand like I was trying to steal his wallet. It was prescription cream for his skin. His face turned redder than the blemishes.

Chris played in most games, but not much, just a couple minutes to give a starter some rest. Still, I voted for him to get the team Hustle Trophy last year, when he was a junior and I was a sophomore. He didn't win, though—I did, which actually was borderline embarrassing. I mean, it was cool to get my name in the school trophy case along with my brother. His name is in there six times (I've counted). It was like I finally belonged. But only sort of. Driving home from the awards banquet, my father said out loud what I was already thinking.

"The Hustle Trophy? Don't they usually give that to some spazzy kid who works his tail off, but isn't very good?"

So winning the Hustle Trophy was nice, but what I really wanted was to someday be chosen Most Valuable Player. Paul was MVP twice for football, and it would kill me if I didn't measure up to him. Well, not *kill* me, but you know what I mean. I actually had the weasel-thought for a second that with Jim missing games I was more likely than him to win the MVP. If I graduated from Newfield without leaving my name engraved on some stupid shiny pieces of metal in that trophy case, I'd feel like a failure. And one thing I had a chance to do that Paul never accomplished, better even than being MVP, was to win a state championship. He was All-State but didn't have enough help from his teammates to go all the way. Paul was on a team that lost in the state finals. But those are the breaks. It wasn't my fault our squad was loaded with good players. I'm not going to apologize that for once I might do something where my brother would be compared to *me*, instead of the other way around.

Riding home in Chris's grandpa-mobile, I started to worry. Why did I tell Coach I'd do it? There wasn't a prayer that Jim's parents would listen to me. I thought of the disaster that Saturday's visit had turned into. Probably I'd only get myself in trouble too, and the team would be worse off still.

"Hey Studly, you gonna get out or just hang with me all day?"

I snapped back to reality. We were parked at my house.

"Sorry. I spaced out thinking about the game tomorrow."

Chris turned down the radio, which he always played too loud. The guy will probably need a hearing aid by the time he's thirty. "Robby, what's the deal with Jim?"

"I wish I knew, Studly," I said and closed the car door behind me.

It was only a little after five, so nobody was home yet. I wolfed down an apple and some chocolate chip cookies, and went to my room still chewing. Lying on my bed, I took that half a concert ticket out of my shirt pocket, and read Pet's phone number. I knew Jim's number by heart, of course. But I dreaded making that call, to ask if I could come over and talk to his parents. First of all, odds were that his stepdad would answer and I wouldn't know what to say. Mr. Powell works at home, doing consulting and stuff with his computer. Second, I wasn't convinced that calling in advance would help anyway. They might even tell me not to come. Most likely I should just show up, ring the doorbell and hope for the best.

The only numbers I found myself pushing were the ones on that Lyle Lovett ticket. My heart was beating fast and my throat was dry and tight—I was calling up a *girl*, after all, one who despite everything I still barely knew—but at least it was a call I wanted to make.

After four rings I expected a machine to answer; after six rings I was about to hang up. You tried, I told myself. You're not a wimp. You went through with it. It's not your fault she isn't—

"Yes?" The voice was like Katherine Hepburn in those old movies on TV.

"Excuse me?" I said. "Is Pet home?"

"Petunia is playing tennis with her stepfather. Please don't make me break their concentration or he'll be cranky all night. I think he's winning for once."

Petunia? "Are they playing at the high school?" I asked.

"No, in the back yard by the pool."

In the back yard? Where did Pet live, anyway? There's only one condominium complex in Newfield with a tennis court, but it doesn't have a pool. So where...? Suddenly the truth managed to sink into my thick skull—she had a tennis court and pool at her own house!

Newfield is not a ritzy town. Sure there's a few rich people, though most of them live somewhere else and just come to their beach houses for the summer. But no one I knew personally had a pool and tennis court.

"Young man, are you still there? Is this a crank call?"

"No."

"Pity. That would be quite exciting, really. Are you Petunia's beau?"

"I'm, uh, her friend."

"Well, that's rather a first. Do you have a name?"

"Robby."

"Robby. How all-American. I'm Marguerite, Petunia's mother."

Marga*reet*, she pronounced it, not *Mar*garet. Over the phone line, I heard ice cubes tinkling in a glass.

"Pleased to meet you, Mrs. Armstrong."

"Marga*reet,* young man. I abhor pretense and snobbery."

"OK," I said doubtfully.

"Do you play tennis? You must come over for mixed doubles sometime."

"I'm not very good."

"Splendid. I'll tell Petunia that you called." And she hung up in my ear.

She sure did like to tell me what I *must* do. The more I thought about it, the more unnecessary it seemed for her to mention the pool in the first place. She probably only brought it up to brag that she *had* a pool, but oh so casually so you wouldn't realize it *was* bragging. It was actually a pretty brainless arrangement, at least if there were any hacker tennis players, because if you hit the ball over the fence it could end up in the water. But maybe no hacks were allowed. Maybe you had to pass a test or something to step onto their precious tennis court.

———◆———

Dinner was hamburgers and frozen French fries. My parents didn't mention Jim and his punishment, which told me they hadn't heard about it yet. No way they wouldn't have brought it up if they knew.

When I asked if I could borrow a car to visit Jim, I got the response I expected—another question. Two questions actually, almost identical and spoken at the same time so the words all jumbled together.

Mom: "Is your homework done?"

Dad: "Did you do your homework?"

High honor roll almost every marking period, and they still don't trust me to do my homework.

"Of course," I lied. It was only a tiny lie, because I had only a tiny bit left to do. Still, though, it was a lie, and on the drive to Jim's the word "trust" stuck in my head and wouldn't budge.

Seven-thirty when I pulled into Jim's driveway, and already dark. There was no light on in the living room so I went around back, and climbed the steps to the deck. I stood looking in the back door. Jim's parents sat talking at the kitchen table, with glasses of white wine. Mrs. Dolan said something and Mr. Powell shook his head, staring at the remains of dinner. It was a whole chicken, now hammered and mostly carcass. Jim's mother got up and I made a quick move back, but she just cleared away some dishes and put them in the sink. They couldn't see me, I knew, unless I was real close to the glass. At night you can only see *in*, where the light is.

Suddenly the porch light went on. I nearly ran, but instantly realized how bad that would look. Instead I stepped toward the door, my fist up like the light just happened to find me as I was about to knock. The door opened before I got there.

"Robby!" Mr. Powell filled the doorway. He peered at me like I was a bug under a microscope.

"What brings *you* over tonight?" Mrs. Dolan said, putting stuff away in the refrigerator. More than ever I knew this was a bad, hopeless idea. Instead of feeling sorry for Jim I was pissed at him for being such a frigging jackass and causing this mess. Get drunk and crack up your car because some ditzy cheerleader uses you—damn, what a moron.

I stood in the kitchen like a nervous geek, regretting being there, wondering how I could possibly begin. I crammed my hands in my pockets to wipe off my sweaty palms.

Mr. Powell sipped his wine. "You do have a reason for coming over tonight, don't you? Beyond checking to see if the deck needs staining."

My best friend's parents, who had always treated me great, obviously did not like me much right then. My throat felt so choked up I was afraid to talk. Only some embarrassing croaking noise might come out. Or worse, it might be tears.

I swallowed hard. "Coach Reynolds told us about Jim."

Mrs. Dolan was wiping the place mats with a dish cloth. "What about him?" she asked.

"That he's…that he can't play soccer for a while."

Mr. Powell swirled the wine in his glass. "I doubt you came over to tell us that. You probably deduced that we knew it already."

I was not used to sarcasm from these people, except for the fooling-around kind that shows you like somebody. This was the real thing, and it hurt.

"Is Jim in his room?"

"Go on up," Mrs. Dolan said. Her voice was softer now, as if she didn't enjoy the tension any more than I did. It's not like they wanted any of this. Mr. Powell was one of our biggest fans and rarely missed a game, so I knew it hurt him to tell Jim he couldn't play. It hit me that Jim's parents were mad for the same reason I was—because none of this should have happened.

"Can I say something first?"

"It's a free country," Mr. Powell said.

"I wondered if there was a chance Jim could come back to play sooner."

"Why?" Jim's parents asked at the same time.

"Because the team needs him. We're hurting without Jim in goal."

"He should have thought about that before he broke the law," Mr. Powell said. His voice was soft now too, not mean anymore. It made me confident enough to continue.

"It's not fair that Jim's punishment should hurt all of *us*."

Mrs. Dolan started, "You see, Robby—"

Mr. Powell cut her off. "*Lots* of life isn't fair. It's not fair that people are killed by other drivers, but it happens anyway. A driver can hurt many more people than himself, or even the person that he hits. What about their family, and friends? If Jim had died in that accident, you'd be hurt a lot more than you are now. Fair has nothing to do with it."

I completely saw his point, and knew he was right. But it didn't change one bit that I still wanted Jim back on the team.

"Sit down," Mr. Powell said. "You're making me nervous standing there like a guy waiting for the hangman." He stretched his leg under the table and pushed a chair toward me. I took it, but I sat on the edge.

"I've been thinking," I said. "What's punishment for? To make someone suffer for 'crimes', whether anybody benefits from it or not? What's the point? Jim's already learned his lesson."

Mrs. Dolan set the cookie jar on the table, and took off the lid as an invitation.

"If it makes you feel any better," she said, "you're not the first person to make these arguments. Half the teachers think we're being too harsh, and Mr. Lee...well, let's just say Mr. Lee really likes Newfield to win games."

Mr. Lee's the school principal, and his family has lived in this town since the Puritans stole it from the Indians. There's a bunch of Lees buried in the old cemetery I went to with Pet. Mr. Lee's at every home game, with his voice like a foghorn cheering us on.

"No," I said. "It doesn't make me feel any better."

Mr. Powell took a cookie. "Robby, did Coach Reynolds put you up to this?"

I thought about telling the truth and I thought about lying, until I realized I wasn't sure which was which. Reynolds had asked and I turned him down, then I decided on my own to do it.

"Sort of," I said.

Mr. Powell's face crinkled like he'd stepped in dog shit. "Can you believe that schmuck, Beth? The coward sends a kid over to do his dirty work."

"He didn't make me. I decided."

Mr. Powell heard me, but he didn't act like it.

"Reynolds couldn't care less what happens to Jim, just what happens to *him*, and losing Jim might mean losing some games. If Jim was a nonathlete, or for that matter a football player,

Reynolds would be screaming for the electric chair. But it's different when it means losing his goalie. Damn hypocrite."

Mr. Powell was red in the face, and sweat had beaded up on his forehead. Meanwhile, all I could think about was results. Mr. Powell was ticked off at Reynolds—would that make him go easier on Jim?

"For a man who talks about role models," Mrs. Dolan said, "Ed Reynolds is setting a pretty poor example."

"There's no getting away with anything," Mr. Powell said. "Whether the world knows or not, *you* know. Your conscience knows." He took his wife's hand. "I'm willing to cut it to two weeks, if you are."

Mrs. Dolan nodded. "I can live with it. But it's probation. One more stunt like this and he's out for the whole season. Minimum." She turned to me. "Why don't you go up and tell Jim?"

"OK," was all I said. "Thanks."

I was halfway up the stairs when I noticed Jim sitting on the top step, his fist in the air and a huge grin on his face.

"You animal," he whispered. "That was awesome. I snuck down and heard it all."

If you told us last Friday Jim was going to miss two weeks we'd have thought it was the end of the world. Now, all it seemed like was a lot better than a whole month.

"It *is* awesome," I whispered back. "I am one silver-tongued devil, ain't I?"

Chapter 11

I N THE TEAM ROOM before the Pearson game, Reynolds stomped back and forth, ranting like some crazed preacher about victory and pride and adversity. I wasn't any more nervous than usual, even without Jim. But my right shoelace was tied too tight so I knelt down to loosen it, and when I stood again I noticed Tommy Francis leaning against a locker with his eyes closed. The kid looked like he'd eaten fried earthworms for lunch, with pond scum for dessert.

Reynolds's face was a fat sweaty tomato as he worked himself up. "Run your tails off, beat 'em to the ball and don't pussy out—ever. You are Newfield Warriors!"

He clenched his big fists. "Do you men want it?" he yelled. "Are you going to take it?"

Normally we'd yell back, going animal and enjoying it. But this time was not normal. This time Tommy let out a groan and bolted into the bathroom, and we heard our backup goalie gagging then blowing chow, and the sick splash as it splattered in the toilet.

Preston the assistant coach headed toward the bathroom. "Ask her if she needs a fresh tampon," Reynolds said. He hammered his fist against a locker. I used to jump at that loud bang, but now I was used to it. After all, he did it before every game.

"OK, men, get out there and make this school proud of you!"

We heard another raunchy retch and a toilet flushing. Not exactly the ideal send-off for a big game. For the first time that season it felt like we were a bunch of individuals doing the same thing, instead of a real team doing it together.

"Listen," I told the guys as we jogged to the field. "If Tommy's dog meat, suck it up and cover for him. Play your butts off and help him out. We've got to hang in until Jim comes back."

Rossi was giving me the hairy eyeball, but in the end he wanted to win as bad as I did. "I don't trust Francis for back-passes," he said. "I'll clear the zone deep most of the time." He looked at me. "So forwards be ready. Keep your fingers out of your asses and we might get a breakaway."

"We'll be ready," I said.

"Then we'll win," Nick said. "'Cause ain't nothing getting by me."

We were running harder as we hit the field, putting together that team energy, getting psyched. The sun was strong, nearly as hot as summer, and I was sweating already. The way our field is laid out the sun glares in one goalie's eyes the whole first half, then drops behind the trees for most of the second. Wind wasn't a factor, so I hoped we'd win the coin toss and pick the goal that kept Tommy's face out of the sun. We did that with Jim too, though with him it didn't much matter. One thing you always had with Jim was confidence.

We ran a quick lap around the field, clapping loud and rhythmic like Marines at boot camp, then circled up for calisthenics. As captains, Rossi and I were the leaders in the center. The Pearson team hadn't arrived yet, so it was more to psych us up than to psych them out that Nick and I called out the repetitions, and the team shouted the numbers to ten in the deepest, baddest voices we could manage:

"ONE, two, three, FOUR!"

"TWO, two, three, FOUR!"

"THREE, two, three, FOUR!"

Mr. Mac says it's like some primitive ritual of ancient barbaric tribes, right down to the war paint—the eye black we smear on our cheek bones, supposedly to cut the glare of the sun. But everyone knows eye black doesn't do anything. We just put it on for show, to try and look savage. It's ridiculous, but so what? It's fun.

Have you ever played a sport? I'm not talking about just messing around for a couple minutes on a field or a court. I mean with something on the line, with uniforms and referees and people watching who care what happens. If so, you know that edgy feeling that grows the whole time you're warming up, how after awhile all you want is for the game to start so that feeling will stop and you can do what you came there for.

The Pearson bus showed up as we finished doing calisthenics, and they took the field trying to look as tough as we did. They even brought cheerleaders. Newfield only has cheerleaders for football and basketball. Our manager Ricky Prentice dumped out the bag of balls for warm-up drills. Ricky was a senior, a decent player himself until he got multiple sclerosis his sophomore year. He could still walk more or less OK, but running was a different story. So he became manager to still feel part of the team. Ricky never complained, but you could see in his eyes how bad he wanted to be out there with us.

He motioned me close. "Is Tommy going to come through or what?"

"Hope so," I said, dribbling away with a ball.

"Me too," I heard behind me. "But you better score a dozen goals to make sure."

Once a game starts you have to keep your head in it, stay focused on the play, but during warmups I sometimes look around and just try to take everything in. It's interesting, all that's going on, and half the time people don't even pay attention. They're into whatever thing they're doing, and hardly notice anything else. For instance, Briann Duffy got nailed in the knee with a ball over at field hockey practice, and looked like she wanted to shove her stick down Jamie Kane's throat. Pearson had some hot cheerleaders—too bad we were going to send them home sad. By the bleachers, Mr. Lee the principal was talking to one of the science teachers, Mr. Folker, who nodded without making eye contact, probably because he was checking out the Pearson cheerleaders. Mr. Powell's car pulled into the parking lot. For a second I hoped Jim was with him, though he wasn't coming back to school until tomorrow. But the passenger seat was empty.

"Yo," Rossi said. "Puke Boy to the rescue."

Tommy was halfway between us and the school, walking between Preston and Reynolds. It was the first time I'd ever seen a Newfield soccer player not running to the field. Preston had a hand on his shoulder. Tommy wore his goalie gloves, and kept punching one fist into his palm, watching the ground and shaking his head at whatever they were saying to him. Suddenly he sprinted away like he'd been stung by a hornet. He left so fast that when Reynolds went to slap him on the butt Tommy was already out of reach, and Coach swatted only air.

Nobody said anything to Tommy about losing his lunch. We pretended everything was normal, everything was cool. Tommy got in goal and we started peppering him with shots so he could warm up. After him our only goalie was Ravi Shankar, a freshman who showed promise but was too small and weak to play varsity yet. (My parents say Ravi has the same name as some musician who used to be famous, but I've never heard of him.) So Tommy was our only real chance. He was doing OK, showing decent hands and stopping more shots than not, but he sure wasn't reminding anyone of Jim. I put a last penalty kick past Tommy in the left lower corner, then went over to the bench to look up at the sky, take a few deep breaths and get focused. I had to find the back of the net today, probably more than once, or we might be in deep.

"Captains!" called out the referees, standing at midfield. Nick and I jogged over. We shook hands with the three Pearson captains, guys I'd played against before. Last year we'd split our two games with Pearson, but the funny thing was we each won on the other team's home field. So I knew they were pretty confident today, especially when their center halfback, Albert Dorsey, gave me a psych-out smile and said, "I hear Jim Dolan can't drive straight after a party."

That surprised me so much it shut me up. I'd been hoping Pearson didn't know about Jim. Not that they wouldn't find out as soon as the game started. The accident had been in the paper, just a little article but it was there, and I bet coaches around the league had made some quick phone calls. Of course you hope he's not badly hurt, but you wouldn't mind Jim missing your game with Newfield, either.

"Visitors call it in the air!" said a ref, flipping a coin.

"Heads," Dorsey said. We watched the quarter land on the grass. George Washington glinted in the sun.

"We'll defend that goal," Dorsey said, pointing to the side of the field where we'd been warming up. He grinned at me. "You can have the ball—and the sun."

Reynolds called the team over, and we huddled around him. "Remember, Rossi," he said. "You shadow Buitano. Stick to that sucker like stink on shit."

Hugo Buitano was an exchange student from Chile, the league's top scorer so far—one more goal than me. Nick scowled. "Don't worry. I'm in his jock."

Reynolds held out his hands, palms to the ground, and we all crowded around to get at least one hand onto the pile. That feeling of togetherness is pretty cool, even if do you look like a bunch of newborn puppies snuggling at their mother for a meal. "One, two, three, NEWFIELD!" we yelled, and the eleven starters ran out to their positions. I almost slapped Tommy Francis on the back, but stopped just in time. I didn't want to have to play around a puddle of puke on the field.

After those nervous but fun moments of anticipation, standing over the ball at midfield and waiting for the ref, he blew his whistle and I kicked off to Mark Lawrie. It's not like a football kickoff; I didn't drill the ball down to the other end of the field. That would only give Pearson the ball. Mark was standing right next to me, and I just pushed it ahead a foot or two. Then we started upfield.

Soon I realized I was going to be shadowed myself. But it wasn't by a defensive player—a halfback or fullback. Hugo Buitano, a center forward like me, a guy who's supposed to be thinking offense, dropped back and stayed with me as Mark passed to Richie Bonnaccorso on the left wing and we tried a quick rush down the side. And I do mean stayed with me. I'm fast, but Buitano matched me step for step. And when Richie crossed a long ball to the penalty box, Hugo got the angle on

106

me, leaped up like Michael Jordan and headed it away. The kid could play.

We knew Pearson's style, a control game of short passes that was disciplined and effective. That was how we played too, for the most part, though we took more chances and often pushed our defenders up to attack because we trusted Jim to cover any mistakes. With Tommy in goal, Coach told us to be more conservative and play by the book unless we had a sure opening.

Pearson played their deliberate style, precise passes that got the ball back to midfield but didn't have me worried too much. That's what we wanted today, to keep the ball in the midfield and the Pearson end, to take the pressure off Tommy. If we scored less than usual, no problem—shut the other team out and one goal is all you need. I stayed close to Buitano, and Nick picked him up before he reached the midfield line. Outside of that header, Hugo had not touched the ball, and that was OK by me. My second wind had settled in. I don't know if it's nerves or adrenalin or what, but the first sprint of a game always leaves me sucking air. Then it passes and I'm fine. Buitano dropped back a couple of yards, toward his own goal, and Nick stuck with him. I edged away to try and shake my shadow, and be open for a pass when we stole the ball.

Then everything went bonkers. Pearson's three halfbacks and two outside fullbacks sprinted forward, leaving only Buitano and their center fullback with the goalie on defense. We completely didn't expect such a reckless move, especially not from a no-chances team like Pearson, especially with their top scorer far away from our goal. They had used Buitano as a decoy to draw our best defender away from Tommy, and had a two-man advantage on the attack before I or our other two forwards could react and get back to help. It took a few seconds to sink in because we couldn't believe they were doing it, leaving themselves totally vulnerable to a breakaway if we stopped their rush. I saw it all as I ran down the field, trying to get there in time. Barry Leeds tried a sliding tackle and almost trickled the ball over the end line for a corner kick, which would have stopped the action and given us a chance to regroup, but instead their right winger got there for a solid cross into the penalty area. There was a scramble in front of the goal, half a dozen guys kicking at the ball. I had closed to within ten feet when Dorsey got off a weak, toe-kick shot. Tommy either was screened and didn't see it until too late, or just blew it. He dove, but the ball squirted under him. It bumped the inside of the post and trickled over the goal line.

The Pearson guys went batshit, jumping on Dorsey, pounding on his back. They were sky-high for this game, and now their huge gamble had paid off early. Tommy retrieved the ball with his head down, and kicked it upfield disgustedly.

Dorsey smirked as he passed me. "Beautiful goal like that, Dolan wouldn't have saved it either."

"Lucky for you," I said, "ugly-ass goals count the same as nice ones."

He laughed and kept going. But he had brought up what every Newfield coach, fan and player—including Tommy—was thinking right then: I bet Jim would have made that save.

"That's only one, Newfield," Mr. Powell yelled from the stands. "Come on, let's get it back!"

I jogged over to Tommy. "Shake it off, T. That was a tough shot."

"It was a horseshit shot and you know it," he said, staring at the ground.

"Is the sun bad?"

He waved me away. Well, at least he wasn't making excuses. On my way back to kick off, Rossi caught up to me.

"What's the deal with Candy Ass?"

"He'll be all right." I didn't like Nick's attitude, but at least he was talking to me. Gut it out, I told myself. One goal is nothing.

Pearson fell back into a defensive formation that was the complete opposite of the one that led to their goal. Instead of sending almost everyone ahead and leaving Buitano back on defense, they used everyone to protect the goal, with only Buitano hanging around midfield as a striker. But I was confident, for two reasons. First, sooner or later we'd break through and score. We were too good not to. Second, the more the ball was on the Pearson side of the field, the fewer chances Tommy would have to blow it. They were playing into our hands by taking the pressure off him.

What can I tell you about the rest of that first half? Pearson played tough and smart, we only had a few scoring chances and their goalie made the saves. Dorsey shadowed me. He wasn't as talented as Buitano, but he was good. He was also irritating, an obnoxious weasel who talked a ton of trash to try and put me off my game. He fouled me a couple of times, hard, and kicked me in the ankle once that I'm sure was on purpose. I almost decked him, which would have been just what he wanted because they'd have thrown me out of the game. I caught myself in time, told myself to ignore him and just play soccer. But it wasn't easy.

Sitting on the grass behind our bench at halftime, we chugged water and caught our breath. There was no sense of panic. We knew we could beat this team. Even Coach Reynolds was calm, hardly raising his voice at all.

"You played a good half, men. Keep the pressure on and wait for our break. They'll never try that crazy attack again."

"At least we shut down Buitano," Ricky Prentice said. He stood with a ball under his left arm, the way he did all game, every game. Who knows where he got that superstition. "Come on, Robby, get us a couple goals and take over the scoring lead."

"Only a couple?" I said.

Ricky pretended to think it over. "Ah, go ahead. Score as many as you want."

I liked it that we were loose. This was no time to start pressing and maybe make dumb mistakes. Even Tommy looked OK. Now that he'd played a whole half for the first time in a varsity game, I think he was beginning to feel more confident. Pearson hadn't pressured him much, and he did let a squibber get by him, but that was his only mistake so far. We couldn't have asked for more, not realistically anyway. Now it was up to our offense. And that meant me.

My right ankle where Dorsey had kicked me was throbbing pretty good, so I walked around to keep it from stiffening up. Putting ice on it might have been smarter, but I was too full of nervous energy. I had to keep moving. And I didn't want Pearson to know it hurt. Behind their bench, Dorsey was staring over at me and smiling like he knew some dangerous secret. It was a classic attempt to mess with my head, and it wasn't going to work. I couldn't wait for the second half to start so I could wipe that smile off his face.

The sun was below the trees now, and not a factor. Jim's mother had joined Mr. Powell in the bleachers, like she always did by the second half after working in her classroom for a while. She's a great teacher. Jim won't take her classes, says it would be too bizarre. Maybe so, but he's missing out.

"Come on, Robby," she yelled, "we need one!"

Speaking of bizarre—how about having the parents who kept your best player from playing, cheering in the stands? Mr. Lee was shooting them looks that said, "Newfield would be winning right now if it weren't for you two." They either didn't notice, or pretended not to.

Pearson stuck to that defensive strategy in the second half. Dorsey shadowed the hell out of me. He talked trash, took cheap kicks at my legs, grabbed my jersey every chance he got. It's an ugly way to play but unfortunately it can work if the refs don't call a tight game. I hate trash talk and rarely answer except by trying to make a good play to shut the guy up. But this time we were losing and I was getting frustrated, especially when Dorsey took me down from behind with a sliding tackle. I fell on top of him, pain shooting through the same ankle he'd kicked in the first half.

"Pussy," he whispered, and gave me the most irritating little smirk in the universe.

I needed all of my willpower not to smack his face. It must have looked like a fight was going to happen because guys from both teams rushed over. But I unclenched my fists and got up to take the free kick after the foul. The ball was six feet outside the penalty area, almost straight-on to the goal, our best chance to score so far in the game. Pearson formed a human wall ten yards away, their hands over their crotches in case I nailed the ball right into them, which I wouldn't have minded a bit doing to Dorsey. My ankle was hurting. I had to blot out the pain and think only of the shot, which I tried to put high into the right corner of the net. I kept my head down, got my body over the ball and hit it square, really drove it, curved it just enough—and it slammed off the bottom of the crossbar. It bounced back out and Richie got a foot on it, but his shot sailed just wide. Goal kick for Pearson.

"Nice gag job, Fielder," Dorsey said. "Thanks for choking."

Choking had nothing to do with it, luck did. I hit a beautiful shot that missed by two inches. Sometimes the breaks don't go your way. So you have to try to make some more.

Pearson began stalling every chance they got. After Richie's missed shot our ball kid on the sidelines threw in another ball right away for the goal kick, and their fullback fumbled it around like it was covered with grease. Then he took his time placing the ball perfectly on the goal area line, more careful than if he was about to take a penalty kick with the game at stake. He stopped to look at the ball as if he had just finished some great work of art and needed to contemplate it. After all that, and setting up to send the ball downfield, in the end he just drifted over to the side. The goalie, after adjusting the ball again to suit himself, finally took the kick.

It's not cheating, not really. It's part of the game. Anyone with a lead over a good team would likely do the same. If we had been trying to sit on a lead our ball kids would have dawdled chasing and throwing in balls kicked out of bounds, to kill a few extra seconds. Now, of course, they were rushing a ball back into play as soon as possible.

We were dominating the game. The ball rarely left the Pearson half of the field, and we kept on the pressure. But if a team drops almost all of its players back on defense, it's really hard to score on them. Provided they're any good, and Pearson was. We had our chances but couldn't quite break through. Their keeper made a couple of excellent saves, and my head ball off a corner kick hit the left post. ("Man, are you overrated," Dorsey said.) Still, it was only a matter of time before we tied the game, especially since Pearson wasn't challenging Tommy in goal. But time was running out. Our fullbacks kept edging up farther from our goal, thinking offense. We needed a score.

And my hamstring kept tightening up from that sprint yesterday with Rossi. Preston was right, I shouldn't have taken any chances with a big game today. But you can't undo the past. All I could do now was go as hard as I could and try not to limp. I didn't want to give Dorsey the satisfaction, or let him think he had an edge on me.

Rossi sent in a high ball from midfield, their center fullback misjudged the header, and suddenly I had the ball at my feet inside the penalty box. I pushed it once to my right to get off a shot, and next thing I knew I was face-down in the chewed-up grass, with pain ripping through my hamstring. Dorsey had chopped me bad with a tackle that took out my legs before he got to the ball. The whistle blew. Penalty kick for us, and the Newfield fans went wild.

I stayed on the ground for maybe fifteen seconds. Normally I jump right up after getting fouled, like in baseball if I get hit by a pitch I jog straight to first base as if nothing happened. But this time it really hurt. Finally I stood up, and gimped around a little. The worst pain had faded, but my right ankle and hamstring were still throbbing.

"You OK, Fielder?" Reynolds yelled from the sideline. "We need this one."

I waved to Coach that I was all right. Dorsey walked by with an oily smile. "Choke, pussy," he whispered. "You know you're gonna choke."

Rossi ran over. "Let me take it," he said. "Your leg's screwed up."

"I'm OK."

"You're limping like a son of a bitch."

Maybe. But I took the penalty kicks for this team. The guys counted on me to come through for them, and I was going to. Still, it was true that I wasn't a hundred percent.

What if I missed?

I chased that thought from my mind. You can't take a penalty kick with even the slightest belief that you could fail, because then you might.

Rossi shot me a look more hostile than Dorsey's. "You damn well better make this," he said.

The ref handed me the ball. It's wild how the same distance feels different, depending on your perspective. With a penalty kick, those twelve yards to the goal feel a lot longer to the kicker than to the goalie. Maybe because the pressure's all on the kicker. You're *supposed* to make a penalty shot. The goalie's a hero if he stops it.

I set up the ball on the penalty stripe and took five slow steps backward. The crowd quieted down, a sudden hush. Only my hamstring was screaming. I worried that it would affect my shot. Maybe you should let Rossi take it, I thought. But you can't bail out now. You'd look like a total wuss, afraid of being the goat.

"Come on, Robby, you can do it!"

I recognized Pet's voice immediately. I forced myself not to look up to see her, kept my focus on the ball and the Pearson goalkeeper. He had set up a step to his left from the center of the goal, trying to get me thinking, daring me to go to the wide side, to his right where there was more room. Then I saw Pet through the net. She was behind the goal, holding up both hands shoulder-high with her fingers crossed.

"You can do it!" she yelled again.

The ref blew his whistle. No way I was going to miss with Pet watching, no matter how much my leg hurt. I ran up to the ball, took the keeper's dare and shot to his right—and smacked it off the post. There was a scramble for the rebound, and the keeper managed to fall on the ball. He punted it away to mid-field. I felt like crawling into a hole. Missing that shot was even more painful than my leg.

My ankle and hamstring were killing me. I knew I should leave the game. But if I did, it would look like I was making excuses for missing the shot. Maybe I should have let Nick kick it. Was it my ego that made me try, or just confidence that I could do the job for the team? Nick might have missed anyway. But we'd never know—all we knew was that I *did* miss. "You can do it!" Pet had said, but she was wrong. No she wasn't. I could do it. I just didn't, not this time. Why did she have to yell right then? I had good confidence till I heard her. Then I started worrying about *not missing* the shot, rather than about *making* it.

Give her a break, I told myself. All she did was cheer you on. If you can't handle that, give up on playing.

Dorsey dogged me up the field. "Thanks, Fielder, you're our best player today. Who's the skanky white rat?"

I punched him right in his filthy mouth. My knuckles exploded with pain. Dorsey tackled me and we rolled on the grass, trying to damage each other. It wasn't just what he said about Pet. It's that he said it when I was frustrated and hurting and embarrassed. So I got in a fight, and became way more of all three.

Frustrated, hurting and embarrassed.

Players grabbed our arms, yanked us apart. We each got thrown out of the game. It actually wasn't a bad deal for us because I could hardly run anyway. But I felt like a punk. I had sunk to Dorsey's level. I don't punch a trash-talker to shut him up, I put the ball in the net. But this time I missed the shot, and knew my body was too messed up to get another chance that day. I let anger and frustration beat me. As I limped off the field to the bench, I saw Pet walking away with her head down. By the time I sat on the bench with ice packs on my knuckles and ankle, she was gone.

We had no choice but to push everyone forward and attack. That kept the pressure on and we got some good shots, but just couldn't manage to score. With our whole team thinking offense we were vulnerable to the long ball, and eventually Buitano got loose on a breakaway, faked Tommy out of his shorts and almost casually rolled the ball into the net for their second goal.

Somebody from Pearson screamed out, "Stick a fork in 'em and turn 'em over! They're done!"

The whistle blew. We had lost for the first time. One game without Jim, and we went down.

Reynolds gathered the team together. He opened his mouth, but nothing came out. He shook his head. "That was *total* horse-shit." He turned around and stalked back toward the school.

We stood there stunned. "Listen," Preston said, "you guys played a fine game, and I don't want to see any of you hanging your heads. Sometimes the breaks go the other way. Hit the showers and we'll see you tomorrow at practice."

Jim's mom and stepdad intercepted me on my way across the field.

"How's your leg?" she asked. "You're walking like it's really bothering you."

"It's OK." The truth was it felt awful, and my hand was worse. I should have known Dorsey would have an anvil for a head.

Mr. Powell glanced at the ice pack I was holding on my knuckles. "Hey, don't worry about that missed penalty. It was a 2–0 game. They'd have won anyway." I nodded. But we both knew Pearson's second goal happened because we were playing desperate, from behind, rather than tied at 1–1. If I had made the shot probably the worst that would have happened was a tie, and most likely we would have won.

"Good thing you're playing Northbrook on Friday," he said. "We should be able to win even without you and Jim."

"I'll be OK by then. I'm a fast healer."

Mrs. Dolan frowned. "Robby, don't you know the rule? Get ejected from a game and you automatically miss the next one."

My heart sank. I had totally forgotten about that, because never in a million years did I expect to get tossed out of a game. That only happened to dirty players, not guys like me. I walked away in a daze without saying good-bye.

In the Team Room I peeled off my sweaty, grass-stained uniform and flung it in my locker. A few guys told me not to get down about that penalty kick, but most just left me alone. Maybe they knew nothing they could say would make me feel better, maybe they were too pissed off that I had choked. Maybe both. I gimped into the showers. For the first time all year the place was quiet. No laughing, no stupid comments that somehow seem funny when you're standing there in the steam. I stayed for a long time under water as hot as I could stand it, letting it beat against my hamstring, then went into the side room where you towel off. A few seconds later I heard Nick Rossi's voice, as clear as day.

"Stupid bitch was right behind the goal." His voice rose to a creepy falsetto. "You can do it, Robby."

I didn't know who he was talking to. I didn't know if he *wanted* me to hear that, or just didn't *care* if I heard it. The couple guys drying off with me watched to see what I'd do. Should I go out and get in Nick's face? I was sick of fighting. And I hurt. I left those guys to think what they wanted, went back in and turned on my favorite shower full-blast, so hard it stung.

Something hurt even more than my body, or missing the shot. Something I didn't want to admit.

Rossi had a point.

I didn't try to or mean to, but I had let the team down. Three times. First when I left Jim at the football game, next when I blew what should have been a sure goal, last when I let that miss frustrate me and got into the fight. And each time Pet had been a part of it. A girl who said, "I don't like jocks," somehow shows up at two games—at least partly because of me—and bad things happen. Not that it was her fault. Not that she was trying to cause problems. But if Pet hadn't gone to the football game I would have been with Jim at the party, and the accident probably wouldn't have happened. If she hadn't come to our game I wouldn't have been distracted, and I probably would have made the shot. If I had made the shot, I wouldn't have got into the fight.

It wasn't her fault. I knew that. But as steaming water peppered my aching hamstring, and blood seeped out of my cut knuckles, I promised that I wouldn't let the team down again. No matter what, I would never let the team down again.

Chapter 12

THAT NIGHT I COULD HARDLY hold a fork, and when my parents saw me spazzing out trying to eat spaghetti left-handed, Dad took me to the clinic for x-rays. Would you believe two broken knuckles? And a cast? The next time you see some movie with two jerks slugging each other's face with bare fists, complete with smack-a-rama soundtrack, just laugh. Or puke if you prefer. Because it's a crock. Skulls and jaws are way more solid than fists. I found that out the hard way—bad pun intended.

My parents knew we had lost, but I didn't explain how I messed up my hand. I just said it happened during the game. I knew they'd find out eventually, but anything seemed better than telling them right then. Most of all I was embarrassed, and didn't feel like talking about it.

Then at breakfast while reading the newspaper, Dad nearly choked on his Cheerios.

"*What?*" He snapped the crease out of the sports section, folded it in half and shoved it across the table to me. "Fine publicity our son got," he called out. "Really something to be proud of."

"That's nice," we heard from her office. She was already on the phone with a client about selling a house.

He pointed to what I was supposed to see, as if I could miss it. The headline practically grabbed me by the throat.

Undefeated Newfield Blanked By Pearson

Leading Scorer Ejected

Unbelievable. High school soccer gets hardly any notice in our paper, usually only a measly line or two until the later rounds of the state tournament. But I lose my cool one time and that's news, a full article with all the gory details.

Then it got worse. No way, I thought, it can't be. Never had they printed a picture of me scoring a goal or doing something good. I couldn't remember seeing a photo of Newfield soccer, period. But there I was, face twisted like an ax murderer, being pulled away from Dorsey.

"Dad, I made a mistake. But the guy was such a creep—"

"We didn't raise you to get into fights."

"I know. It won't happen—"

"Your brother played *football*, and he never got into fights."

"Yes, and football's so much manlier. How could anyone fight in such a wimpy sport as soccer?"

"I didn't say that."

"You didn't have to. I know it's what you think."

"It must be nice to be sixteen years old so you know everything, Robby."

"Would you two please keep it down? This is an important phone call!"

Dad rolled his eyes. "All I'm saying is that it wouldn't kill you to pick up a few pointers from your brother's example. He's a darn good model to follow."

"Dad, you're absolutely right. But you're forgetting one small thing."

"What's that?"

"Paul's perfect. I'm not. Sorry about that—bad break for both of us." I looked down at the new white cast on my hand.

Neither of us spoke for a while. Then Dad cleared his throat. "Your mother and I only want what's best for you, Robby. You have too much potential to throw it away."

Potential! That word again!

I stood up from the table. "Gotta hurry or I'll miss the bus."

That was a lie. I wasn't late. But I was afraid that I'd say something I would really regret, or that would get me in trouble. And most of all I was afraid that he'd see the tears of frustration filling my eyes.

———

After first period I was walking in the swarm of bodies down the hall, wishing Jim was back at school. But last night when I'd called to tell him about the cast he said his parents were keeping him out till tomorrow. Suddenly Mr. Lee stepped out of the principal's office.

"Robby, could I have a word with you?"

I stopped. Nearby kids checked me out, wondering how much trouble I was in and whether it would be a good show to stick around for.

Mr. Lee nodded at my cast. "What's this, the walking wounded?"

At least he was smiling, not looking like he wanted to put a hurt on me. Lee's a decent principal, after all. At least he likes soccer.

His smile disappeared. "Step into my office for a minute."

I looked at my wrist as if I was wearing a watch—which I don't. "But, second period…"

"I'll give you a pass," he said and gestured with his arm, like he was inviting me into his house. Ms. Schipke, the young secretary who skydives on weekends, gave me an encouraging smile, but ancient Mrs. Barnett who's been there forever kept right on typing like a machine gun. I followed Mr. Lee past the secretaries' desks to his office in the back. The door clicked shut behind me.

In thirty seconds I had gone from the freedom of the hall to the bad news of the principal's office. It didn't have to be bad news, but come on. No kid goes to the office for fun. It's enemy territory.

Mr. Lee sat at his desk and stared at me. He's a thin, tall guy, with a chrome dome he tries to hide by combing his hair over from the side.

"Coach Malfetone is lobbying for a longer than one game suspension for you, Robby."

My stomach dropped down around my knees. "How *much* longer?"

"Three games—two at least. He says we have to set an example that fighting won't be tolerated."

"He just wants revenge because Jim and I won't play football for him!"

Mr. Lee lowered his voice. "Look, it wasn't my idea for Jim to miss any games. That was his parents' decision. And what that Dorsey punk was doing—if I was you I'd probably have socked him long before you did."

He fiddled with a paper clip. The bell rang for second period. "But I have to do something to keep the wolves off my back. So you're suspended from practice the rest of this week too. It's actually not that bad an idea, to heal those beat-up legs of yours. Fair enough?"

"I guess." Considering how worried I'd been about coming in here, this was nothing. I felt bad about missing practice, being captain and all, but not *that* bad. Reynolds was going to be a demon after that loss. And my legs *were* a mess.

"All right then." Lee stood up, rubbing his hands. "Good thing it's only Northbrook on Friday. Our jayvees could whup those turkeys. And good thing you don't need your hand to play soccer."

He opened the door. "Ms. Schipke, a late pass for Mr. Fielder, please."

Out in the empty hall, I noticed someone had slapped a FIREMEN HAVE BIG HOSES bumper sticker on the magazine drive thermometer. That wouldn't be there long.

For a principal, I thought, Mr. Lee is all right. The guy doesn't like to lose.

"Me neither," I said out loud, and took my time walking to class.

———————

The thing was, hardly anyone even noticed we had lost. What was so important to us didn't even register on the radar screen to most of the school. A loss by the soccer team didn't affect their lives. About the only reaction I got was from idiots who said junk like "Way to kick ass!" when they heard about the fight. Mouthbreathers who had never been to a soccer game, but would go in a second if there was guaranteed to be a rumble. The kind of cretins who watch NASCAR just waiting for a ten-car pileup. They never wonder how it would feel to be in the car that's flipped over and on fire.

I was thinking about that in the lunch line. I had sat with Pet again yesterday. She didn't mention anything about going to our game, which is why seeing her there had shocked me. Now, as Mrs. Bogart ladled me a plate of rice casserole, my throat tightened like when I ask a girl out on a date.

But this was the exact opposite.

You have to understand something. I want to go to college on a soccer scholarship. *Really* want to. My brother got a full athletic scholarship, and I'd feel like a loser if I don't. Yeah, I know, I wouldn't really be a loser, barely anyone gets a full scholarship, etc., etc., blah blah blah. My brain realizes that. But I'm talking about feeling, not thinking. And I'd feel like a loser.

I came out holding my tray mostly in my left hand, because I didn't trust the hand in the cast. I went straight over and sat at the soccer table. Pet's head was down, reading *Catch-22*. I took a seat with my back to her, only two chairs away from Nick Rossi. My first loyalty had to be to the team. I was the captain, and I had let them down yesterday. I wanted to win and I wanted to get a scholarship. Fighting wasn't going to cause either of those things to happen, and certainly sitting on the bench wasn't. Our great season was starting to come unglued, and I had to do what I could to put it back together.

It's not like Pet was my girlfriend. I was under no obligation to eat lunch with her every day.

Then why did I feel like such a scuzzball?

"This lice casserole is skunk shit." Rossi stuck in his fork and it stood up like a straw in a milkshake. He scooped out a lump of gooey red rice.

"Time for the mighty catapult," he said, looking for a target. He glanced at Pet a couple of times. He was practically admitting he was the one who nailed her with the gingerbread on Monday, and was daring me to do something about it.

"Nick, man," I told him, "don't do it. If you get caught they might suspend *you* for a game."

"That would totally suck," Barry Leeds said. He stared at the spoonful of green Jell-O he'd been thinking about heaving, and shoved it in his mouth instead.

"We need you bad," I said. "I don't care if it *is* only Northbrook."

Rossi smirked. "Sure you're not just protecting someone?"

I'd have loved to grind a plate of rice casserole in his face, with lime Jell-O for dessert.

"Yeah," I said. "I'm trying to protect *us*. The team."

Other guys joined in.

"He's right, Nick."

"Don't chance it."

"Chill out, dude."

Rossi enjoyed the attention. After making us wait, he splatted the rice casserole back on his plate.

"Good point. We'd be screwed without me." He looked me in the eye. "And somebody's got to take penalty kicks."

"Shut up, OK Nick?" Barry said.

Rossi got up to bus his tray. "Don't worry, I won't let anything distract *me*."

The bell rang. I joined the kids busing trays at the last minute, and figured I might catch up to Pet on the way to Mr. McLaughlin's class. I didn't know what I would say, but I had to say something. I remembered sitting in a tree with her, hugging her with a weathered gravestone between us, kissing her. It was good, real good—it was great. But soccer was too important not to come first. She had to understand that.

But I knew she wouldn't.

Her white hair was far ahead down the hall. I couldn't get to her without plowing through half the people in the school, so I told myself I'd talk to her after class and tried to relax. Then I passed the girls' room as she was coming out and we almost collided. Unlike that first time in Mr. McLaughlin's class, though, this one was pure chance. And this time we didn't touch.

"Hi," I said.

"Hello." Her voice was so cold it had frost on it. She walked faster.

"Hey, come on. I'm sorry I didn't sit with you at lunch."

She reached her locker and spun the combination. She wouldn't look at me.

"I mean it, Pet. I'm sorry."

"Don't be sorry for what you are. You can't help it."

"And what's that?"

She finally looked me in the eye. "A boy, like all the rest of them."

That was an even bigger stereotype than her comment about not liking jocks. But I remembered what had happened to her, and that photo. I couldn't help it. Team or no, I couldn't stand to see her like this. "I'll sit with you tomorrow," I told her.

"Thanks for the charity, Saint Robby. But maybe I don't want to sit with you." She snapped shut her lock and strode away.

I stood there stunned. Part of me wanted to tell her off, but the other part felt sorry for her. I had to run to Mr. McLaughlin's class.

I took a desk as far away from Pet as possible. Mr. Mac raised his eyebrows, because yesterday we had come in together from the lunchroom, and sat side by side. But fortunately he didn't say anything. Nothing about us, that is. He faced the class from the front of the room.

"OK, folks. Character quiz."

Everyone paid attention. We all liked Mr. Mac's character quizzes, when he asked us to imagine some sort of dilemma or tough situation. That's what writers do, he says. Give characters problems and choices and see how they react.

"Remember, a character quiz isn't to show whether you're a good person or not, it's to get you used to putting conflicts in your stories. OK—what would you rather do, play the best match of your life but lose the Wimbledon final to someone who played even better, or choke, play a terrible match, but win because your opponent was even worse? If tennis doesn't work for you, pick any event you want."

Skunk Darwin jumped right in. "Just win, baby. That's all that matters."

Mr. Mac made a steeple with his index fingers, and rested his chin on it. "So if you don't win, you wasted your time?"

"I guess." Skunk scratched the roll of fat on the back of his neck, looking like he'd rather be out on the field crashing into somebody than sitting here trying to think.

Mr. Mac pressed him.

If that was true, the Newfield High football team sure was wasting its time. Pet was looking down at her notebook with her chin in her hand, doodling or writing, I couldn't tell. Like I couldn't tell whether I was more mad at her or sorry for her.

"I don't know." Skunk shrugged his shoulders. "I just play."

Pet spoke without looking up. "If you win, the trophy says Champion, not how you won."

"But are all wins the same?" Mr. Mac sat on his desk. "Aren't some wins more satisfying than others? Being the underdog, for example."

Pet finally looked up. "No doubt. But the worst win is better than the best loss." She lowered her eyes again. "Ask Robby, he'll tell you."

Mr. Mac glanced at me, then nodded slowly the way he does when he's debating a couple of possibilities. "You might be wondering why we're talking about sports in creative writing class. Because we're not really talking about sports! We're talking about winning and losing. It's the biggest conflict there is in life—and therefore in fiction. All conflicts come down to some variation of winning or losing, success or failure."

I raised my hand. "So reading is like being a fan watching a game?"

"Bingo," Mr. McLaughlin said. "Rooting for certain characters to win, or at least play well, and hoping other ones don't."

Pet frowned. "But it's not the same. You can close a book whenever you want."

"Hey," I said, "you can leave a game, too."

"What about the players?" Skunk asked. "Don't we count for anything?"

Mary Ann Nunn rolled her eyes. "I don't know how to break this to you, Skunk, but the characters in a story aren't real. That's what fiction means."

Most of the class laughed. Skunk pouted. "They seem real while you're reading," he said.

"Yes!" Mr. Mac said. "That's the magic of stories—they *do* seem real while we're reading. But back to the character quiz. Would you cheat to win?"

He held up one hand like a traffic cop. "Don't answer. I'm not interested in how honest you are, I want you to see how complex winning and losing can be. Maybe you cheat and win the game, but lose self-respect. Or win the match but lose a friend, or your reputation. Maybe you lose the game but win something more important to you, like the respect of others. Or the knowledge that you're strong enough to lose with class."

"If the final score of a game is the most important part of a story, it's not much of a story. That score only matters insofar as it affects characters—why they *care* what the score is. One character would rather sit on the bench for a state championship team than be the star on a team in last place. One roots for the teammate who took her place in the lineup, while another wants her to mess up even if it costs her team the game. Fiction is about winning and losing, and what those words *mean* to the characters."

Mr. Mac always says that without conflict there's no story, because unless there's trouble readers won't care. But I'd never thought of it in terms of winning and losing. Jim wanted to win a ditzy cheerleader and instead lost part of a soccer season—and almost his life. I wanted to win a college scholarship. What would I be willing to lose to get one?

Pet was still doodling in her notebook, as if she wasn't paying attention. But I knew better. I thought of her going to that drinking party as a freshman, trying to win popularity and be cool, and instead losing big-time.

"I want you to write a scene," Mr. Mac said, "or a whole story if you get inspired, concerning conflict and a sporting event."

"That's not fair," Candace Martin whined. "I *hate* sports."

Mr. Mac pretended to play a violin. "Oh, the injustice of it all. Seriously, folks, no problem if you hate sports. Because whatever you do, don't make winning or losing the game the main conflict. Imagine that you're the wife of the guy who tried to kill himself because the pro football team he liked fumbled five times in one game. Or that you're tall and the basketball coach tries to get you to go out for the team, but you're not interested. Or you want to watch a movie on TV and your girlfriend wants to watch a game."

Candace blushed. "Mr. McLaughlin, I don't have a girlfriend."

The class burst out laughing. Mr. Mac sighed and shook his head. "It was just an example, Candace."

Even Pet smiled a little. But when she noticed me looking at her, the smile faded. Fine, I thought, be that way. I only punched that butthead because of you. I only missed that penalty kick because you—

"One last thought before you start," Mr. Mac said. "In 1968, huge underdog Harvard made a miracle comeback to tie Yale on the last play of the game. The next day's headline, in huge letters? 'HARVARD BEATS YALE, 29–29.'"

Skunk looked lost. "What do you mean, beat? It was a tie."

Mr. Mac bit his lip not to smile. "Skunk, let's just say that in life the winner isn't always the one with the best score. OK, citizens, dip those quills in the ink and start scribbling."

I opened to a blank page and stared at it. Most of us did the same. Mr. Mac clapped his hands three times.

"Don't think—write. Spew words and don't let your brain get in the way. No matter if it reeks to high heaven, you can fix it later. That's why God invented revision."

My hand was awkward with the cast but I started cruising anyway, blasting down words about a kid with a hurting leg who lets his teammate take a penalty kick and the guy hits the post and their undefeated team is in big trouble but the kid with the bad leg steals the ball from this jerk with a big mouth and ties the game with a spectacular goal in the final seconds. Pitiful, I know, but that's what came out when I didn't let my brain cut in and tell me it *was* pitiful. The thing is, the kid is only semi-happy. It's just a tie, not a win, and this girl he likes who had cheered for him to make the penalty before he let the other kid kick it had left and didn't see his goal. He looks for her as the whistle blows to end the game, expecting a hug maybe or some sort of semicelebration for at least avoiding the loss. But she's gone. And the team's still undefeated, but their winning streak is history. And the kid keeps thinking if only he'd taken that penalty kick, bad leg or no bad leg.... Maybe what he thought was smart and best for the team was really just wimping out.

Their coach, a really cool guy only one year out of college, calls the team together around him. The sun is going down over the trees. "Well, guys, they say a tie is like kissing your sister. I only have brothers so I wouldn't know, but I imagine it's better than not getting kissed at all. Good comeback, and we'll get 'em next time."

Meanwhile, the kid is remembering kissing that girl who left and missed the best part of the game. He's thinking of how she blew it, leaving like that, or maybe he blew it, anyway someone did or maybe they both....

The bell rang. Notebooks snapped shut and bodies surged for the door. I tried to finish the sentence then gave up. I didn't know where it was going anyway. I glanced over at Pet. She was already gone like the girl in my story. I started to rip the page out of my notebook, then saw Mr. McLaughlin watching me and left it in.

"Robby," he said as I passed by his desk, "is something wrong? Outside of discovering that boxing is a tough way to make a living?"

"I guess I don't like losing." I held up my cast, already covered with kids' signatures and drawings.

His fingers tapped on the desk. He didn't smile. "Well, keep in mind that there's more than one way to win."

"I guess," I said, not feeling like much of a winner, and hustled on sore legs to make my next class.

Chapter 13

I WAS USED TO BEING AT PRACTICE every day after school, not catching the bus and finding myself alone in an empty house at 3:00. I tried writing out back on the deck, but the Indian summer weather was so perfect I couldn't stay focused. I wondered how hard Reynolds was working the team right then, how loud he was yelling. Missing that part was no great loss.

I kept thinking of Pet. I unzipped my backpack and dug out that half a Lyle Lovett concert ticket. I looked at her phone number a long time, debating whether I should call.

In the end I wimped out. I shoved the ticket back in the pouch, jumbled up with keys and pens, Tic-Tacs and an emergency Snickers anti-starvation bar that I have to replace about twice a week. Not that I called it wimping out. I was mad at her, after all, with her snotty attitude and bogus remark about boys.

I did make a call, finally—to Jim. "Nice photo in the paper," he said. "You looked like you wanted to rip the dirtbag's head off."

"Yeah, well I did."

"I'd probably have helped you. Stupid as hell, though."

"It gets worse." I told him about my hand, and what happened in Mr. Lee's office.

"At least you can play with a cast. Not like me in goal."

"Reynolds would just put you at another position."

"Yeah, great. And we're stuck with Tommy 'The Human Swiss Cheese' in goal."

Neither of us said anything.

"Listen," Jim said after awhile. "How bad was Francis?"

"It's not that he was so bad, it's just that you're an animal. The goals weren't really his fault."

"No shit. They were *my* fault."

"Come on, it's nobody's fault."

"Robby, cut the crap."

I couldn't BS Jim. He knew he had let the team down, just like I knew I had. Words couldn't change that. Which is why he was smart enough not to try and cheer me up over that missed penalty kick.

"OK," I told him. "We both screwed up royally. But that's history. Now we gotta come back."

"I'm just pissed off I did something so frigging dumb."

"I'm pissed too. We're all pissed."

"At least you only miss one game. And you're not grounded till the end of the season. And your car's not in the junkyard."

It might as well be, I thought. I don't have a car. But what I said was, "See you in school tomorrow."

I did see him. But not Pet. She had to be sick—or faking sick, though I doubted that was her style. Either way, I figured it was a good excuse to go to her house. I wanted to see her and put things straight, one way or the other. Back to friends, or whatever we were, or just say "sayonara means goodbye" and forget about it. I wasn't psyched for the second option, but it was better than dancing around like dipshits the way we seemed to be.

After school I stopped by the principal's office to ask for Pet's address. "I'm not supposed to give that out," Ms. Schipke said with a flirty smile. "You're not a stalker are you?"

"No way. I'm a good boy." I was trying to be cool and flirt back, but I could feel myself blushing.

"I'll trust you, Robby. Just this once." She wrote the address on a yellow Post-It. "Don't let me down like so many heartless men in the past."

"Thank you." Before my cheeks could turn any redder I stuffed the Post-It in my shirt pocket. I walked out to the student parking lot, and for the first time got into the driver's seat of Chris Bolger's Taurus.

Chris is such a good guy I didn't even have to bribe him to lend me his car. "No prob, Studly," was all he had said when I asked him after American History that morning. "Just be back by the end of practice." Chris didn't even ask why I needed his wheels, just reached in his jeans and handed me his beat-up New York Yankees key chain. I'm a Red Sox fan, but I kept my mouth shut.

The buses had all left, and the student lot was pretty cleared out too. I smoothed out the wrinkled Post-It and read Ms. Schipke's neat printing: 171 Keller's Pond Road. Must be down by the dam, I figured, somewhere over there. I stuck the note on the dashboard and pulled away.

I drove north along Keller's Pond Road, checking numbers on mailboxes. Many of them were gleaming new, not yet crunched by snowplows or beaten up by New England weather. Other lots were only half-cleared of trees, with a bulldozer working or maybe a foundation recently poured, and the framing just getting started. There'd be mailboxes in front of those places soon enough. I know it was an illusion, the way we used to pretend the woods were wild when I was little. But now you can't even pretend.

171 had to be on the left side of the road, with the other odd numbers. I passed 159 near where Jim's grandfather got hit by a car and died ten years ago. They never caught who did it. It was the first time anyone I knew ever died, and I remember being jealous of Jim because it was so exciting.

I found 171 painted in white on a big wooden mailbox shaped like a barn, sitting on top of a stone and cement base. I'd never seen that mailbox before. It was new. The freshly paved driveway cut through a high stone wall and curved away into the trees. Somewhere back there was the Keller mansion, invisible from the road, where the richest family in Newfield used to live. They made a fortune buying cheap land during the Depression, and from a factory just up the road that used water power from the dam at Keller's Pond. Eventually the factory was a sad, boarded-up skeleton, vandalized to the max and ready to collapse. They tore it down when old man Keller died and left the lake to the state.

I sat there idling in front of the open wrought iron gate. Come on, Fielder, don't wimp out. I started crawling up the driveway. Tree branches arched overhead, forming a shady canopy, and as I moved deeper into the property I was glad I wouldn't have to rake all those leaves in a few weeks, or clear that long driveway when the snow fell.

When I got out of the woods I saw a two-story white Colonial house, and a red barn that looked like the mailbox out front. Maybe it was the mystery because it was hidden, or the stories about the fabulous Keller wealth, but I was surprised not to find a palace back there. Still, it was really nice, and with land that ran down to the pond the place must have cost a fortune.

I parked in front of the barn, that was now a three-car garage. A gleaming black Mercedes was in there, and Pet's BMW, so I figured she was home. I was nervous, but had to do this sooner or later. Better now in private than at school with who knows who listening.

A path made of slabs of slate the size of children's gravestones in the old cemetery led to the front porch, whose steps were two big rectangles of granite. I pushed the bell but didn't hear anything. I tried the knocker. It was an antique horseshoe, though maybe it had been there so long the horseshoe was new when they put it up. Maybe Newfield still had a blacksmith then. I gave it three good raps, each harder than the one before. Nothing. If Pet was in bed, she was either really sick or a very sound sleeper.

She might be out back, I thought. Even if she wasn't, it gave me an excuse to snoop around, after years of wondering what the mystery mansion might be like. If someone stopped me I could seem legitimate, not like a trespasser.

I went around the corner of the house, walking softly on my aching legs. I saw that Pet's mother—I mean, ahem, Marguerite—hadn't lied to me on the phone. There was the bright green tennis court, surrounded by a high fence, and about ten yards closer to the lake, an inground pool with a diving board.

A woman was sitting on a deck chair at the pool. She had her back to me. I saw a pink sun visor and dark brown hair past her shoulders, so it wasn't Pet. She sipped from a tall glass, then set it on the low table next to her and went back to reading something in her lap. A boom box was playing classical music.

I could have backtracked to Chris's car and bolted, but I needed to see this through. I started across the lush grass—not full of weeds and dandelions like our lawn—as she added another piece of paper to the stack on the table, and kept reading. Not wanting to startle her, I coughed and said "Excuse me" while still twenty feet away.

She held up her hand without turning around. I stopped. Then another page joined the pile on the table, and the hand gestured me forward. I was almost to her when she finally looked up from her reading, and turned her head. She had on wraparound sunglasses and not much else, just a green bikini.

"Can I help you, young man?" She looked great, like she spent a lot of time doing aerobics or something.

"I was, um, is Petunia feeling better?"

She smiled, and slipped off her sunglasses. "I assume she feels fine, unless her favorites are losing at tennis. She's in New York with her stepfather at the U.S. Open. I'd be there, too, but I have a deadline to proof these galleys."

Galleys? Aren't those the boats Roman slaves used to row?

My face must have looked clueless because she held up the printed pages. "Galley proofs. To check for errors before the book is published. It's my new novel, *Harvest Moonshine*."

She put the papers on the table. "Would you care for a drink?"

"No, thanks."

"Are you sure? How about a gin and lemonade without the gin?"

"No, really."

"Do you have a name?"

"Robby Fielder."

"Ah, the lad who phoned the other day."

"If Pet's not here, I guess I'd better go."

Marguerite punched a speed-dial number on her phone, and held up a finger. "Darling, could you snag Petunia? A beau is here to check on her welfare." She handed me the phone.

"Mother," I heard, "I'm mortified! His phone rang in the middle of a point!"

"Hi," I said. "I didn't do it."

"Who is this?"

"Me." I guess that was my ego talking. I wanted her to recognize my voice.

"Robby? Where are you?"

"At your house."

"Where?"

"I came over because I thought you were sick."

"Where at the house?"

"Out by the pool."

"Oh, no. What does she have on?"

What was I supposed to say with her mom right there?

"She'd better be wearing something!"

Marguerite picked up her glass and walked slowly past. She pointed to the drink, then me. I shook my head, politely I hoped, and she kept on going.

Pet sighed. "What's wrong with that woman?"

"Nothing that I can see," I said.

Pet hung up.

I stood there like a geek statue. Why didn't I keep my mouth shut? If your mouth is closed, you can't put your foot in it.

I turned over the top page of the galleys.

Her knees quivered at Elrod's virile touch, and Morgana gave a silent prayer of thanks that she was already on her back or she might have collapsed. The chauffeur's brawny passion was a carnal crescendo, driving her into ecstasy's penthouse suite. Sweet penthouse, she gasped in her brain. Oh sweet, sweet! Drive me there, lover, and don't worry about speeding. I'll pay the tickets!

Wow. That sure seemed to fit into what my mom calls trash (yet reads sometimes), and Mr. Mac calls junk food literature. "Scarf it down occasionally if you must," he told us, "but a steady diet of it is definitely not healthy."

I put the page back on the stack and set the phone on top. There was only a tiny breeze, but I didn't want the blame if a sudden gust blew the papers into the pool. I had no reason to be there anymore, now that I knew Pet was in New York. Should I take off before her mom came back? It's not like she even knew me. But what if I ever went out with Pet again? You don't want a girl's parents ticked off at you, or thinking you're a slouch. Especially when your best friend's parents already feel that way. Or your own.

"Yoo hoo," I heard from an upstairs window. "I saw you peeking at *Moonshine*! That's fine—feel free to enjoy. Wait a moment, I have a surprise for you."

No way I could leave now. She came out carrying a tray with two tall glasses on it and, I saw when she got closer, a hardcover book in a bright-colored jacket.

"*Tiens*," she said. "Be refreshed in body and spirit."

I reached for a glass.

"No, the other one. The gin and lemonade without the gin."

I took the drink and glanced at the book. *Passion's Trigger*, by Marguerite St. John. There was a guy on the cover dressed in buckskin like Daniel Boone, carrying a woman who must have been wearing the ultimate Miracle Bra under her pioneer dress. Her arms were wrapped around his neck, yanking him down for a lip-lock. They definitely looked ready to find a motel, or at least a secluded spot in the wilderness.

"The novel is yours," she said. "With compliments from the author. I know I'm considered a 'woman's writer,' but *Passion's Trigger* has a powerful, sensitive male lead that I'm sure you'll relate to."

Both my glass and I were sweating. Marguerite sipped her drink. "Read the inscription," she said.

I opened the book, and saw these words in beautiful, flowing handwriting:

> *To Ronnie,*
> *May your voyage be full of romance.*
> *Affectionately,*
> *Marguerite St. John*

"Thanks," I said. No sense telling her she got my name wrong. I chugged my lemonade. "I'd better get going. I'm glad Pet's not sick."

"Take a dip with me first."

I held up my cast. "I can't. Thanks anyway."

"Next time, then." She crooked a finger at me. "Come here, young gentleman caller, and I'll sign your cast."

As she wrote with my arm practically pegged against her chest, I finished my drink and tried to fake being nonchalant.

"*Voila!*"

"OK," I said, edging away. "Give Pet my best when she gets in."

"I'm afraid that I'll be in dreamland by then. They're staying for the evening matches."

"Pet's breaking curfew on a school night?" I said, pretending to be shocked.

Marguerite grimaced. "My daughter does not have a curfew. Petunia is free to make her own decisions."

Then why did she tell me she had a curfew, standing at her car across from the cemetery? I wasn't about to say anything to her mother, but I sure asked myself that question as I limped away.

So this is Pet's life, I thought, rolling down the driveway. To escape a McDonald's ad, I hit a different preset on Chris's radio, and suddenly was listening to a story about a family of refugees trying to make a new life in America. As I drove back to school I heard how their home was destroyed in a war. They had seen their uncle dragged out and shot in cold blood. Only one of them, a kid my age, spoke any English, and I could barely understand him. They were grateful to be here, but didn't know what to do, or what was going to happen next.

"You're listening to *All Things Considered*," the announcer said, "on National Public Radio."

All things considered. I thought about that, sitting in Chris's Taurus in the parking lot, waiting for practice to end. I was going through a crappy time, but at least my house wasn't getting blown up. No one was shooting at me or my family.

I looked down at my cast. *Happy healing, Ronnie. A basket of kisses, Lady Writer.*

It's a crazy world when some people are killing each other, while other ones read galleys by the pool and give books to kids they just met, whose names they got wrong. All things considered, it really is.

Chapter 14

FRIDAY WAS GAME DAY, and I woke up psyched to play—then remembered that I was suspended. I couldn't even travel to Northbrook on the team bus. Pet looked tired in school after getting home late from New York. Since her last move had been to hang up on me, all day I pretended she didn't exist, and she did the same to me. And we both did a decent job of it.

I was glad the game was away. Jim and I weren't allowed to be with the team, and being stuck on the sidelines with a bunch of people from Newfield sounded miserable. I could just imagine the comments.

From adults:

"Why aren't you out there, Robby? Are you hurt?"

"I hope this teaches you a lesson. Fighting doesn't solve anything."

From kids:

"Dude, what did that Pearson asswipe say to get you so pissed off?"

"Good thing it's only Northbrook, or you'd have really fucked up."

Actually, I felt the same way about that last remark. We were lucky to play the weakest team in the league while we were shorthanded. "Northbrook's a punching bag," I'd heard Coach tell Preston. "They couldn't beat the Little Sisters of the Poor." They hadn't won a game, and rarely managed to even score. I'd return next week, aching legs healed, and we could get back on track.

Chris came through again, and lent me his Taurus. He was psyched because in blowout games like Northbrook he usually played quite a bit. Even coaches like Reynolds, who want to bury the other team, feel obligated to give the scrubs some decent minutes in a slaughter. Plus it makes sense to give your bench guys and jayvees some experience.

Jim rode with me to Northbrook. At first his parents weren't going to let him watch the games he couldn't play in, then changed their minds. Maybe they figured it would be harder for him to be there and see what he was missing. Whatever the reason, Jim wouldn't be driving. His parents had taken away his license for the rest of the year. He'd get it back on January 1—at the earliest. "If you've earned it," they said. Jim wasn't happy about that, but he was in no position to argue.

Northbrook is a few towns inland from Newfield, on the Connecticut River. It's a pretty place, rural mostly (though some of the last farms have been subdivided into McMansions), so we call the Northbrook kids hicks and hucklebucks and shit-stompers. Not to their faces, but it's fun to laugh at in the locker room or on the bus. It's totally ridiculous, but that's the way people are. Like we're so sophisticated in Newfield.

"I wonder what those hucklebucks call us," I said in the car.

Jim snorted. "How about 'winners'?"

"Conquerors."

"Gods of the soccer field!"

"What the hey, I'm a generous guy. I'll settle for 'sir.'"

"Sir, yes sir!" Jim said. "Now drop and give me twenty, you mangy shitkicker!"

"But sir, I'm the valedictorian and president of the Still Have Half My Teeth Club!"

"I don't care if you're the only member of the Haven't Done My Sister Yet Club—drop and give me twenty!"

We were laughing like lunatics when I pulled into the high school. Then we saw the Newfield bus, and the players in their uniforms, and it wasn't funny anymore. Both teams were huddled up for the coaches' final instructions, guys leaning forward to stack their hands together. In a few seconds someone in each group would bark "One, two, three," the players would yell "Newfield!" or "Northbrook!", and the piles of hands would break apart. Everyone's heart would be racing, ready to go. And Jim and I would be going nowhere.

"This sucks," Jim said.

"Just one more week," I said. "Only two more games."

"Three. This sucker hasn't even started."

"It has now."

Soccer is a game of control, and you can see right away whether a team has it or not. Northbrook didn't. Crisp passes, clean traps of the ball, cutting to open spaces and anticipating your teammate's next move—that's how a good team plays. Bad teams boot the ball as far as they can away from their goal and run after it. There's no control, you're just hoping to get lucky. If you have no skills, though, it's as good a plan as any. If the ball's moving toward the other end of the field, at least for a little while it's not shooting past your goalie.

"Man," Jim said, "these shitkickers yank the crank."

As we sat on the hood of Chris's car, another bummer hit me. Northbrook was so bad I'd probably have scored twice in this game, maybe more before Reynolds put in the scrubs. Missing a chance to feast on these turkeys could cost me the league scoring title. Buitano would be hard enough to beat, and he had hung a hat trick—three goals—on Northbrook earlier in the season. More important, my stats would be less impressive for college coaches deciding on scholarships.

And missing those goals would make it harder for me to be voted Most Valuable Player of our team.

I glanced at Jim. He would never stoop to such punk BS. But I guess you never can be totally sure of anything. After all, would he ever think that I'd sink to that level? But he doesn't have an older brother's name on half the hardware in the school's trophy case, either. If he doesn't win awards, so what? If I don't win awards, I'm the loser of the family.

"Yes!" I jumped up to celebrate our first goal, then leaned back against the car. Somehow their goalie had smothered the ball an inch before it rolled over the line.

"Merry Christmas," Jim said.

"Talk about lucky. That dipstick should buy Lotto tickets."

As the game wore on, it reminded me of fishing in a pond so full of bass you expect to catch one on every cast. But somehow, despite strike after strike, you can't manage to hook a single fish. We were dominating the game, always on the verge of scoring, but hadn't actually put one in the net. Four shots slammed off a post or the crossbar; a couple of others barely missed. Two head balls off of corner kicks sailed just high over the goal, and Northbrook's keeper made some spectacular saves. Then a goal was disallowed because Richie Bonnaccorso was offside.

"Come on, ref," Jim yelled. "Open your eyes, you tool."

Seconds later the whistle blew. First half over. No score. Reynolds stalked the sideline, looking ready to explode. The only good thing about not playing was escaping his halftime tirade. He was screaming and flailing his arms, while Preston stood there calmly rolling a ball under his foot. Preston seemed to be staring our way so I gave a little wave. He nodded. Reynolds noticed and glared over at us, then went back to reaming out the team.

"What the hey," I said, "we dominated those losers. This half we bury 'em."

Jim touched the bandage on his head. "Dude, tell me it wouldn't be cool to have Preston for a coach."

"We do."

"Head coach, you freak."

"You mean a guy that we actually like and respect, instead of a Nazi?"

"Exactly."

Reynolds chucked down his clipboard and stomped on it.

"I think it would be friggin' great," I said. "Know a good hit man who works cheap?"

"He's gonna give himself a damn heart attack, but with our luck not until we graduate."

The teams switched ends for the second half. Now Tommy Francis was in the goal closest to us. "Yo, T.F., you're kickin' butt! Keep it up!" Jim yelled. Tommy turned around for a quick grin at us, then put his game face back on. He had hardly been tested in the first half, just a couple of easy saves off long desperation shots.

"Think he blew chow before the game?" I asked.

"Buckets," Jim said.

For me, watching a game is more nerve-wracking than playing one. When you're playing you're in control of your own destiny, but a spectator is helpless. You can cheer and boo, but those are just reactions to what happens; you can't *make* anything happen. Which is why ten minutes into the second half, I started to feel the pressure and sweat a little. I rolled up my sleeves to cool off.

"Who the hell's Lady Writer?"

Last night I'd thought about covering Marguerite's words with a magic marker, then decided a big black patch on my cast would be worse. It would be a blatant sign I was hiding something, and sure to get people wondering—beginning with my parents. As long as my sleeves were down, you couldn't see much anyway.

"Confess, sucker. Sarah Malinowski? Jessica Funk?"

I shook my head.

"Don't be a tubesteak." He grimaced as the Northbrook keeper handled Rossi's mediocre free kick from outside the penalty area. Suddenly he grinned and wagged his finger at me.

"It's that new girl!"

"Maybe." Hey, no lie—Marguerite was a "new girl."

"You animal! You played the right card ditching my ass at the football game."

"Better than taking off with Lisa Birnbaum, that's for sure."

Jim stared at me. "For my best friend, you sure are a dickhead."

"No way!" I jumped off the hood of the car. Northbrook had just taken a corner kick, their first of the game, and when Tommy leaped up and stretched to catch the ball it slipped through his hands. In the scramble, some Northbrook guy toe-kicked it into the net.

"Are you shitting me?" Jim said. "That's only their third goal this season."

"We should have had three in the first half."

It took the Northbrook fans a couple seconds to start cheering, as if they couldn't believe what just happened, but once it sunk in they went berserk. Not one person there, either on the field or watching, would have bet an hour ago that Northbrook would be leading us in the second half. Even without Jim and me. It just could not happen.

If you think Pearson stalled against us last game, you should have seen the slow-down Northbrook went into. And while Pearson was good and these guys were hacks, Northbrook had the advantage of playing at home, with their own ballboys. Every chance they got they pounded the ball far out of bounds, where the ballboys would dawdle after it to kill as much time as possible. Every throw-in or free kick they practically had a committee meeting to decide who was going to take it, then changed their minds twice after that. Minutes kept ticking by, we kept getting great scoring chances, but somehow nothing quite worked.

Meanwhile, their keeper was playing the game of his life. Even Jim would have had trouble with some of the miracle saves this kid was making. Once he was so out of position he was facing into his own net, yet Rossi's hard shot caromed off his spine right to one of their fullbacks, who creamed it out of bounds. And the ballboy casually strolled after it.

You could see confidence building in Northbrook's eyes and body language. They were starting to believe that maybe, somehow, they were not only not going to get destroyed but actually might win. The momentum was shifting, our guys getting tight—not scared, but tight and frustrated—as the game wore on. When you're the better team and totally dominating a game, yet still are losing, you start to wonder if you're ever going to catch a break.

The Northbrook crowd screamed like banshees, smelling blood. "How much time's left, do you think?" I asked.

Jim's eyes didn't leave the action on the field. "Enough," he said. "There's got to be."

Suddenly Barry Leeds got taken down in the penalty box. The whistle blew and I pumped my fist in the air.

"Penalty kick!"

Jim whistled. "Whoa, that tackle looked clean to me."

A sliding tackle is perfectly legal if the defender first hits the ball. "Who cares?" I said. "It's about time something went our way."

Jim shrugged his shoulders. He hates to lose, but he can't stand it when a game gets decided by an official's call, rather than by the players. "Swallow the damn whistle," he likes to say. "Just let 'em play."

The Northbrook fans were going batshit, booing and whistling at the ref.

"How much did Newfield pay you?"

"Open your eyes, you bum!"

"Nice call, Stevie Wonder!"

Rossi set the ball on the penalty stripe. He was going to score, of course he was—but I had thought the same thing before my kick against Pearson. Rossi stepped backward away from the ball.

"Nail it," Jim said. "Back of the net."

"Piece of cake," I said. But a snake-thought slithered into my mind: part of me hoped Nick would miss. I didn't want us to lose, no way, but seeing Rossi succeed after I'd let down the team would hurt. Especially after his scummy remarks about me and Pet. Maybe Reynolds would even have him kick all the penalties from now on. I felt like selfish slime, even though I mostly wanted Rossi to score. I looked at Jim, glad as hell that he couldn't hear me thinking.

Nick ran to the ball, kept his head down and buried a rocket in the lower left corner. The keeper dove but had no chance. "Yes!" Jim and I yelled. Our guys mobbed Rossi, then headed back upfield. It was only a matter of time before we put this team away.

But we ran out of time. We dominated the rest of regulation and the two five-minute overtimes, and Gil Gigliotti was sprinting to take yet another corner kick when the final whistle blew. Northbrook fans stormed the field like they'd just won the World Cup.

"Are you shitting me?" Jim said. "A tie with *Northbrook*?"

"We played OK," I said. "We just had no luck."

"We had a ton of luck—all of it crappy."

I thought back to Mr. Mac's class and that newspaper headline he told us about: "HARVARD BEATS YALE, 29–29." Zero doubt about it, Northbrook felt like winners right now. And we felt like losers..

"Let's get out of here," Jim said.

"Maybe we should say something to the guys before they reach the bus."

"Like what? All we'll do is get in range for Reynolds to ream us out new assholes."

"But we're the captains."

Jim spat in the grass. "Some captains. Royal screwups costing the team games. There's no way we'd have lost today if we were out there. That goal Francis let in was pitiful."

"We didn't lose," I said. "We tied."

"Don't kid yourself. We didn't get beat, but we lost."

So we left. We didn't feel much like captains right then, and after that disaster it would have been too easy for somebody to say the wrong thing. Better to give it a rest over the weekend, then come back strong on Monday. Me anyway. Jim still had another week of exile.

There was a traffic jam on the way out, Northbrook car horns tooting in celebration. I remembered sitting up in that tree with Pet, cars inching along below us, horns blaring. And the sick words those punks had yelled at her.

"What are you doing this weekend?" Jim asked.

"I don't know. Maybe go to the football game. I could use some comic relief."

Jim stared glumly out the window. "Dude, after that damn game we got no right to talk about comic relief."

Chapter 15

I TOOK JIM HOME and went back to school. Things were falling apart. The team a mess because of me and Jim, my relationship with Pet curdling like milk in the sun. It was nothing compared to getting your house blown up in a war, but it still hurt.

I was sitting on the hood of the Taurus when Chris came out. His face was all red, as if his acne had flared up. Reynolds must have really reamed them out. It was even worse for Chris because he'd expected decent playing time against Northbrook, but in the close game he didn't even get in.

"Thanks for the wheels." I flipped him the keys. He spazzed and dropped them.

"No problem, Studly," he said as he picked them up off the cracked blacktop. But his voice was full of this strange quiver that scared me.

"You OK?" I asked.

Chris coughed to clear his throat, and glanced around. "Robby, it was *bad*."

"I know, I can't believe it. I mean, Northbrook—"

"Not Northbrook! You don't...." Chris shoved the key in the door, which was already unlocked. "Come on, let's get out of here."

He talked all the way to my house, definitely shook up. Reynolds had come unglued on the bus, he said, stomping up and down the aisle and screaming about how embarrassed they should be for losing to such a piss-poor bunch of pansies. Nobody dared correct him and say we had tied, not lost, first because they didn't want their head bitten off, and second because it did feel like a loss. They had all seen Reynolds go ballistic before, and you just had to suck it up and deal with it. But then he called a special Saturday practice tomorrow, 8:00 A.M.

"In case any of you girls expected different, be ready to leave your breakfast on the field. It's going to be a Purgatory Practice."

Chris said the bus stayed dead quiet, though I know every guy was groaning inside. Coach's Purgatory Practices were sadistic sprint and calisthenic sessions that were about punishment, not soccer. Purgatory is where Catholics believe souls go to suffer and work off their sins before being allowed into heaven. It's just one step this side of hell, Reynolds likes to say.

"Any of you ladies got a problem with that? Monthly period is no excuse."

Harlan snorted at that, Chris said. Harlan is often our driver to away games. He's around fifty, with a belly so huge it slops over the steering wheel. He puts a cloth between his gut and the wheel to keep it from leaving a stripe of grime on his shirt.

Reynolds wheeled around. "You think that's funny, Tammy?"

At first, Tommy didn't realize Coach was talking to him. But the next thing he knew, Reynolds was leaning over him in the front row, right behind Harlan.

"Are you deaf, Tammy? I said, do you think it's a joke that we lost?"

"No, Coach."

"Then why are you laughing, sweetheart? Are you up here giggling about your new makeup, or nail polish? Maybe met a cute boy at the mall?"

Harlan spoke up. "I'm the one who laughed, Coach."

Reynolds ignored him. "That's good. Because I'd hate to see Tammy laughing after she let in another easy goal. I couldn't understand that. You'd think she'd be weeping her eyes out."

Chris was across the aisle. He said Tommy fought real hard, but he already felt so bad about giving up that goal that he couldn't help it. His shoulders started shaking and a few tears spilled over.

"Aww," Reynolds said. "Poor little girl." He stood up and announced to the team, "Miss Francis has taught us an important lesson today. You can't grow balls, especially brass ones. You either got 'em or you don't."

Preston stood up. "Come on, Coach," he said, putting a hand on Reynolds's shoulder. "Cool off. Don't say something you'll regret later."

Reynolds slapped Preston's hand away. "The only thing I regret is hiring a girl for a coach. Why don't you get a haircut, missy?"

Chris made a full stop at a sign he usually rolled through. "The guy snapped, Robby," he said. "I mean, you just don't do that."

I wiped my palms on my pants. Two seconds later they were sweaty again. "What did Preston do?"

"Get this. Preston sits back down and says, 'Coach, are you sure we're allowed to have Purgatory Practices? You know, with the separation of church and state and all. I wouldn't want us to have to forfeit any games.'"

"On this team, bucko," Reynolds growled, "I'm Pope *and* President."

Chris pulled into our driveway. "Thanks a lot for the ride," I said. "And for lending us your wheels."

Chris waved it off. He hesitated, then asked, "You going to practice tomorrow?"

"You kidding me, Studly? I wouldn't miss it for the world."

———

"You lost to Northbrook?" Dad asked at the dinner table. "They're the worst team in the league." Dad doesn't know squat about soccer, but he does check the standings in the paper.

Mom wiped sauce from her mouth with a paper napkin. She had sold a house that afternoon, so was in a bubbly mood. She brought home a pizza from Caddy's Shack, and she and Dad were celebrating with a bottle of champagne. "Anyone can have one good day," she said.

"Or one bad one," I added.

Dad refilled their glasses. "How did Reynolds take the loss?"

Should I tell them about Reynolds bullying Tommy? I didn't like the guy, but I'm no squealer either. I couldn't decide which plan was better for the team. I had called Jim as soon as I got home to talk it over, but no one answered.

"Chris told me he called practice for tomorrow. Eight A.M."

"He has quite a nerve to spring that at the last minute."

"Mom, I'm a captain. I'm scum if I don't show."

The phone rang. I answered.

"Robby? This is Rachel Bonnaccorso. Is your mom there?"

Mrs. Bonnaccorso's voice sounded tense and urgent, not friendly as usual. As I passed the phone over I had a feeling I knew why. Then Mom's face pinched together as she listened, and that feeling turned to no doubt about it. Besides, Mrs. Bonnaccorso has one of those voices where you have to hold the receiver a foot from your ear not to go deaf, so I heard most of what she was saying.

Her kid Richie had told about Reynolds ripping Tommy on the bus.

Dad seemed concerned, until he was sure it was Mom's "surprised angry" look, not "surprised worried." "Surprised angry" is only a problem if you're the target.

"So, Robby," he asked, "are you going to the football game?"

"I guess. Could I use one of the cars?"

"Why not just go with me? I think Mom's coming too."

Although I tried to be cool, my face must have showed what I thought of that idea.

Dad chuckled. "Just kidding. Hey, I'm only offering you a lift. God forbid, you don't have to actually sit with your old man."

"It's not that. But I'll probably go out after, and I'll need the car to get home." I decided to take a chance. "I could maybe get a ride from somebody, but my curfew's earlier than most of the kids."

"Most?"

"Well, some."

"Robby, your curfew is very reasonable. Your brother—"

"No child should be punished for losing a game! Has the man lost all sense of proportion?" It had been a while since I'd seen Mom that ticked off.

"What's going on?" Dad whispered, but Mom held up a hand and kept her attention on the line. A few seconds later she said, "OK, fine, I'll see you at the game," and handed me the phone. I decided it was the wrong time to comment about not being her servant, so I just went over and hung it up.

When Mom filled Dad in she didn't use Reynolds's language. Maybe that's because I was there, or because Mrs. Bonnaccorso hadn't told her. Maybe Richie hadn't told Mrs. Bonnaccorso. Whatever, when Dad heard the story he didn't exactly have the reaction Mom expected.

He broke out laughing.

"Come on," he said. "That's funny. Tammy!"

"Ed Reynolds demeaned that boy in front of the whole team! He's a bully and a coward!"

"My high school football coach said worse than that and we didn't go crying to mommy."

"Tommy didn't say a thing. It was some of the other kids who told their parents."

Dad got serious. "Well, that's different. I can't stand a whiner, but if it was other guys who complained it must have been pretty bad."

"Thank you for your sensitivity, Mr. Neanderthal."

Whoa. My mom doesn't usually talk like that. My parents rarely even argue, at least with me around.

Dad hesitated, then reached over and filled both their glasses. "But honey," he wheedled in his Homer Simpson voice, "I thought you liked my hairy back."

That line was so pitiful Mom had to laugh. So I laughed too, out of relief, and also because hey, it was actually pretty funny. In a totally lame way, of course

"All right," Mom said. "If you guys were as good at not getting into trouble as you are at BS'ing your way out of it, I'd be a happy woman."

"Come on, Mom," I said. "How could you be any happier?"

She took a big sip. "I'll answer that after I talk to people at the game about a certain pig-headed coach."

"Who shall remain nameless?" Dad asked.

"Oh, no, he has a name. I just can't say it with my son sitting here."

"Be my guest," I said.

"I am not a guest in my own home, smarty-pants." She got up and tossed her paper plate in the garbage. Then she picked up the bottle and checked the wine level before putting it in the refrigerator. "I don't want to see this any emptier when we get back."

"But it'll be flat by then," I said.

"Then I'll pour it down the sink."

"But I know how you hate to waste things."

"Not as much as I'd hate for *you* to get wasted."

"Don't worry, I don't even like champagne. It tastes like sour ginger ale."

"How do you know?"

"Paul gave me some of his at cousin Denise's wedding." I knew that would cut off the questioning. Nothing Paul did was ever wrong. Little did my parents know about the times I'd covered for him when he was in high school, protected his butt. Like the Saturday morning I found the cookie jar in the refrigerator. Paul's team had won a big football game, and he must have celebrated hard and come home with the munchies. You'd have to be pretty hammered to put a cookie jar in the fridge. Mom was making coffee and I snuck the jar out while her back was turned. She caught me with it, but just said, "Have a decent breakfast, Robby, not cookies. Don't you want to grow up big and strong like your brother?"

Dad drank the rest of his glass and stood up. "This is a fascinating discussion but if we don't get moving we'll miss the opening kickoff. Brenda, let's take your car. I told Robby he could use mine."

I listened to Mom's car back out and the garage door close. There was one piece of pizza left in the greasy box, but suddenly I didn't feel hungry. Pet was on my mind. I pushed up my shirt sleeve and checked my cast. Marguerite's words were gone, covered by a black splotch of magic marker. People could think whatever they wanted, but the evidence was buried. And the person I most wanted to hide it from was the daughter of the woman who wrote them.

Before I could talk myself out of it, I dialed Pet's number. No, I didn't need to check that Lyle Lovett ticket. I had the number memorized.

I was getting more nervous by the second. After four rings I expected a machine, and almost hung up. On the fifth ring a gruff voice said, "It's your nickel, so start talkin'."

It must be her stepdad.

"Hello, may I speak to Pet, please?"

"Betty," he called. "Is Petty still here?"

Petty? Betty? Maybe Betty was the maid.

"Sorry, amigo," he said. "No can do. Apparently she's off gallivanting somewhere."

I heard Marguerite in the background. "Gallivanting? I *hope* she's gallivanting. It's about time that child *did* more gallivanting."

"Do you know where she might have gone?"

"Wherever the four winds blow, is my guess."

"How sweet," Marguerite said. "A reference to one of my titles."

"Who should I say called?" That's kind of a pushy way of putting it, different from just asking if you'd like to leave a message.

"Robby. A, uh, friend from school.".

"Do you have a last name?"

"Fielder." I was beginning to not much like this guy. In the background I heard Marguerite, her voice rising: "Is that Ronnie, Petunia's gentleman caller?"

"Betty, will you stop interrupting? I can't hardly hear myself think." Then to me, "OK, she'll get the message. Hasta la vista, baby."

The line clicked in my ear. I held the phone for a few seconds, sort of stunned. Say what you want about my parents, at least they would never embarrass me by quoting Arnold Schwarzenegger to a kid on the phone.

I felt about as decisive as that last piece of congealing pizza. A dozen thoughts swirled around in my head, and I couldn't seem to pin anything down. Pet, Reynolds, Preston, Tommy, Mr. Mac, Jim, Chris, Rossi, losing to Northbrook (I mean tying—man, Reynolds was right, it *did* feel like a loss), Purgatory Practice.... What should I try to do about any of it? What *could* I do?

Another thought sneaked in—maybe I should nab one of Dad's beers. He always has a case of bar bottles, the kind you have to use an opener on. He only keeps two or three beers in the refrigerator. Whenever he drinks one he replaces it and drops the empty back in the thick cardboard case, which most of the time is a mixture of full and empty bottles. Unless the case was just bought or almost gone, if I switched a warm beer for a cold one and put away the dead soldier, he'd never notice.

I'd done it before, and more than once. Paul taught me the technique one year when he was home from college for Christmas. "But not when I'm around or your ass is grass," he warned me. "If we both take one Dad might catch on."

So I'd always been smart about it, and tonight would be no different. Unless the case was around half gone, where a beer wouldn't be missed, no way I was touching it. I jumped down the steps two at a time to the unfinished half of the basement. I opened the case and counted thirteen bottles with their caps still on. Good thing I'm not superstitious, I thought, and pulled out a Schlitz. Upstairs I traded it for a cold one in the fridge, and pried off the cap with the opener on a corkscrew.

I put the cap in my pocket, so Mom or Dad wouldn't see it in the garbage. I took a long swallow. The beer tasted bitter, and lingered on my tongue after it was gone. I wasn't psyched to go to the football game alone. It's not like Jim was my only friend, but I was so used to starting out the night with him that the whole situation still felt really weird. I took another hit off the bottle, looking at the mess of graffiti on my cast.

What did Marguerite say to her husband on the phone, about a reference to one of her titles? Beer in hand I ran up the stairs to my room. I got on my knees, reached under the bed and dragged out the metal safe Dad gave me on my twelfth birthday. The top was dusty. I spun the dial left-right-left, lifted the heavy lid and took out *Passion's Trigger*.

I checked out the "Also by Marguerite St. John" page at the front of the book, and there it was: *Where the Four Winds Blow*. *Blow* was the second of four books listed, after *Outback Maiden* and before *Love in the Palm of Her Hand* and *Angel on Tiptoes*. I knew from seeing the galleys that *Harvest Moonshine* wasn't far behind. Marguerite may not have been the world's best writer, but you had to give her credit for churning them out. Six books! That's a ton of writing.

The phone rang.

I took my time going to my parents' room. If you answer right away it can look pitiful, like you've got nothing to do but wait by the phone. So though I wanted to rush, I sauntered in, sat on the bed, put my beer on the nightstand, and didn't pick up till the fourth ring.

"Hello," I said, keeping my voice low and even, trying to sound at least halfway cool. You never know who it might be.

"Hello?" I said again. Stupid. If there's a pause, odds are 99% it's a telemarketer—what Mr. Mac calls "human horseflies."

"Good evening. Mr. Fiedler?"

"Close but no cigar."

"I'm sorry. Is *Mrs.* Fiedler home?"

"No Fiedlers under this roof. If you're going to bother people at least get their name right." I hung up, but softly. Part of me felt sorry for him for having such a crappy job.

And part of me felt sorry for myself. Maybe that's why I zoned out, and cracked my knee on the edge of the nightstand when I stood up. The beer bottle toppled over and dropped before I could grab it.

I ran to the kitchen, grabbed some paper towels and a bottle of Formula 409. I sopped up the beer, sprayed on cleaner and rubbed hard. The beer smell disappeared, but the 409 aroma was not exactly subtle. Neither was the damp spot on the carpet. Unless that sucker dried fast I was going to have some explaining to do.

Why did that human horsefly have to call? Why was I so lame as to take a beer into my parents' room, then knock it over? What really bugged me was all this hassle over what should be nothing. So what if I had a beer? I didn't hurt anyone. I remembered Anders, the Dutch exchange student from last year (who to our disappointment was terrible at soccer), saying in class that kids drink a little beer all the time in Holland, and in France and Italy they drink wine.

"But teenage drinking is *dangerous*," said Sue Gilmore, who is a babe and a half but an incredible goody-goody.

Anders smiled politely. "It is bad to get drunken, yes. But I am finding it amazing that Americans think for me to drink a beer is dangerous, yet have stores where people buy guns. This I do not understand."

I opened both windows in my parents' room to air out the smell. It was out of my hands now. I was either going to get in trouble or I wasn't, and worrying wouldn't make one bit of difference. I drank the last swallow of beer, rinsed out the bottle and returned it to the case, then gargled with some chemical-green mouthwash Mom bought at a warehouse store. Who knows, that stuff might have worked better on the rug than the 409. I backed down the driveway, not sure where I was going.

Chapter 16

I WAS CRUISING IN THE HONDA, just floating along till I hit a junction then flipping a coin in my head for which way to go. I even shut off the radio, and not because Dad had it on a lame classic rock station. I just wanted quiet. After awhile I realized that instead of the football game I was heading in the opposite direction, down toward the Boston Post Road and the beach.

I poked along the Post Road past Taylor Rental and toward the marinas and the center of town. A horn blasted as I crossed the little bridge over the Menagonquit River, and I expected to see the grille of a tractor trailer filling my rearview mirror. But it was a boat with an air horn signaling it was about to pass under the bridge. Only one boat can fit at a time, and has to shoot through fast to buck the current. Without the warning horn there could be a nasty collision.

I came up on Jake's Place, this seafood joint with tables on the river that's always jammed in summer, and it was packed tonight too. Summer people were probably around for the weekend, maybe to start shutting down their beach cottages for the winter. I crossed the Singing Bridge over the river. The bridge doesn't really sing, it just makes a whiny hum as cars drive across. People like it as a local landmark, but it's actually a crummy bridge that makes your car sway back and forth as the metal grids grab your tires, and is so low only a dinghy can pass under it at high tide. They should tear it down and build a decent one.

I took a right toward the town beach, through a neighborhood of cottages with a stop sign about every ten feet. At the last one, facing Surfside Avenue with Long Island Sound spread out in front of me, I suddenly remembered something I once heard my grandfather tell my mom. A friend of his had just died of a heart attack the week after he retired.

"Honey child," Grandpa said, shaking his head as he poured a big glass of whiskey, "if you want to make God laugh, make plans."

I hope God's not laughing at me, I thought, because right now I sure don't have any plan. I drove along Surfside, cottages to my right, beaches and wooden jetties to my left. Surfside is kind of a joke of a name, because there's no real surf in the Sound except during a storm, or at least high winds. Long Island blocks off the Atlantic Ocean, which makes for a boring beach—no waves, no surfing. But it's a sweet place to take a girl at night.

With memories of Sarah Malinowski in my head I pulled into the town beach lot and parked at the north end, closest to the boarded-up snack bar. There were a couple of cars at the opposite side, as far away from the entrance as possible. Probably kids smoking dope down on the rocks. That's the last thing I needed. I walked in the other direction, past the pay phone and book with ripped-out pages where I'd wasted my time looking for Pet's number.

The dunes behind the beach only run for a couple hundred yards before flattening out, and soon the sidewalks start above the narrow private beaches. Private because access is restricted, not because you have any privacy. The dunes are the place to go for that. Sarah and I would pick a spot and climb barefoot up the soft sand, then spread out a towel on the coarse, sparse grass behind the crest. Sometimes we'd find a McDonald's bag or other litter, or worse, a pile of dog crap. But usually there was nothing but inviting empty spaces.

You might expect it to be make-out city with a bunch of kids there, but it's not. Hey, *I* never thought of it. It was Sarah's idea. I don't kid myself that I'm the first guy she went there with. She even parked her dad's Oldsmobile at a friend's house down the street, to not worry about getting locked in when the cops close the lot. Obviously she'd had practice. But now it was over, and Sarah had dumped me for slime-king Billy Hagan.

I sat on the dune watching the sunset. Already days were shorter than when I came here with Sarah. We'd lie on our stomachs on her huge Old Navy towel, shoulders and hips touching, and peek over the dune to see the night happen: moon shimmering on the water, lights of Long Island glittering in the distance. And then we'd turn to each other. Summer suddenly seemed like a long time ago.

A sleek sailboat glided silent as a dream in the fading light, and disappeared behind Gull Island. I wished I had someone to share the sight with. I wondered what Pet was doing, and felt a little jealous that it was without me. Then some idiot drove by blasting rap with the bass cranked so loud it sounded like the speakers were shredded. The noise rumbled into the parking lot and stayed there, thumping and vibrating. Brutal. I stood up, swiped the sand off my butt and headed toward the noise in order to escape from it.

The music was erupting from Jason Jones's rancid old Ford. The doors were flung open and the hatchback lifted so the distorted noise would carry even farther. Jones and Mike Krozel were leaning on the fender trying to look bad, white-boy wannabes at the beach with their ultra-baggy jeans and gangsta rap, pretending they were boyz in da 'hood.

"Yo, homey," Jones said, arms crossed over his scrawny chest and big medallion on a chain that I bet he takes off and hides before going into his house.

I waved and got out of there. On the Post Road I veered toward the Civil War–era cemetery, turned right past the fire-house and basketball courts and parked behind one of the Little League dugouts. I opened my door and sat sideways to shake sand out of my sneakers.

Between the dugout and the grandstand I could see part of the infield. I remembered our Little League All Star team. With Jim and me alternating pitching and playing shortstop we won three games in the World Series tournament before we got bounced out. Jim's dad flew in from Utah to watch the games. He sat with Jim's mom and stepdad, which seemed pretty strange, but that's nothing—he was also best man at their wedding, the same way Mr. Powell was at his. They just traded places, groom and best man, with the same woman. Bizarre. But Jim is cool with it. He says that as long as you like them both, two dads are better than one.

I walked over and leaned against the dugout, one shoulder on the cinder-block wall. Man, that field seemed small, the outfield fences ridiculously close. Only four years ago but a different world and a different person already.

I went out to the mound and toed the rubber like I was about to pitch. The empty stands stared at me. Four years ago I'd peer in at batters and see those bleachers packed to the gills, crowds as big as at our soccer games now. And after every game the people go home, their shouts and applause vanish into the air and nothing is left. Nothing but ghosts. Or memories. I turned around to where Jim would be at short, telling me to blow it by this guy, he can't touch my stuff. It was weird how real it all felt as I nodded back at nobody, at Jim's vacant position.

Out beyond the center field fence I saw somebody on the soccer field. Was it a guy on our team? If so, what an animal to work out after the game with Purgatory Practice in the morning. I headed closer, keeping my mouth shut till I knew for sure.

The odd thing was this guy didn't seem to be doing anything, just standing there. Maybe he wasn't such an animal after all. I was in front of the ad on the fence for the Talit Insurance Agency before he finally moved. And I saw three things.

He had no ball.

He was standing at the penalty kick stripe, staring at the goal.

He wasn't a he.

From this distance, even in the dark I could see Pet's white hair. Peeking over the fence I looked out to the tennis courts across the road. Parked under the lights was a silver BMW, top down. So this is what Pet does when her mother thinks she's out partying. I almost called out to her, but I caught myself. First I had to watch this. What was she doing, at night, on the field of a sport she didn't even play?

With both hands Pet placed an imaginary ball on the penalty kick line. Keeping her eyes on the ball that wasn't there she took a few slow steps back and to the side, more like a football field-goal kicker than a soccer player. She seemed totally focused, as if it were an important game with people depending on her.

As if she were pretending to be me at the Pearson game.

She ran up and kicked the air. Pretty good form, head down and weight forward, though too much side of the foot. You can only punch a ball like that, not really drive it like you can with the top of your foot. Still, I bet it would have been a goal, the keeper sprawled on the grass after a useless dive.

But Pet's shoulders sagged. She scuffed the ground with her tennis shoe. Obviously she thought she had missed. Dorsey would be spitting trash talk at her by now. Her teammates would be saying no problem, get the next one, but she knew they only half meant it. She had let them down. Watching her brought me back to my own blown penalty kick—not alone in the darkness but for real, in a big game with people watching and teammates expecting you to come through for them. The cast on my wrist felt heavy and wrong. I wanted to tear it off.

"Sir, what are you doing there?"

Nobody calls me sir unless I'm in trouble.

"No quick moves. Keep your hands where I can see them."

I stood up and turned around. A powerful flashlight shone in my face. I flinched and squinted.

"Is there a problem?" I said, trying to keep that laser beam out of my eyes.

"Officer Perkins, Newfield Constabulary. We had a report of a stalker on the ball field."

Oh no, not *that* guy. Rich Perkins was the biggest hard-ass of the local cops. At least that's what I'd heard; I don't exactly spend quality time dealing with the police. Once Perkins nailed Jim's stepdad for speeding—35 in a 30 mph zone—and Mr. Powell stomped into the house with smoke pouring out of his ears.

"Richie Perkins was a punk in high school and he's still a punk! The little weasel used to deal pot, and now he arrests people for it. Goddamn hypocrite!"

Perkins took a step closer and the light got brighter. My eyes felt like they were cooking in a microwave.

"What are you doing out here, sir?"

"I haven't done anything wrong."

"I asked a simple question, sir, I'd appreciate a simple answer. Or is it a complicated thing, why you're crouching behind a fence in the dark?"

"I didn't want to bother anybody."

"And just who would you be bothering out here?"

Nobody, I thought. That's exactly the point. So why are you hassling me?

"I think that might be me, officer."

Perkins swung the light over and trapped Pet in the beam, ten feet away on the other side of the fence. She was wearing a navy blue sweatshirt with QUESTION AUTHORITY in big white letters.

Pet raised her forearm to shield her eyes. "Officer, if I go blind from that flashlight can I sue the police department?"

To my surprise he lowered it a little, out of her face. "Is this the man who's been stalking you?"

Pet came over to the fence and leaned over to stare at me. I felt like a bug on a microscope slide. She shook her head.

"No. That guy was ugly as sin. This one's halfway handsome, at least in the dark."

"You're sure?" Perkins asked, sounding disappointed that he wasn't going to slap the handcuffs on me.

Pet hesitated, and I realized she was enjoying jerking both of our chains.

"Positive," she said.

Perkins snorted. He aimed the light at me. "Keep your nose clean, pal. I'm going to remember you." He strode away across the outfield, flashlight beam bouncing back toward the parking lot and the police station in the town hall.

Where's Pet?

There are two gaps in the fence, where it overlaps but doesn't connect, so outfielders can retrieve home run balls. I squeezed through the one in right center (I fit through easy when I was twelve). Amazing. Is that girl fast or what? Pet's BMW was still by the tennis courts but she was nowhere in sight. Could she possibly already be in the car?

"Who? Who?" The last time I'd heard that noise it was coming from a leafy maple tree, and I got ticked off thinking I was being made a fool of. This time it was coming from an outfield fence and I just smiled.

"Who? Who?" Pet stood up from where she'd been crouching behind the ad for Pack & Mazzaccarro Used Cars.

"You, you," I said. We faced each other from thirty feet away. It was too dark to know who took the first step, but we started walking closer, and didn't stop till you could have barely fit a gravestone between us.

"How did it feel," I said, "taking that penalty kick?"

"I can't believe you saw that."

"Don't be embarrassed, I was impressed. You've got good form. But...maybe I'm crazy, but I swear you acted like you missed."

"I did miss. I had to."

Had to? "In my fantasies I *never* miss," I said.

Somehow, both of her hands were in mine. Or was it the other way around?

"But this wasn't a fantasy. I wanted to understand how you felt. You know, when you—when the ball didn't go in."

"Go ahead and say it. When I blew that penalty kick."

Pet squeezed my hands. "The most pressure I ever faced in sports was when I was a freshman, second serve, down match point in the league championship."

"What happened?"

"I got the serve in but she won the point." Pet put her head on my shoulder. "A penalty kick is like having to serve an ace, with anything else a failure. I tried to imagine being you in that game. The ball, the goalie, the people screaming—"

"Including a person standing right behind the goal?"

Pet's head left my shoulder. Her hands stayed in mine briefly because I gripped them tight. But then she pulled them away too. "You're blaming *me* because you missed that kick?"

"I'm not blaming you. I wouldn't have said that in a thousand years if I'd thought it through. Really. I'm sorry."

"I'm not talking about *thinking*. You said it because that's how you *feel*. And that's what I need to know." She started walking away, fast, then stopped and turned back toward me. "To hell with thinking. And you know what, Robby? To hell with you, too. I could have been playing tennis or writing a story for Mr. Mac, something I wanted to do. Instead I went to that damn game to support you. Well thanks a lot, and you're welcome." She spun around and took off again.

It was the first time I'd ever heard her swear, and having it aimed at me was about as much fun as chewing tinfoil.

"I'm a bucking brasspole," I called out to her. "But I only punched that creep because of you."

Pet stopped short. "What?"

I walked toward her and I didn't say a word until we were face to face again.

"I hate fighting," she said. "I hate it."

"I know you do. But he said something so scummy I just snapped. Something about you."

"I bet you wouldn't have smacked him if you'd made that goal. No matter what he said."

Maybe she was right and maybe she wasn't. But she made me wonder. Pet being so smart made life harder at the same time it made life better.

I decided to challenge her right back. "Why did you say you have a curfew when you don't?"

Slow seconds went by. I stared at her in the dark. She stared at the ground. Finally she looked me in the eye.

"Can I show you instead?" Pet leaned forward and kissed me, as soft and deep as the night sky over our heads. Only our mouths touched, no other parts of our bodies, but it felt like everything. When she spoke, her warm breath brushed my cheek like fingertips.

"*That's* why," she said.

A golden chance for me to say something smart and sexy. So what *do* I say?

"I don't get it."

"I wanted you to like me, Robby. You already knew about my car and...what happened at that party. I was afraid you'd think I was some spoiled rich chick and get turned off."

"So you pretended you had a curfew."

"Yeah. And after I dropped you off I drove back to the cemetery and walked around for an hour, visiting my friends. I even stood at that gravestone where you kissed me, and imagined you were still on the other side."

"That's funny," I said. "I remember *you* kissing *me*."

Pet laughed, a tiny laugh like the beginning of a song. "Maybe at first, boy, but it sure ended up even."

This time our kiss was even all the way, with no gravestone or anything else between us. And though it was with a girl who liked to visit cemeteries and make friends with dead people, it was the best kiss of my life.

Pet broke it off. "Uh oh," she said.

"What's the matter?"

She grabbed my hand, the one without the cast. "Come on."

We ran through the night. One false step in a hole and I could turn an ankle—with Purgatory Practice tomorrow. But I held on and trusted her. As we got nearer to the tennis courts and the streetlight on the corner Pet picked up the pace.

"You see?" she said.

Two junior high kids were on the courts, smashing balls all over the place. They weren't even trying to get the shots in, but just to see how hard they could nail them, preferably at each other.

"What's the problem?" I asked.

Pet pointed, her finger bouncing as we ran. I looked through the wire fence and noticed a camcorder set up on a tripod.

"If I come home with that in pieces my stepfather will kill me."

"I don't know, I bet he'd just buy you a new one."

"But he'd kill me first."

We rescued the camcorder before the mental midgets could break it. They were laughing like unstable hyenas. Probably they had raided their parents' liquor cabinets.

I stood guard as Pet disconnected the camera from the tripod. She wasn't sucking wind, though we had sprinted over here. This girl who told me she didn't like jocks *was* a jock.

"You were taping yourself?" I asked.

"Serving. I wanted to see if I'm bending my knees and arching my back enough. It's amazing how something can feel so different from the way it really is."

"Maybe I should tape myself kicking penalties."

Pet looked me in the eye again. "It can't hurt," she said, and started for the car. "Could you grab that ball hopper, please?"

I picked up the wire contraption that tennis players use to carry a ton of balls around. As Pet stowed the camcorder in her trunk she nodded toward the two kids. One of them launched a ball high into the air, way out across the road. The racquet flew out of his hand and smashed into the fence. He rolled on his back, laughing like a lunatic and kicking his feet in the air while the other kid slammed shots at him, trying to nail him between the legs.

"Drunk people," Pet said, "are not a pretty sight."

You're right, I thought. But what about someone like me who drinks, but not to get drunk? We're not ugly, are we?

Suddenly things got awkward. We had to make a decision: what next? And neither one of us knew. I had no answer, but I had a question. I leaned against her car.

"You've got your own court at home. Why'd you come here?"

Pet joined me on the car, so close you could barely fit a sheet of paper between us. But not touching, either. "Well, for one thing our court doesn't have lights. But mostly I couldn't handle listening to my mom. She's got to be the only parent who lectures their kid to *go* to parties."

I thought of a certain sick photo, and why Pet was so set against drinking. "Even after, you know…?"

"You don't know my mom. Here's her quote for everything: 'If the horse throws you off, get right back on.'"

"Nothing wrong with that," I said.

"I didn't say there was anything *wrong* with it. I just didn't feel like having to listen to it."

"I'd rather listen to you," I said. I put my arm around her and scooched over to hold her close. Pet squeezed me tight, and even with those two idiots on the court, for a few moments life was perfect. Then she pulled back.

"Ouch, what's that?"

She pressed her fingers against my thigh, on the sharp circle made by that beer bottle cap. The cap's ridges faced outward so it wouldn't dig into my leg, and I'd totally forgotten about it.

"Nothing," I said.

"It feels like a bottle cap."

"What's the big deal?"

"I'm not saying it's a big deal. Why are you acting guilty?"

"I'm not guilty."

"Then why are you acting that way?"

"What way?"

"Like you're hiding something."

OK, Fielder, you can weasel around or you can be honest. I stuck my hand in my pocket and held it out to Pet, slightly bent cap sitting upside down in my palm. She took my hand like a gypsy about to read my fortune. I waited for her to turn the cap over and see the word Schlitz—and for the trouble to start.

"It *is* a bottle cap." Pet closed her fist around the cap, walked ten feet and held her arm out over a trash barrel. She smiled at me as the cap plinked into the garbage.

I can't even come close to telling you how much I liked her right then.

Pet came back from the trash can. She put both arms across my shoulders and locked her fingers behind my neck. I locked mine behind her waist, thinking this was about as good as it gets. "Hey," she said.

"Hey what?"

"Let's go for a run."

"A *what*?"

"A run. You know, one foot in front of the other, faster than usual."

"That would be cool, but I'd better not. I have Purgatory Practice at 8:00 A.M."

"Purgatory? Is it some religious ritual?"

"Sort of. Mostly it means wind sprints till you drop."

Pet laughed. "Run yourself into the ground to get to heaven. Talk about twisted theology."

"Tomorrow will be the worst. That's why I can't show up hurting. I'm the captain, and some guys might need protection."

"Can't the coach protect them?"

"You don't understand. They need protection *from* the coach." I told her how Reynolds had gone ballistic after the game today.

"That is so wrong." She took her arms from around my neck and drifted away a few steps. Suddenly she kicked a pebble, hard, and sent it skittering across the road.

"Why do you put up with him?"

"What am I supposed to do? If I want to play I have to deal with him. And he's not going anywhere."

"Why not?" There was a real edge to Pet's voice, a bite.

"Because his teams win. If you win, people will forgive an awful lot."

Pet glared at me. "Do *you* forgive him?"

"Sort of." It wasn't what she wanted to hear, but too bad. It was the truth. "I don't like the guy, but I don't like to lose, either."

"So if you lost you'd want to get rid of him?"

I thought of the framed, autographed photos on Reynolds's office wall: "Just win, baby! Al Davis" and "For Ed Reynolds—A Winner! Bob Knight".

"I *do* want to get rid of him. But I have to be realistic."

"If you told people how he treated Tommy Francis today, I bet he'd get fired."

"Maybe. Maybe not. I'm not going to find out, though, because I'm no rat."

Pet looked like she wanted another pebble to kick. "How is it being a rat if you're doing the right thing?"

"You don't squeal on someone, you just don't. It's like a code of honor."

"Men!" Pet almost screamed the word. Even the drunken dweebs on the court shut up and stared. "You actually believe there's honor in letting an injustice happen?"

I'd never thought of it that way before. To me a rat was always a scumsucker, what when you were five years old you called a tattletale. It meant you couldn't fight your own battles, but had to go running to mommy and daddy or the teacher. But could claiming you weren't a rat sometimes be a cop-out, because you were afraid what people would think of you? Was I keeping my mouth shut because it was the right thing to do, or because I couldn't face dealing with what people would say? There goes Robby Fielder, the pussy who whined and got his coach fired, the most successful soccer coach in Newfield High School history. And what if Reynolds *didn't* get fired? I'd have stuck my neck out for nothing, and he could make my life miserable. He could give lousy reports on my attitude to college recruiters and kill my chances for a scholarship.

Every option seemed shakier than the last. "I guess there's no honor at all," I said. "But I'm not positive there's injustice, either."

"You're not *positive*?"

"Give me a break, Pet. There's a difference between bad, and so bad you have to do something about it."

"All I know is Reynolds is exactly the kind of guy who took that picture of me. And I bet he'd keep a copy for himself, stuffed in a drawer behind his underwear."

I didn't doubt she was right. I could see Reynolds pawing through a jumble of tighty-whities to get at the wrinkled photo. But what did that have to do with whether or not he should be our soccer coach?

Pet walked toward me wearing a wide smile, and I smiled too, ready to hold her again, and hopefully to make her forget that idea of a run and hang out with me instead. But her smile passed right by mine and got in the car. "A picture is worth a thousand words," she said.

"Would you use that cliché in a story for Mr. Mac?"

"You know I wouldn't. But that doesn't mean it's not true."

Pet started the car. "Get some rest. Tomorrow sounds dreadful."

I nodded, trying not to sulk but not having much luck.

"Robby?"

"Yeah?"

"If I asked you politely would you kiss me good night?"

That put my sulking to bed. I leaned down for a soft, sweet kiss that I enjoyed big-time, despite the snickering and fart noises coming from the court behind me.

"Thank you," she said.

"Just being a gentleman. Answering a lady's request."

She rolled her eyes and started to drive away.

"Pet?"

She braked and looked back at me.

"You forgot your soccer ball out there in the field."

Her eyes sparkled under the streetlight. "If you're such a gentleman, how about chasing it for me?" And she and her smile drove off into the night.

Chapter 17

I WATCHED HER TAILLIGHTS DISAPPEAR behind the firehouse, heading toward Route One. Then I cut back across the dark field—gently dribbling Pet's imaginary ball that I found on the grass. Until I reached the lights at the basketball courts, that is. I mean, it was fun, but I didn't want anyone to see me doing it.

Above the trees I could see the clock on the Congregational church steeple. Only 8:30. The sensible thing was to head home and get to bed early. But I knew I'd have Pet too much on my mind to be able to sleep for awhile.

In the end I did something pretty weird. I drove to the high school and walked to that maple tree again. After a check to make sure no one was looking I climbed up to the limb where I had sat with Pet. What a strange feeling—just like that night yet totally different, at the exact same time. I sat alone on the limb, my back against the rough bark of the trunk, watching the night through the quivering leaves. Suddenly the crowd went wild and the P.A. blared out that Billy Hagan had scored a touchdown. Even after botching the conversion Newfield was actually ahead, 12–10. Maybe a miracle was in the making, though they were only playing South York, whose record was as bad as Newfield's.

I heard myself saying something before I even realized I'd thought it. "She had to know," I whispered. Pet and that beer cap—she threw it away without looking, but just about every other drink comes with a plastic twist-off top. She must have known what it was, or at least been *almost* sure. But she didn't say anything. That was cool, right?

"Definitely," I whispered again. "Definitely cool."

I wished I was still with her. I wished my coach wasn't such a jerk. I wished I didn't have to decide if I should try to do something about it. I wished I had a beer. I was a walking example of Mr. Mac's favorite vocabulary word—ambivalence. It means to be confused because you're torn in different directions.

Mr. Mac. I debated for a couple minutes then started down the tree. The crowd roared again. The P.A. announced that Billy Hagan had just intercepted a pass. Talk about ambivalent. Couldn't Newfield win without him being the star? Lisa Birnbaum would be bouncing up and down with the rest of the cheerleaders, ready to jump all over Hagan the Football Warrior. Good thing Jim wasn't there.

As I dropped the last few feet to the ground the crowd erupted again, so loud I felt the vibration through my shoes. Newfield had held on to win. I sprinted to my car before anyone saw me, especially my parents. I knew where the party was going to be, so I could roll over there later if I wanted. But for now I pointed the Honda toward Mr. Mac's.

By the time I turned onto his road, doubts were starting to get to me. I slowed down, then pulled into the Guenivere Gardens Nursery. Maybe the visit was a bad idea. My headlights shone on peat moss bags piled high on a pallet. I killed the lights, shut off the engine. It's a five-minute walk, I told myself. Go check it out. On foot in the dark Mr. Mac won't see you—and if it's not cool you can slide away without embarrassing yourself.

My feet crunched on the millions of seashells that paved the parking lot instead of asphalt. Shells are one thing you never run out of on the coast, and I wondered why more places don't use them. I went out to the road and walked in the grass, as far as possible from any cars. Suddenly I realized how odd this would look. If anyone I knew saw me they'd probably stop, think something must be wrong, ask if I needed a ride. The game had just ended; there'd be plenty of traffic soon. So for the second time that night I found myself running in the dark, hoping I didn't step in a hole.

Four cars passed, two in each direction, but they kept on going. When I reached Mr. Mac's I stood in his side yard out of headlight range, one hand on the rough bark of an oak tree as I caught my breath. I walked around back, softly, as if the earth could squeak like an old floorboard and give me away. Mr. Mac's car was there but the house was almost dark. Just one light in the living room. But that didn't mean much. Mr. Mac always talks about conserving energy and recycling, paying attention to the environment.

I was all the way to the door, my fist raised and ready to knock, when my nerve went south. So Mr. Mac's your favorite teacher, what right does that give you to bother him on a Friday night? What if he's doing something important? I thought of one good reason for having the lights down low—man, what a loser I'd be if I bothered him while a woman was there.

I backed away off the low granite porch into the grass. Scattered leaves, damp with dew, hardly crackled when I stepped on them. I stood still and listened. Was that music? Maybe Mr. Mac was playing his guitar, singing Woody Guthrie songs, or his own. Maybe he'd like an audience, or at least not mind one.

Or maybe he already had an audience, and the last thing he needed was some kid coming by and messing up his date.

I moved toward the window, crouching low. A quick peek wouldn't hurt anyone, and then I'd know what to do. Simple. The window had venetian blinds but the slats were open. A hydrangea bush reached almost up to the windowsill. I felt pretty protected, only the top of my head showing over the leaves as I peered inside. Come on, I thought, be playing music by yourself. I'd really like to talk tonight.

He *had* been playing. But now he sat on the couch with his guitar in his lap, looking straight ahead the way you do when you're not really seeing anything. Suddenly his face just kind of collapsed. At first I couldn't believe it, because it was the last thing I expected to see.

Mr. Mac was crying.

I wanted to help him, but what could I do? This was private pain, nothing some kid could fix.

Mr. Mac took off his glasses. He put them on the wicker-trunk coffee table next to a half-full glass of beer. I remembered the cool coasters he had used for our apple juice, souvenirs from bars all over Europe—and how much I wanted to travel to Europe myself someday. He dried his eyes with the cuffs of his flannel shirt, then used his sleeve to wipe away tears that had dripped on his guitar.

Standing here was wrong unless something good came of it, and I didn't see how that could happen. With my hands in my pockets I shuffled across Mr. Mac's lawn, feeling cheap, like I'd spied on him then let him down. Keeping as far off the road as possible I walked back fast to the nursery.

I was almost to the Honda before I saw the cop car. The cruiser was parked on the other side of my car, lights off. I froze.

Rich Perkins was standing there with a ticket book in one hand and a pen in the other.

He stared at me with his head cocked sideways. With the ticket book he pushed up the brim of his hat.

"You again? Is this your vehicle?"

"It's my dad's."

"How would he feel about it being left on private property?"

"I didn't think there was a problem. There aren't any signs."

"Tell me about the spray-painted vandalism on the wall over there."

"What spray—"

"Did you sell the bags of peat moss you ripped off? Who helped you?"

"I don't know what you're talking about! If I did that would I be dumb enough to park right here?"

"People on drugs do dumb stupid things."

"Drugs! What?"

"Sir, lean over and put your hands against the vehicle. Slowly. No sudden movements."

I put my palms on the Honda's trunk and gritted my teeth as Perkins frisked me: my pockets, the inside of my legs, and rougher than he had to. It felt like a violation. My heart jumped for a second—the beer cap!—till I remembered Pet had dropped it in the garbage at the tennis courts.

"Sir, I'm asking your permission to search the car."

I told him to go ahead. It was easier than arguing. I'd get at least a little satisfaction from watching him play Hawaii Five-O for no reason. He soon gave up.

"You're free to go. But keep your nose clean."

I didn't say a word, just put on my seatbelt and started the car. As I drove away I could feel him watching, waiting for me to screw up, and I made sure to use my blinker as I turned on to the road. Forget Melissa's party. If there was anything I didn't need, it was a chance of meeting Perkins for a third time that night, especially after having a beer or two. I took a zigzag route through the back roads, half hoping to see Pet on her run. but it didn't happen.

At least Mom and Dad weren't home yet. They were probably having a drink over at someone's house, the Pozorskis' maybe, or the Hikels', to celebrate the football win. I took the stairs two at a time and closed the windows in my parents' room. The cleaner stink wasn't bad and the wet patch on the rug was mostly gone. Chances were they'd only notice if they stepped on it barefoot.

I brushed my teeth and got into bed. I put on a CD Mr. Mac had lent me, *A Tribute To Woody Guthrie*, and turned the volume down low. It was a live album from 1968 and 1970, a bunch of people like Bob Dylan and Joan Baez, and others I'd never heard of singing Woody Guthrie songs at Carnegie Hall and the Hollywood Bowl.

I listened to "Deportee," a song about migrant farm workers whose plane crashed as they were being deported back to Mexico. True story. One minute those people were there, the next minute they weren't. It got me to thinking about something Mr. Mac had told Lori Peplowski last week: "Remember that you're a human being, not a human doing." We all groaned because it sounded so corny, but now it was making sense to me—still corny, but making sense.

Lori spends all her time studying and building her résumé. She joins clubs she doesn't even care about, to make her college application look more impressive. She'll be valedictorian of our class for sure—yet I've seen her cheat on tests.

Odetta was singing "Why Oh Why." I was wondering the same thing as I hit the stop button and killed the light.

Pet's imaginary penalty kick.

Mr. Mac crying in his living room.

Why oh why.

You just never know what you're going to see. I pulled the covers up to my chin and waited for dreams (nightmares?) of wind sprints and Purgatory Practice. Or whatever was coming next.

Chapter 18

I T WAS SATURDAY, so I couldn't take the bus to school. I needed to borrow a car again or catch a ride. I called Chris Bolger at seven, talking quietly on the downstairs phone.

"No prob, Studly," he said, sounding like he'd already been awake for a while, unlike me. "I'll swing by."

Funny—Chris drove me home every day after soccer, but I never rode with him to school. This was the first time. I don't know why. Things just work out certain ways, I guess. Or don't work out.

Chris grinned as I got in. "Did you bring a barf bag, Studly?" He was trying to be cool, but we both knew he probably *would* puke today. It happened to him a lot.

"I skipped breakfast," I said.

"That's worse, man. Dry heaves."

I smiled, though it felt creaky on my face. We drove a mile or so without talking. Each of us had things on his mind. Chris was probably wondering what his breakfast was going to look like on the grass. I was worried about practice, too, but mostly my head was full of Pet—and Mr. Mac crying all alone.

"Yo, Studly, how was Melissa Mentzer's fiesta last night?"

Chris tried to ask the question real offhand. I knew Melissa hadn't invited him, and even if she had he would've been too chicken to go. I mean, what kid calls a party a "fiesta"? One who's trying too hard. And when you try too hard you come off as a geek. A nice guy, maybe, but still a geek.

"I wouldn't know. I sacked out early."

"Self-preservation instinct?"

"Something like that." I wondered how many soccer players did go to the party, and if any of them would be hurting today. Most of the guys either didn't drink or were real careful, but a few could get crazy once in a while. Jim was one of those guys. But what do you expect from a goalkeeper? You have to be deranged to play that position.

Chris got a thrill pulling into a faculty parking space. It was barely 7:30 and we were probably the first kids there. The school was open. The locker room was open. But the door to Reynolds's office was shut. Through the picture window we saw him and Preston talking—actually it was Reynolds talking, with Preston staring at the floor. Coach looked over and gave us an acid glare.

"We're toast," Chris said and ducked into his row of lockers.

Reynolds crooked a finger at me. Uh oh, I thought. Other guys were rolling in now, and as I walked past in the wrong direction they asked what was going on. "Purgatory," I said. They saw where I was headed and kept moving. No one wanted to be late on to the field. Running extra laps at Purgatory Practice would be suicide.

My hand was an inch from the door knob when I heard Rossi's voice.

"Going in to kiss ass?"

I felt like punching him, but I didn't need a cast on the other hand, too. I tried to be friendly. "Only if you are. I'm sure he wants both captains in there." I opened the door.

Reynolds nearly took my head off. "Didn't your mother teach you to knock first?" He hawked and spat into the wastebasket. "I changed my mind. Get the hell outta here—I can't stand the sight of you two right now. Captains!" The last word came out sounding like he was still spitting.

"Son of a bitch," Nick said as we walked together, for a few feet at least. "We're on the shit list."

"Welcome to purgatory," I said.

Nick half smiled. "Call it Hell. It's easier."

The locker room was dead as we dressed, the quietest I'd ever seen it. Guys were zombied from the early wake-up and dreading what was waiting for us on the field. It wasn't all Reynolds's fault, either. Shame can shut you up, and there wasn't a kid on the team who wasn't ashamed that we didn't beat Northbrook.

Tommy Francis raced into the room. He was so nervous and rushed that he kept messing up the combination on his lock. He swore and slammed it against the locker.

"Take a deep breath," I said. "Like right before a penalty kick."

Tommy flashed me a smile so weak it said the opposite. But after a deep breath he did get the lock open. He tore off his clothes and jumped into his uniform, but was still fumbling with his cleats when Reynolds stomped in.

"OK ladies, on the field! Double-time! I want to see you girls sprint out there, as if you actually gave a shit!" Guys took off, cleats clicking on the concrete. Reynolds grimaced at Tommy and folded his arms.

"That time of the month, Tammy? We'll see what we can do to help you out." His voice wasn't loud, just sarcastic. It got louder when he looked at me.

"Are you deaf? Or doesn't the captain lead the team anymore?"

"I—"

"You'd rather cuddle up with your girlfriend here? You got a thing for Tammy, Fielder?"

"Back off, Coach!" Preston's voice was at the far end of the locker room, but coming closer. "I mean it," he said. "That's *enough.*"

For a second Reynolds seemed too surprised to be angry. Then he got that red face that looks like an instant heart attack and puffed out his chest.

"You telling me how to run my team? How many winning seasons have you had, bucko?"

"That's not the point."

"It is as long as I'm the coach here." He jerked his thumb toward the door. "Move your ass, Fielder! And take your girlfriend with you."

I looked at Preston. He nodded.

"Now!" Reynolds said. "And I want twelve laps out of everybody before you even think about doing cals!"

During Purgatory Practice balls weren't even allowed on the field. No playing, not even drills, just calisthenics and running—mostly running. We looked forward to the cals as a break for our burning lungs, though sometimes Coach could get sadistic with the pushups. Plenty of guys pointed out that strong arms aren't much use in soccer. But not to his face.

I told Nick what Reynolds said about the twelve laps, and we led the team around the field, careful not to cut the corners. Coach hated cut corners. It was tempting to skip a few laps to try and not kill ourselves, since he wasn't there to see, but we all knew about the famous team who tried that maybe ten years ago. Reynolds was watching—and counting—from a classroom window. Every guy on the team's heart sank when they saw him come out of the classroom wing near the field, instead of the gym.

It's hard to believe, but supposedly his voice was calm. Maybe it was worse that way.

"Obviously you girls are either too stupid or too lazy to be Newfield High soccer players. It's my job to change that. Give me twenty laps—and yell out the count each time around so your lazy, stupid heads don't forget." He slowly scanned the guys, one by one. "After that, ladies, we'll do some *serious* running. Now take off."

What followed was the legendary Hell Week: Purgatory Practice three days in a row. I didn't even want to imagine that torture. So we ran the twelve laps and ran them hard, without cutting corners, though Reynolds was nowhere in sight.

When we finished the laps we were panting like dogs in August. A dozen laps might not sound bad, but try it sometime and then tell me what you think. Especially since it was only the beginning. We formed a big circle for calisthenics, Nick and me in the middle.

"Where the hell are they?" he whispered.

"Maybe Preston strangled him."

"Dream on, dude."

I usually think "dude" is a pretty lame word, but hearing it from Nick felt good. Maybe he wanted to be at least semi-friends. We started doing jumping jacks, counting loud, like before a game. As we went through each exercise, though, guys started throwing glances toward the locker room. If no coach came soon, Rossi and I would have to decide what to do next. And since the big mesh bag of balls was inside, none of our options were too inviting. We could stretch for awhile, but then what? I didn't want to be the one who made us do wind sprints. Besides, Reynolds might not believe that we did them and make us start from scratch. Then again, maybe he was watching and this was a test to see what we'd do on our own.

"Stretches?" I asked Nick.

"I guess. Should somebody go check inside?"

"You volunteering?"

He squinted into the sun. "Stretches," he said.

Stretching might be thought of as dogging it, except Reynolds always stressed doing a lot of it to avoid injury. So when I saw him coming—alone—while we were all flopped out on the ground I didn't worry about him going ballistic over that. And he didn't over that.

We were all on our feet when he reached the field. He stared at us for what felt like a minute, though it was probably ten seconds. I forced myself to look him in the eye. I wished Jim was there.

"Is there anyone here who's not man enough to be a Newfield soccer player?"

No one said a word.

"I *said* is there anyone here who doesn't have the pride to do what it takes to be a Newfield soccer player? Because if there is, pack your purse right now and go join a long-haired quitter who doesn't have the guts to coach here. You'll probably find him weeping in the girls' room."

My heart thumped and my stomach felt sour. Preston quit? Not good, not good at all. Dazed looks on guys' faces told me they felt the same way. We all liked him, every single one of us. Maybe more important, we respected him. Preston was a scholarship player who had started for three years at UConn. He knew what he was doing.

"A quitter never wins and a winner never quits," Reynolds said. "Ladies, in case you haven't noticed, I'm a winner. Losers make me sick. If you *are* one then haul your sorry ass out of my sight before the going gets tough. Because it's about to get tough."

He dragged his eyes over us again. "Anyone got something to say?"

I felt like I was letting Preston down. But what could I do, or any of us? We didn't have any power. Anything we said would just get shoved back down our throats.

"Captains?"

Probably most guys on the team wished we'd stand up to him, but nowhere near as much as they wished we'd keep our mouths shut, or this Purgatory Practice might be the worst ever.

"We're going to miss Preston," I said.

"Right," Rossi said.

Reynolds smirked at Tommy Francis. "Not as much as Tammy will."

I don't know if Tommy looked more scared, or more embarrassed. Whatever it was, Reynolds was enjoying it.

"Get those twinkle-toes on the goal line, ladies. It's killer time."

Nobody even bothered to groan. We all knew what we were here for, and we knew what we were in for. Any complaining would just encourage Coach to pile it on worse.

"Seniors first, " he said, then added the words we were dreading. "Suck hind tit and you win a second chance."

That was his way of saying that if you came in last you had to run again. Not with the next group, because they left as soon as the last guy crossed the line, but with the group after that. Hitler or Vlad the Impaler probably invented the idea, but it was one of Reynolds's favorites. It turned wind sprints into not only torture, but competition. No one wanted to finish last and have to run double. And sometimes not being last wasn't enough. If Coach thought you were dogging it, or looking around to see if you were ahead of other guys instead of just running balls-out, he might make you go again anyway. "Run *through* the line, not *up* to it like some friggin' pansy! Like when you reach a ball at the same time as a girl on the other team! *Through* the ball!"

I was glad the seniors were first, though we juniors were next and it all worked out the same in the end. They spread out along the goal line, legs tense and ready, waiting for the word from Reynolds. Because in this case it *was* a word, not the usual blast on his whistle.

"Killer!" he yelled.

"Killer!" they screamed and took off like delinquents with cops on their tails. If you don't remember, a killer is what Reynolds calls a sprint from one end of the field to the other and back again. Our soccer field is 110 yards long—you do the math. One killer is brutal enough. Nobody on the planet wants to do two of those monsters in a row.

Chris Bolger was a candidate for last place with the seniors. It wouldn't be the first time. Coach made us yell "Killer!" when we crossed the finish line, too. So when a kid who's last says "Killer!" he knows full well that's practically what it's going to do to him. Chris was in a dead heat for hind tit with Steve Cohen when their shouts of "Killer!" mixed with ours as the juniors took off.

It doesn't matter what kind of shape you're in, if you run your hardest it will hurt. Your lungs will burn, your heart beat so hard the thumping fills your chest. It might even hurt more the better shape you're in because you're used to pushing yourself. You don't let the pain stop you. You keep testing your limits and those limits keep expanding. It's never easy unless you coast. And if Reynolds caught you coasting, he soon made you wish you hadn't.

When you hit the far goal line you had to stop and reverse direction. That's not so tough in hockey, when you can dig your skates into the ice, but when you're running full speed your momentum carries you past the line. Which means you have an even longer trip back. Anyone turning right on the line was asking for trouble, because it showed you weren't going all out. But sometimes guys would risk it, especially after doing so many killers they thought they were going to die anyway. I don't care anymore, they figured, just put me out of my misery.

My legs were still sore, not quite a hundred percent from the beating they took in the Pearson game. It only made sense to ease off a bit. If you've ever pulled a hamstring you know what it's like. You're worthless. No matter how much you try to gut it out, you just can't move. That was the last thing I needed. So though I'm the fastest guy on the team I finished second in my group, half a step behind Dave Cappella. Not exactly a disgrace—Dave used to run cross-country before he switched to soccer.

"You call that a captain's effort, Fielder? You sucked hind tit, girlie. Run with the freshmen."

I wanted to tell him off but that would only get me in deeper. I'd been hearing the same thing, in nicer language, from my parents my whole life. Some people jump for joy if they got second place, but for me it wasn't good enough. So I just stretched my hamstrings then lined up with the freshmen. They'd been in high school less than a month, and looked stunned and scared that the captain and leading scorer could finish one foot from the leader and still get the shaft. That was

Reynolds's point—no one was safe. Matt Ciscel, the junior who straggled in last, joined us too, but I was the real sacrificial lamb and example to the rest.

I was thinking all this as the sophomores came nearer. Chris Bolger had lost with the seniors and was bringing up the rear now, but that was normal. Even a Nazi like Reynolds couldn't expect a guy running double to keep up with guys who hadn't. After you did it once you stayed with your new group to get regular rest before the next killer.

The problem was Tommy Francis. He was dragging at the back of the pack. I was rooting for him like crazy because of all the crap he'd taken, but in the end only Chris was behind him.

"That time of the month, Tammy?" Reynolds screamed. "Suck it up! A girl has to learn to deal with PMS!"

Chris stumbled across the line. "Killer!" we yelled, and ran.

That prick, I thought. I knew how Reynolds's mind worked: he blamed Tommy for Preston quitting. According to his logic, if Tommy had only been as good as Jim then he wouldn't have forced Coach to go ballistic and ream him out to teach him a lesson, and Preston would never have shown his weakness by defending the wimp. Of course that meant it was really all Jim's fault for having the accident, but Jim wasn't there to take abuse. Besides, Reynolds could forgive something stupid, like reckless driving, a thousand times before he'd ever forgive you for not being what he called a man.

Though Reynolds had ticked me off and I knew I was playing into his hands, I was determined not to finish last with this group. Not just ahead of Joey, which would be cake, but in front of most the freshmen. It wasn't for macho reasons, and certainly not to please Coach—though I knew it would. But I wasn't going to not do something just because a person I didn't respect would like it too. I wanted to prove to myself that I could do it, not to mention prove it to the team. A small payback for missing that penalty kick.

So I ran like a fiend, all out, ignoring the twinge in my hamstring and the fire in my lungs. 220 yards seemed like a mile, a mile with a knife stuck in my side. But I bellowed "Killer!" with the first guys over the line, third place out of nine. This time it truly felt like a killer. When my momentum died I collapsed on my knees to suck air. For a second the world was spinning, till I shut my eyes and straightened it out. I wasn't sure what I had accomplished, if anything, but pain or no pain I was glad that I'd done it.

And you know the sick thing? When Reynolds said, "That's a man! That's the way a captain runs!" I felt good. Despite what I thought of him, the praise felt good. Until I made it to my feet and saw none of the team was paying any attention to me. And the seniors weren't running their second killer yet. What was going on? Was Reynolds actually going to make a Purgatory Practice more humane?

His whistle shrieked. "Listen up!"

We came closer, warily, hoping for something decent to happen but not really expecting it. Reynolds gave us the evil eye without saying a word. Then he reached into his jacket pocket and pulled something out. He held it up like a hunter with a shot rabbit.

"Behold the Tampon Tiara, ladies. At least that's what my coach in college called it. But ours is going to be named after the first girl who played weak enough to wear it. Get your pansy ass over here, Miss Francis, and try on the Tammy Bonnet."

Tommy blushed like a sunset. I wouldn't have blamed him if he'd told Reynolds to shove it and quit on the spot. Then we'd have a freshman third-string keeper till Jim got back. Did we have a prayer of winning with Ravi Shankar in goal? I wondered if Reynolds had thought of that, or if he was too busy showing who was boss to care.

"I'll wear it, Coach," I said. "I'm the one who missed the Northbrook game."

Reynolds looked blown away. He obviously never figured someone would volunteer to put that thing on. But then he remembered why he was doing this in the first place.

"I make the decisions around here, Fielder. Miss Francis wears the bonnet. Though play your cards right and you'll earn your chance." He held out the sick pink headband in both hands, like it was a crown waiting for a king. "Tammy, front and center!"

Tommy swallowed hard. He started walking and guys got out of his way. He stood in front of Reynolds, his lip quivering, fighting not to cry.

Reynolds stretched the band around Tommy's head. Half a dozen tampons were tied to it, hanging like snow white dread-locks. One dangled right in his face.

"Suck it up, crybabies. Start playing like men again and the bonnet disappears." He paused for effect. "Until then—seniors line up for Killers."

I could take you through the rest of practice, but it would be as boring for you as it was for us—minus the pain. Unless you're as big a sadist as Reynolds and you'd love the details: sprints, laps, figure-eights of the field, pushups and squat thrusts till we were gasping facedown on the field, sweat smeared with dirt in our nostrils. It was the hardest ninety minutes of my life. Preseason conditioning sessions were nothing compared to this.

But not one guy quit. All of us could barely jog by the end, and some could barely move, but not one guy quit. No matter what trash Reynolds heaped on us, and he heaped it like he had a shovel. Maybe that meant we had no self-respect, but I think it meant we loved soccer so much we'd put up with almost anything to play.

If any guy deserved to fold, it was Tommy Francis. I've never seen anyone dumped on like that. No matter how he turned the headband, at least one tampon was always bouncing in his face. None of us laughed, though, because it wasn't funny. Reynolds rode his butt like a witch on a broom. But Tommy took the abuse. He ran his hardest every sprint, screamed the loudest every time across the line. He took the abuse and didn't quit.

My legs felt like cramps with feet at the end. We were all half dead, but Tommy was more like three-quarters. He looked like he might pass out any second. The headband was dirty and sweat-stained, the tampons not snow white anymore. Although I had volunteered to wear that thing, I'd be a lying dog if I didn't admit I was glad not to be in Tommy's shoes.

The whistle blew. We practically crawled over. Reynolds nodded as if deciding our fate.

"Winning isn't everything, it's the only thing. A winner never quits and a quitter never wins." A big grin broke out on his face. "I didn't see an ounce of quit in you men today. I'm proud of you. Now hit the showers."

We turned toward the building. The whistle stopped us. No, I thought. You *can't* make us run more. Not now, not after what you said.

Reynolds slowly strode over. He stopped in front of Tommy.

"You've got a pair of brass balls, Francis. I heard 'em clanking all practice." He held out his hand, palm up. "You proved you're a man today so take that goddamn thing off."

Tommy peeled off the headband. Exhaustion, pride and hatred mixed equally on his face.

"But remember, the Bonnet is waiting for any girls who try to join our team." Reynolds held it up and gave us a long look, then shoved it back in his jacket pocket.

"What doesn't kill you makes you stronger. I'll see you men Monday. You did a helluva job—go ahead and walk it in."

That was a first. We *always* had to run to and from practice. After a couple steps I had a feeling Nick was looking at me. I was right. One glance and I knew what he was thinking. I nodded, and together we started jogging, not fast by any means but not walking either. I heard a few whispered swears but every guy picked up the pace and followed. Coach stayed on the field, his arms crossed and legs spread wide apart, watching us. He was still out there when we reached the building.

"What a friggin' nut case," Nick said.

"The man is Satan," Chris Bolger said.

Other guys said stuff a lot stronger. Yet the sick thing was, whether or not they admitted it, not a guy on the team wasn't celebrating a little inside at what Reynolds had said about us. About us being men, and how proud he was. There was a feeling of camaraderie for surviving this together, like Marines who make it through boot camp.

Tommy Francis muttered something.

Nick cupped a hand to his ear. "What was that? Those brass balls are clanking so loud I can't hear!"

"Clank! Clank!" Half the team joined in, including me, chanting and slapping Tommy on the back. Which is how he became "Clank" Francis. Clank doesn't mind; he actually kind of likes it. I guess no matter how stupid it is, no guy complains if people say he's got a pair of brass ones.

In the locker room no one had much to say, partly because we were too tired to talk but mostly because we were paranoid about Reynolds. Who knew when he'd walk in? We all had Preston on our minds, and if Reynolds could hear what we were thinking we'd be back in his doghouse. We owed it to Preston—and ourselves—to do something. But what? What power did we have?

Most of us spent a lot longer than usual in the showers, and cranked them up really hot and steamy. My muscles were screaming for the warmth. I could practically have slept standing up under the spray, like a horse in the rain. But no matter how beat my body was, my mind was working overtime.

We could rat on Reynolds to our parents, but that would only tick him off again. Nothing else would happen. "So Preston quit," people would say. "So what? The longhair obviously was too big a wimp for Newfield soccer." Reynolds had been a winning coach for twenty years. People like coaches who win. It makes them feel proud of their school and their town, even if they have nothing to do with the team. And tons of Coach's former players still live in Newfield or close by. To them we'd be whiners and sissies instead of the tough guys they remember themselves being. Nobody on *their* teams went crying to mommy and daddy over Purgatory Practice. They'd laugh us out of town, and nothing would change.

I saw Chris Bolger peering into the steam from the shower room door. Chris is one of those guys who wraps a towel around his waist on the way to and from the shower room. Why bother? You're going to be just as naked as the rest of us under the water.

He waved me over. I shook my head.

"No way, José. I *need* this shower." My skin felt red as a lobster from the boiling water. Chris hung up his towel and came over.

"Coach is back," he whispered. "He's in his office."

"Chris, you forgot to take off your glasses." They were fogged up like a bathroom mirror.

"Duh, Bolger." He slapped himself in the head, then put on the towel to go to his locker.

Rossi had a shower in the far corner, next to Bonnaccorso. I went over and told Richie to trade places with me. He grabbed his soap and did what I said, partly because he was a freshman but mostly because he knew Nick and I needed to talk.

"OK," I said, "what are we going to do?"

"What *can* we do?" He closed his eyes, and steaming water streamed down his face. I let it beat against the back of my head.

One decent thing about this lousy day—Nick and I had somehow become at least halfway friends. "Damned if I know," I said. "I'll call Jim later."

"Hey, great plan. That drunk will get shit-faced and run the bastard over."

Oh no, I thought. Is he going back to his old ways?

Nick laughed. "Come on, I'm kidding. Can't you take a joke?"

"I can take a joke. But this Preston stuff isn't funny. What are we going to do without him?"

"Win, same as before. It just won't be as easy or as much fun." Nick's voice was serious, hard-edged. He turned off his shower and stood there dripping.

Tommy Francis showed up at the door, already dressed. He cleared his throat.

"Coach wants to see you both. In the office."

I killed my shower. "Thanks, Clank."

"Hey Clank," Nick said. "Don't walk near any magnets unless you're wearing a cup." Clank grinned and got out of there.

"What do you think he wants?" I spoke softly because the showers were off and I couldn't be sure Reynolds was still in his office.

Nick peeked around the corner for privacy before he answered. "Probably wants to pin a medal on us. But he'll make us take our shirts off first."

We went to our lockers. Chris came by, ready to leave. I told him about the meeting.

"No prob, Studly, I'll be out in the car." He started to walk away, then added, "Take your time if you're having fun."

"Munch feces," I said.

The other guys were gone. I dressed quickly, figuring that making Reynolds wait would not be our best move. Nick's locker slammed shut.

"Ready?" he asked.

"When you are."

As we walked out we could see Reynolds through the plate glass window. He was sitting at the desk, writing something.

"His resignation letter," I said under my breath.

"Dream on."

Though the door was wide open, I knocked. Reynolds ignored us and kept writing on a yellow legal pad, scribbling fast with a stubby pencil. Finally he flipped away the pencil and waved us in. He didn't ask us to sit down, or tell us to. He spun the ancient office chair around to face us. It creaked like fingernails on a blackboard.

"You two guys don't like me much, do you?"

What could we say to that? Any answer was a loser.

"Of course you don't. No man on this team does. And if I'm doing my job, they never will. I'm not here to be your friend. I'm here to lead you to victory and make this school proud. That's how a man earns respect. I could care less if anyone likes me. All I care about is respect."

Maybe he expected some comment from us now. If so, he was disappointed. But if I was crazy enough to spill the truth he'd have learned that the respect he counted on wasn't there either. Not after what he did to Tommy and Preston. That junk at the end of practice about us being men and him being proud of us—well, that was something, and not one of us wasn't glad to hear it. But you can't kick around a dog, then just throw it a bone later and think everything is OK.

Reynolds smiled like a politician caught in a lie. "I'm counting on you two men. And Dolan when he gets back. With captains like you, we don't need an assistant coach."

"But it would be better if we had one," I said.

"Preston's a good coach," Nick added.

Reynolds nodded. "No one's saying Bass doesn't have the skills. But does he have the guts? If it was up to him, Francis wouldn't have had the chance to show his brass balls today. But now we know he has 'em. More important, *he* knows he has 'em. We're going to get the job done and we're going to kick ass doing it, because we're Newfield High School Warriors." He leaned back in his chair. "So, are you two with me?"

I wasn't psyched to be with Reynolds in anything. But even worse was the thought of losing and having our hard work go down the drain. The team came first—with trying for a college scholarship a close second.

"Yeah," I said, after a pause just long enough to be uncomfortable.

"Right," Nick said.

Reynolds seemed satisfied. "There's no 'I' in 'team,'" he said, as if bestowing great wisdom on us.

But there's an "I" in "cliché," I thought.

Reynolds picked up the pencil and walked to the far wall of the office. When he turned his back I saw Nick sneak a quick look at the pad.

Reynolds tapped the eraser against the glass of a framed photo of a middle-aged guy with a crew cut and hornrim glasses.

"Vince Lombardi. The greatest coach who ever lived. What the greatest coach said should be good enough for the rest of us. Do you know what that was?"

Of course we knew. Every kid on the team knew, because Reynolds constantly quoted it. "Winning isn't everything," Nick and I started, then Coach joined in like we were praying together in church, "it's the *only* thing."

"I'm proud of you two warriors. You're all this team needs. Go home and think about that. And show up on Monday with your game faces on."

I glanced at the pad on the way out, and couldn't believe it. We waited till we were outside the building, and still kept our voices low.

"Did you read it?" I said. "'Pansies Need Not Apply' written about a million times? The whole paper was covered."

Nick whistled. "So our coach is a friggin' whack job. What else is new?"

Chris came over, limping from all the sprints. "What's going on?"

Nick put a hand on Chris's head. "Nothing you can't handle, Bolger, because you are a Newfield High Warrior. Bless you, my son." He started giggling and I did too. It was better than crying.

"Take it sleazy," Nick said with a wave, and headed for his dad's Rossi Plumbing and Heating van.

"Always," I said.

Chris looked like someone who'd studied hard for a test, then didn't know a single answer. "What happened in there, Studly?"

I wasn't sure what the answer to that was. "A little more purgatory, I guess." Reynolds's dirt-brown Monte Carlo was parked a few spaces away, and I got a huge urge to bolt before he could come out.

"Let's roll," I said. "I'll tell you all you want to know in the car, and then some."

Chapter 19

THERE WAS A NOTE on the kitchen table when I got home, on a pad advertising the real estate agency where Mom works. Under her smiling picture and the slogan 'You're Home Free With Premier Properties' I read:

Roberto,

> I'm showing a casa on River Road, Dad's playing golf. Hope you had a fun practice. If you want to mow the lawn, no one will complain. Una muchacha named Pat called and said she'd call back mas tarde. She seems muy simpatica. Is there something you're not telling us???

> Hugs and besos, Mom

I shoved the note in my pocket. Man, were my legs beat. *All* of me was beat. Who was Pat, anyhow? Ah—Pet, of course, Mom just screwed up the name. Should I call her? Maybe my stretch of bad luck was over. Suddenly even Nick was almost my friend, and soon we'd have Jim back on the team.

Then I remembered the Preston situation and didn't feel so optimistic.

I gulped about a gallon of water and scarfed two tuna sandwiches and a greasy pile of potato chips, then had an apple and a couple of cookies. I plodded upstairs and dropped onto my bed. I tried to read, but before I could turn a page, I was out.

I woke up with my face smooshed into the pillow. 2:27, said the green numbers on my radio. I heard a lawnmower. I had to tell Jim about what happened with Preston, but to give Dad less ammunition for comments about his lazy son I decided to help cut the grass first. I looked out the window. Fortunately he'd just started, puttering over the fat part of the lawn on the rider mower. I went to the shed out back, gassed up the push mower and began doing the edges and under trees. After the first pass Dad noticed me and gave a wave. Judging by his grin I guessed he'd had a good golf game.

I did a lot of thinking as I mowed. The cut grass smelled sweet in the clear fall air. Yet soon winter would come and cover it with snow. And this soccer season that meant so much to us now would be history. I'd have only one year left to play in high school. I remembered coming in as a freshman, how the seniors seemed so much older and grown-up. Somehow I was already closer to being a senior than to being a freshman. It hardly seemed possible.

I raked up clumps of cut grass and rolled the cart out back to the compost pile. I noticed a tomato plant growing in there, a foot tall, product of some overachieving seed in a tomato tossed away to rot into fertilizer. It even had a couple of yellow flowers. In May, or even July, I would have dug it up and put it in the garden. But now was too late in the season for the plant to mature. For some reason I felt sorry for it, I guess because it was trying so hard. So instead of just dumping the grass on top

I spread it around the stem like mulch. The plant was doomed, but I figured it might at least have a decent run before the frost killed it.

"Robby," Dad said behind me, "you're an incredible softie."

I started to make some lame excuse but he cut me off. "I'm not putting you down. It's good to be a softie in some things." He put a hand on my shoulder. "Come on, let me buy you a drink."

In the kitchen he poured me a lemonade and opened a beer for himself. He was smiling and I figured golf was the reason. I asked how his round had gone. Dad's cool about not boring people with golf stories, but he couldn't hide the pride in his voice.

"89, Bucko. First time I ever broke 90. And no mulligan, either."

"That's great, Dad. What are you going to buy me to celebrate?"

"You're a funny kid, you know that?" He handed me a tall glass tinkling with ice cubes, then clinked it with his sweating bottle of Schlitz. I thought of the one that spilled last night, how close I had come to landing in trouble

"To low scores on the golf course," he said, "and high ones on the soccer field."

"High scores for *our* team, anyway."

Dad took a swig and smacked his lips. "Once Jim's back, high scores for the other team ain't going to happen." He clinked my glass again. "Want to go watch the news? Let's see if my 89 is the lead sports story."

"Are you kidding me? It'll be the lead story, period. What could be bigger news than that?"

"Keep talking. Maybe I *will* buy you something." Laughing, he went into the den and turned on the tube. I wondered where

Mom was. I wondered why Pet hadn't called me back. I wondered what I was going to do tonight.

I picked up the phone and hit the speed dial for Jim's number. I filled him in on the gory details: the Tommy situation, Purgatory Practice, Reynolds climbing all over Preston's case, Preston quitting. And the one good thing, the truce with Nick. Once in a while Jim cut in with a question or comment, but mostly he just listened. We'd been best friends forever, and I had never heard him listen so hard before.

Finally we were both quiet. Then Jim asked the big question.

"So what do we do now?"

"Maybe go visit Preston," I said. "Tell him we're on his side."

"Fat lot of good that does him."

"It won't do any good. But he might at least feel better."

"Where does he live?"

"I have no idea."

"He didn't have to quit," Jim said.

"Do you blame him?"

"No. But he didn't *have* to."

"Look, we put up with Reynolds because we get to play. What's in it for Preston?"

"But the guy bailed on us, dude. He friggin' bailed!"

It was my turn to pause. Then I said, "You know something, Jim? We're the last two guys who can hammer anybody else for letting the team down."

"Robby!" Dad yelled, so loud it scared me.

"What?"

"Get in here!"

"I'm on the phone."

"Just get in here!"

"What's his problem?" Jim said.

"You can hear him?"

"*Now*, Robby! Move it!"

I jogged into the den, taking the phone with me. One look at the TV and I practically screamed in Jim's ear, "Turn on the tube! Channel Two!"

"What are you talking—?"

"Do it! Now!" I hung up.

"What the hell is this?" Dad said.

My eyes were glued to the screen. It was unreal, like some crazy dream, but I knew I wasn't going to wake up. There it was. There *we* were. And most of all, there Tommy Francis was.

At Purgatory Practice. Wearing the Tammy Bonnet. It was clear what was dangling from little white strings, bouncing around Tommy's head and in his face as he ran a Killer. I heard the voice of Burlin Barr, Channel Two sports reporter.

"Motivational technique from a seasoned and successful coach? Or degrading abuse that has no place in interscholastic sports? A shoreline community debates."

Debates? I thought. Who even knows about it? Then an even more basic question hit me. Who took that video?

"Robby," Dad asked sharply, "what's this about?"

Coach Reynolds came on the screen, peeking out his half-open front door, looking ambushed and wishing he'd never answered the bell. Barr asked about Tommy and practice today.

"That's an internal team matter, and we dealt with it as a team. End of story."

"But these are serious allegations, Coach. Did you cross the line?"

"If the question is do you have to be tough to be a Newfield Warrior soccer player, the answer is yes. The weak are weeded

213

out—and the men on my team wouldn't have it any other way. Now if you'll excuse me...." With a forced smile he stepped back inside and closed the door.

Still standing on Reynolds's porch, Barr turned toward the camera. He's one of those pretty-boy news guys you know is angling to move to a bigger-market TV station the first chance he gets. He's no slouch, though.

"Efforts to contact Tommy Francis and Newfield assistant soccer coach Preston Bass have so far been unsuccessful. We'll have an update on this breaking story tonight on Channel Two at eleven. Reporting live from Newfield, this is Burlin Barr."

Back in the studio, co-anchor Heidi Hartwig shook her head. "The pressure that we put on kids to excel. I don't think we've heard the end of this story."

Gray-haired Rob Dowling nodded grimly. I think he's been on the news since TV was invented. "Not by a long shot, Heidi," he said, then turned back to the camera and gave the audience a 100-watt smile. "Stay tuned for Beverly's Super Duper Doppler forecast, folks."

"Well," Dad said, his fingers drumming on the arm of his chair. "I'm waiting."

I started to tell him the story. I hadn't been talking ten seconds when the phone rang.

"Let the machine get it," Dad said. "I have a feeling we know what that call's about. And before either of us talks to anyone I want details."

So I gave him details. Not all of them by a long shot, but probably more than he expected or wished for. Three more phone calls came in the next few minutes. I heard low voices leaving messages.

It was weird, telling Dad the same stuff I'd just told Jim. Because I realized it wasn't quite the same stuff, and I didn't tell it quite the same way. For one thing, I didn't want to seem like a wimp or a whiner to my Dad, where with Jim that wasn't a factor. I knew he'd never think that. But it's no secret Dad wishes I played football like my brother, and some people think you have to be tougher to play football than soccer. Dad would never say so, but he's one of those people. So part of me was afraid of seeming like a wuss, or making the team look that way.

Mostly, though, I was no rat. Only rats squeal, right?

Dad stared me in the eyes. "A man has an obligation to his team and his teammates, but he has a bigger obligation to the truth. I'm only going to ask once, and I want a straight answer. Was that news report fair? Did it show what really happened, or blow it out of proportion?"

You have to know something about my Dad: though he watches the news he doesn't trust it. Once he saw a news crew shooting video of a swollen stream after some big rains. It was no big deal, but that night the news showed a close-up of the muddy rushing water that made it look, according to Dad, "like if you didn't have Noah's Ark you were a goner." He figures if the news trumped up that story it probably does the same to lots of others, too.

The phone rang again.

"I guess it was fair," I said. "Everything they showed really happened."

"I don't doubt that it happened. What I'm asking you is whether this is just high water in a stream, or a legitimate flood."

He knew I'd understand what he was talking about. I'd heard that story enough times.

"I don't know."

"What's not to know?" Dad sounded pretty annoyed.

Suddenly there was only one possible answer. "It's a flood," I said.

Dad sighed. "That's what I was afraid of. Do me a favor—go check the messages. Let me think this through for a minute."

I pushed the button on the answering machine and listened to tape rewind for a long time. Then I got a surprise, a voice I wouldn't have recognized if I hadn't just heard it on TV.

"This is Burlin Barr of Channel Two, calling about an incident at Newfield High soccer practice today. I was hoping that Robby would care to comment about the treatment of Tommy Francis. Please call back as soon as possible. It's 2:44 Saturday afternoon. Thank you." He left a number.

He must have called while we were mowing the lawn. Should I call him? First I had to deal with the other messages:

Burlin Barr again, 4:03 P.M., still "looking for a statement about the Tom Francis situation." That was the first time I'd ever heard him called Tom, not Tommy.

A hang up, probably a telemarketer horsefly.

A client, looking for Mom, with a corny comment about playing telephone tag.

Mom, looking for the client, asking if she'd called.

Another hang-up. Those telemarketers don't give up without a fight.

Mrs. Bonnaccorso, wanting to talk to Mom about closing on a house, not about practice today.

That was all. I couldn't believe it. Didn't anyone in this town watch the news, or at least hear from someone who does? But then I thought, hey, it's not like I've called anybody, either, and I hardly ever watch the news.

"What are people saying?" Dad called from the den. I could hear the weather report: partly cloudy, seasonable, nice.

"A lot of nothing," I told him.

"Huh?"

The phone rang. I picked right up.

"Hello?"

"Robby? Coach Reynolds."

Reynolds's voice was the last one I'd expected to hear, and the last one I *wanted* to hear. I wiped my palm on my pant leg.

"Hey, Coach. What's up?" I hoped my voice sounded steadier than it felt.

Reynolds cleared his throat. "Did you see the news?"

"What news?"

"Somehow that traitor Bass filmed practice today and sold it to Channel Two. Of course they played it up all sensational, like the Bonnet was going to turn Francis gay or something. I told you Bass was bad news! Because he's not man enough like you guys he's jeopardizing our whole season!"

I had a feeling Coach was more worried about his job than our season. "How do you know Preston did it?"

"Who else *could* it be?"

It made sense. But lots of things that make sense aren't true.

"I guess," I said.

"Listen, I need your help. And Jim's and Nick's—all the guys who are real Newfield High Warriors. Guys who care about our tradition, who know what it takes to win and aren't afraid to do it. Robby, they're going to call you, and I need you to back me up. You'll do that, right? For the team?"

"Who's 'they'?"

"The principal. The superintendent. Reporters sticking their noses in. Worthless parents whose kids wouldn't know discipline at all unless they got some at school. Maybe a pony-tailed whiner who doesn't have the guts to just quit, but tries to take our team down with him. We're not going to let that happen, are we?"

What was I supposed to say? "No way I'll let the team down, Coach."

"Good man." The shaky relief in his voice almost made me feel sorry for him. Almost. "I'll see you Monday at practice."

"OK."

"And Robby?

"Yeah?"

He sounded choked up and quivery. "I'm proud as hell of you guys." I heard a click, then the sick, flat buzz of a dial tone.

Why did he have to say that? Nothing was changed, not really. I still wanted him gone, wanted a different coach. But it was harder now. I felt sorry for him.

Dad found me staring at the kitchen counter. "Who was that?" he asked from the doorway.

"Jim."

"You don't usually look like that after you talk with Jim."

"We don't usually have something this messed-up to deal with."

The phone rang. Dad made a "be my guest" gesture and I picked up.

"Hello?"

"Dude, I've been calling for half an hour. Who you been talking to?"

I hoped Dad couldn't hear Jim's voice. "Yeah," I said. "Can you believe it?"

I walked as far away as the cord would let me. Why didn't we have a cordless phone in the kitchen?

"I don't know," I said. "What do *you* think we should do?"

Dad held out his hand. "I'll hang it up if you want to talk on a different phone."

"That's OK," I said, feeling like a geek since it obviously *wasn't* OK. Why didn't I just tell him the truth in the first place? Who cares if he knows Reynolds called? But I was embarrassed to be caught in a lie.

Dad went back in the den, shaking his head.

"I'll call you right back," I whispered. "Let me get to another phone."

"Dude, what kind of drugs are you on?"

I hung up. Within a minute I had a cordless phone in my room, dialed Jim's number—and it was busy. This was turning into a joke.

I flopped back on my bed. I wondered if Mr. Mac had seen the news. Not likely. Most of the comments I'd heard him make about TV news were, to use his words, "less than charitable."

What about Pet? It didn't take much imagination to know what she'd think of the Tammy Bonnet. Should I call her? Maybe she wants to do something tonight.

A date, you mean? Like an actual date?

I suppose. Yeah, I guess that's exactly what it would be.

What if she says no?

My heart picked up speed. I dialed Jim again. Still busy. I rolled over and grabbed a book off my nightstand. *To Kill A Mockingbird*, a really great novel, and I only had two chapters left. I slipped out the bookmark—a crinkled Lyle Lovett concert ticket—far enough to see Pet's writing. Her phone number stared at me from the edge of the pages.

We'd had a good time last night. She liked me. So why was I nervous? I don't know, I just was. I get nervous every time I call a girl. I wish I was cooler, but I'm not.

Pet's number kept repeating in my head. I even imagined the beeps it would make when I hit the buttons. But I didn't hit them, not yet. I had to at least come up with a decent first line, something better than "Hi, what're you doing?"

How about, "Hey, did you see the news?" No, too direct.

"How's your serve?" Sounds like a bad pick-up line at a country club. Not that I've ever been to a country club.

"Hey, Pet. How was your run last night?" Yeah, that's it. Go with that one. If you ever get up the nerve to actually dial, that is.

The phone rang. "Hello."

"Mr. Fiedler? How are you this evening?"

"It's *Fielder*!" I said and pressed the "OFF" button like I was squishing a horsefly.

I tried Jim. Still busy. Maybe his mom was talking to his grandmother, or Mr. Powell was on the line with a client. But that wasn't very likely on a Saturday, especially this late.

Come on, you wuss. Just *call* her!

Mom's car pulled into the driveway, and the noisy garage door rumbled open. The phone rang. If I were alone I'd have gone down and screened the call with the answering machine, but privacy seemed a better plan under the circumstances.

"Hello."

"Hey media star, can I have your autograph?"

It took me a second to recognize Pet's voice, probably because those weren't words I'd ever expect to hear from her.

"I guess you watched the news," I said.

"Robby, that stuff with Tommy Francis was the sickest thing I've ever seen."

"It was pretty bad. And the news only showed a little. You're lucky you didn't see the rest."

"What do you mean, 'lucky'? Too much for a girl, is that what you're telling me?"

"No, no. Not really. It's just…"

"Just what?"

"Look, I wish *I* hadn't been there, OK? So all I'm saying is I'm glad *you* weren't."

"You can stop feeling glad."

"Huh?"

"How do you think Channel Two got that video?"

"I'm not sure. Reynolds thinks Preston—" My brain cut off my sentence.

"No way," I said.

"Way," she said.

"You?"

"Me."

"How?"

"From the woods on that little bluff by the field. It's not like it was hard. The only tough part was holding the camcorder steady, I was so mad at that troglodyte coach. What's *wrong* with that man?"

I was disgusted with Reynolds, but splashing those pictures on the news, making Tommy's embarrassment public—that was kind of like playing God. Is it the right thing if following your conscience hurts someone else?

"He's old school," I said.

"How old? The Spanish Inquisition? Slavery?"

I looked down at my cast. "Pet, I'm not defending the guy. I'm just saying the right thing isn't always black and white."

"No argument. But where's the gray area here? What Reynolds did to Tommy was awful."

I remembered last night's kisses, and wanted more. But I couldn't lie to get them.

"It *was* awful. Tommy was probably the most embarrassed he's ever been in his life." I took a deep breath. "Until now."

"Now?"

"Do you think he feels better after thousands more people have seen it happen to him?"

Dead silence. *Long* dead silence. I wasn't sure if I should break it, or how. Finally I heard a sniffle, then another.

Great job, Fielder. You didn't have to make her cry.

No. But I did have to say what I did.

"Well," she said in a quavery voice, "that area got gray real fast."

"I'm sorry."

"For what? Telling the truth? I'd be the sorry one if I didn't want to hear it."

"Listen, Pet, I understand—"

"So do I, that's the problem. I have to think this over. I'll call you back, OK?"

"Sure."

More nothing, and more, and more. Then Pet said, "The worst part is that nobody knows better than me the power of a picture."

Oh, man. I hadn't even thought about that terrible photo of her.

"Thanks for being the only real friend I have, Robby."

Suddenly my ear was full of dial tone, and my mind was swirling like snowflakes in the wind.

Chapter 20

THE PHONE RANG AGAIN five minutes later, and steadily for the next few hours.

I wanted to cut short every conversation to open the line for Pet, even with Jim. Normally we'd have barked for half an hour about this craziness, but after only a couple of minutes I told him I'd better contact some of the other guys. I didn't, though, not yet anyway. When adults called I wished my parents would hang up. She probably keeps trying, I thought, but can't get through.

Burlin Barr caught me at dinner, one bite into my second hot dog. I was prepared to ignore him, but at the sound of his voice on the answering machine Mom got up and answered.

"Hello?... Yes, this is his mother, Brenda Fielder. I'm a sales professional at Premier Properties.... Robby? Certainly, he's right here. It was a pleasure talking to you." With her hand over the receiver she whispered, "For heaven's sake be nice to him. Rumor says he's in the market for a house around here."

At least it was the cordless phone, so I didn't have to sit there and be stared at as I reached for the right words. I said hello as I headed up to my room.

"Hello, Robby. Burlin Barr, Channel Two. How are you?"

"OK," I said, and closed my door.

"Any comment on the situation with Coach Reynolds?"

"What situation?"

His voice tightened. "The one concerning Purgatory Practice and a player humiliated by being forced to wear a headband of tampons. We broke the story on the six o'clock news."

The words "Purgatory Practice" showed that he had talked to at least one person on the team. Nobody else would call it that.

"Boy, that's wild. How did you know about it?"

"A source who prefers to remain confidential."

"A student?"

"I'm sorry, I can't reveal—"

"What's her name?"

"Look, if you want to tell your side of the story on camera, I can be there in an hour."

What would Pet want me to do? What *should* I do, for the good of the team? I wished Reynolds weren't our coach, but I couldn't help feeling sorry for him. He was pathetic but he didn't know any better. I thought of Mr. Mac's advice about writing our short stories: "Remember, gang, the villain doesn't *think* that he's a villain."

Some would say I wimped out, but every time I think back on it I decide the same thing. No way was I going on camera. I wasn't some loser who'd do anything to get on TV, and for Tommy's sake I hoped the publicity died down in a hurry. If I kept my mouth shut maybe that would help.

"Won't you at least give a statement?" Barr said. "You're the captain, after all."

"I'm *one* of them."

"Well, Jim Dolan won't comment because he wasn't there, and we haven't been able to locate Nick Rossi. So either let us know what you think, or don't complain if tonight's story doesn't reflect your point of view."

What could I say? Negative remarks about Reynolds and I've got a coach who hates me, which is the pits for me *and* the team and hurts my scholarship chances. Words of support and I'm a liar. Neutral comments and I'm just a spineless politician.

"OK, you can quote me on this. Preston Bass is an excellent coach and I hope he comes back to the team."

"Bass left the team?"

Unbelievable. Barr was so focused on the tampon stuff he didn't even know about Preston. Maybe he needed videotape before he cared about anything.

"I have to go, Mr. Barr. Thanks for calling." I hung up with relief.

There were more calls later, including from other TV stations who figured they couldn't ignore the story though Channel Two had scooped them on the video. We screened through the answering machine and talked to no one.

"Look," Mom said, "we've done all we can for tonight and I don't want to discuss it anymore. Let's watch the movie. Are you going out, Robby?"

"I'm not sure yet."

"Why not join us?"

"What did you get?"

"*The Bridges of Madison County.*"

Behind her Dad pantomimed shoving a finger down his throat. I grinned.

"What's so funny? It's got Meryl Streep and Clint Eastwood. They don't make junk."

"Thanks anyway, Mom. But if I don't go out I think I'll catch up on some homework."

"Suit yourself. Dad and I will have all the fun."

Judging by the expression on his face, Dad's only fun would be laughing at the corny parts.

Mom got out the popcorn popper. "If you need to use the phone please do it now, because I'm going to turn it off. I'm absolutely fried from working all day then coming home to this nonsense. I don't need interruptions every five minutes during the movie."

Normally I'd be fine with that, but today wasn't normal. Pet could call any time.

"But there might be important calls," I said.

Mom rattled a cupful of kernels into the popper. "You didn't seem thrilled about getting calls before, Roberto."

"I'll keep the phone by me. I promise to pick up on the first ring."

Mom smiled and gave me one of her Mom looks. "Hmm, could it be that a certain Pat is supposed to call?"

"Come on, Mom."

"What are you waiting for, *hombre*? Call her!"

Dad snapped the cap off a bottle of Schlitz and looked sorry for me. "Movie's starting, dear. I know how you hate to miss the coming attractions."

"Things haven't *totally* changed since your father and I were in school. Last I checked it was still acceptable for a boy to call up a girl."

I didn't need this, especially since they might start putting pieces together and wonder if "Pat" was that girl Dad saw me with at the maple tree that night. Though maybe not, because Mom's note said she seemed nice on the phone. My parents might assume a lot of things about a freaky-looking girl like that, but "nice" was not one of them. Neither was that her name would be Pat—nice, normal Pat. Good thing Mom heard the name wrong.

"I'll be in my room." I held up the phone. "Like I promised—first ring."

"Remember," Mom said, "you can *make* calls with it too."

If my door had a lock I would have used it. But my parents don't believe in locks except on outside doors, in case there's a fire or other emergency. Not even in the bathrooms, which has led to a few embarrassing (or amusing, depending on your perspective) incidents over the years. I called Nick but his father answered, slurring like he had hit happy hour at some bar after work. He yelled to his wife but neither had a clue where Nick was. I'm not sure the guy knew where *he* was.

So that wasn't happening. I flipped the phone on the bed, got on my knees and pulled out my safe. A few seconds later I had *Passion's Trigger* in my lap. I don't know why I took that book out, I just did. I guess it made me feel a little closer to Pet as I waited to hear from her. Which is insane, because she said her mother's novels made her skin crawl.

Those suckers sure paid the bills, though. The cover boasted that over a million copies of Marguerite St. John's books were in print.

I vowed to read ten pages—though I wanted to bail out screaming after one. Could you imagine writing, "'If you want to break my heart then spit it out!' she spat"? Well, Marguerite did. *Passion's Trigger*, page four; look it up if you don't believe me. To get through the ten pages I tried imagining Pet and me as the main characters, but that was just too pitiful.

The phone rang and I grabbed it.

"Mr. Fiedler? How are you this evening?"

"Good, till now!" I slammed the phone in her ear. Well, I guess that's an exaggeration—but I stabbed the OFF button pretty hard.

I broke out my Trig book and did a problem, but my head wasn't into it. American History, same deal—I read half a chapter, but though it was interesting stuff on the lost colony of Roanoke I couldn't concentrate. Pet was the only problem and the only history on my mind.

I looked at the phone on my pillow, just a dead hunk of plastic waiting for words to arrive. It was past 9:00. The only calls since that telemarketer had been one for my mother (I scribbled a message), and Chris Bolger ("Hey, Studly, didn't expect to catch you home on Saturday night. Did you see the news?"). I cut the talk as short as I could without being rude, trying to keep the line open.

Then after a while I started to write.

Believe it or not it was Marguerite that got me going. I was thinking about how much her book stunk when it hit me that anyone can criticize, but unless you can do better maybe you should keep your mouth shut. Otherwise you're like some out-of-shape fan screaming "You suck!" at a professional athlete. Does buying a ticket (or a book) give you that right? Maybe, but I didn't want to be one of those fans. So, like a challenge I suppose, I turned on my computer and started to write.

Well, sort of. I stared at the blank screen and blinking cursor. Not exactly putting Marguerite to shame, are you Fielder? I got up and put on Lyle Lovett's first CD—a gift from Pet. I skipped ahead to "Closing Time" and listened with my eyes shut: "It's closing time/unplug them people/and send them home/it's closing time." The song made me feel mellow and melancholy, probably the way I'll be when I look at my NHS yearbooks in ten years, wondering where the time went.

I opened my eyes. I typed THE STORY OF PET and started writing. I wrote like a demon, totally lost in what I was doing. No track of time, no awareness of anything but the world I was making. It was *my* world, but still it felt like I was creating it. I was so absorbed in writing I even forgot about Pet calling me. So it was a shock when I noticed it was past 11:30. Doubtful to the max that she'd call now.

I'd forgotten to watch the news. Ah, so what. I'd find out soon enough what Barr reported. I scrolled through the pages and felt a surge of pride. You did this, I thought. That's pretty cool. And it's no slouch of a story, it really isn't; there's some halfway interesting stuff going on here.

What I didn't know—what I didn't have a clue about—was how the story was going to end.

Chapter 21

I WOKE UP IN gray morning light. Rain hammered on the roof. In the hall I saw my parents' bedroom door was closed. It usually isn't. I wondered if they'd gone to sleep late because that loser movie put them in the mood. Oh man, what if they're in the mood right now? I motored downstairs in a hurry, got an umbrella and went out to the box for the paper.

Most of the time I read a newspaper in order. I don't start with the sports section. But today was different, today I was checking for something. I buttered a bagel and started looking, and it didn't take long to find. High school soccer doesn't usually get squat for coverage until the state tournament, but there we were on the front page: "Bad Hygiene or Bad Taste?" by Randy Turcotte, the sports columnist. Turcotte loves controversy, but the article was pretty fair overall, if you call it fair to try and heat up the issue on both sides. Turcotte quoted three former NHS soccer players, who said mostly positive things about Reynolds and implied that we were a bunch of whining pansies who couldn't have hacked it in the old days, when men were men—like them. Sam Castro, Newfield's Third Selectman, even claimed that he hoped his daughter (who's only two years old) would someday "marry a guy with old-fashioned integrity like Coach."

The article ended, "Yes, Ed Reynolds went overboard. Yes, there must be consequences. But we also need to ask what kind of kids our society is producing nowadays. Ones with gumption, or ones who cry to Mommy at the first challenge to their precious self-esteem? In our politically correct era is there still a place for sucking it up, taking one for the team—and maybe, just maybe, growing stronger from the experience?"

I read box scores and glanced at articles but they hardly sank in. My mind kept creeping back to Pet and Tommy, to the whole weird mess this had become.

Suddenly I went blind.

"Guess who?"

"Mom, what are you doing?"

She took her hands off my eyes. "Oh, you guessed right! It's Matchmaker Mom wondering, 'My oh my, did my Roberto call Pat yet?'"

"Can't I have a little privacy around here?"

"Come on, silly, don't be shy. If you wait too long, someone will ask her first and you'll kick yourself."

"Will you please give it a rest?"

"Oops. I didn't realize you were so sensitive." She pantomimed zipping her lip.

I tried to make it a joke. "I hear girls like sensitive guys."

Dad walked in shaking his head. "Yeah, that's what they *say*. But what they really *want* is an alpha male stud like me."

Mom rolled her eyes.

"Deny it all you want, baby doll, but you're wearing my wedding ring!" Dad started punching his fists toward the ceiling and singing, brutally off-key, "Macho macho man, I wanna be a macho man!"

It was way too pitiful. Two minutes later I was back in my room.

The rain hardly let up all day. I hung around resting my beat-up legs, watching football, doing homework—and writing another chunk of my story. The soggy hours dragged by. The writing went OK, but I wasn't in a trance like last night. Around 3:00, in the middle of the Giants game, I almost drove over to Pet's house but either chickened out or thought better of it, I'm not sure which. I used to think that there was right and there was wrong, and I was a decent person who would do the right thing. But sometimes it's not easy to know what's right. No player ratted on Reynolds, not even Tommy, and guys like Sam Castro would say we did right. But other people would blame us for covering up what they called abuse. Who was right?

The phone rang around 4:30. I would have answered but it caught me in the middle of a sentence and I was afraid I'd lose the thought. I don't have to tell you who I hoped it would be. But I knew it wasn't Pet, because Mom had no annoying tone in her voice when she yelled for me. And no seventh-grade smile on her face when she handed me the phone.

"Who is it?"

She shrugged. "No sé."

"Hello?" I said as I started up the stairs.

"Hi, Robby. It's Tommy."

The name didn't register for a second. I mean, Tommy Francis had never called my house before. We weren't even friends, just teammates. I closed the door of my room.

"Hey, Clank. What's up?"

I wasn't sure if Tommy liked his new nickname, but he didn't seem to mind.

"You heard the news?"

"I saw it."

A couple of seconds went by. "What did you think?"

What could I say not to embarrass him—and to keep his mind in shape to play goal in our next game? "Same as everybody else. I was blown away."

"Robby, I swear I didn't hear about it till my cousin called last night. I didn't tell her anything."

"Who's 'her'? What didn't you hear about?"

"All of this. That somebody outside the team knew what happened. I didn't rat to her or anybody else. But then that reporter guy came to the house."

"Barr? What did you say to him?"

"Nothing. You know that, you saw the news."

"Huh? Barr said they couldn't find you."

"That was before. We were with my grandfather."

Finally it hit me why this wasn't making sense. "I only saw the early news," I said. "You must have been on the one at ten."

"*I* wasn't on it. Well, except for that video of practice. The TV guys showed up and I wouldn't talk to them. I didn't want to sound like a whiner. They asked my mom some questions and she started crying. She's stressed out because my grandfather's so sick. But people don't know that. They only know it looked like I squealed and told her what happened, and she freaked out. I didn't, though, you got to believe me."

"Hey, I believe you."

He seemed relieved, at least a little. "That's why I called. So you'd know this wasn't my fault."

Wow. Here was the guy who got dumped on the worst, worrying what the team would think. Suddenly I really liked this kid. "How come you didn't call earlier?" I asked.

"We were at the hospice all day. My mom's still there."

"Hospice?" The word sounded nice, like hospitality or the youth hostels Paul stayed at when he backpacked through Europe.

"It's a hospital where people go to die. Like my grandfather. That's why my mom started bawling last night, not because of stupid tampons on my head." Now Tommy was crying, not a lot but I could hear it. "You should see him in that bed, all shrunk up like a mummy. Throat cancer. He can't even talk. So what does my mom do? Smokes a pack a day, same as he did. And she's a nurse!"

I was pretty sure no one else on the team knew about this. Tommy kept mostly to himself, not really a loner, just quiet. If Reynolds *had* known, maybe none of this crap would have happened. Coach wouldn't have picked on a guy when he was down. Would he?

"Can I do anything, Tommy? Should I tell Reynolds?"

"No way!" Five seconds went by. Then Tommy said, "I wonder who shot that video."

It wasn't a direct question, so I had room to weasel. If he'd asked if I *knew* who shot it, I'd have had a quick choice: lie, or tell about Pet.

"Pet Armstrong." I heard the words before I realized I'd said them. What did I just *do*? But Tommy deserved to know, right?

"The one with the white hair? The magazine girl?"

"Yeah."

"Why'd she do it?"

"Because I told her about Purgatory Practice and she thought it was sick."

"You *told* her?"

"Not after practice. Before. So she wouldn't think I was a wuss for not running with her on Friday night."

"Friday night? What is she, your girlfriend?"

"No, we're just—" I cut myself off, feeling like a coward. "You know what? Maybe she is."

"Really?" Tommy said. "Want to talk to her?"

You don't *know* how much I want to talk to her. I've been waiting all day for her to call, and it's real nice of you to offer to hang up.

"Thanks for asking. Listen, Clank, you sure there's nothing I can do to help?"

"I think you already did," Pet said.

Huh? Where did she come from?

"Pet, where are you?"

"At Tommy's house. I gave him a ride back from the hospice."

This was getting weirder. "What were *you* doing there?"

"I volunteer on Sunday afternoons."

"Since when?"

"Since that trouble I had freshman year. So I could help people with real problems and stop feeling sorry for myself."

"Why didn't you tell me?"

"I was afraid you'd think I was bragging. You know, that I was such a good person or something. Besides—there's a lot people don't tell each other, right?"

"I've been finding that out lately."

"Why did you call Tommy 'Clank'?"

"It's just some guy thing," I said.

"There was a kid on my Little League team they used to call Clank. Because he was such a crummy fielder the ball always bounced off him."

"Pet," I whispered, "drop the nickname stuff. Trust me. Tommy's been embarrassed enough this weekend."

"I see," she said. "It's a pen name. Like Marguerite St. John." She pronounced the name in a hokey British accent and started giggling. I heard Tommy laughing too.

You know the weird thing? Not that they were laughing, though I sure hadn't expected it. But that I felt jealous they were laughing together, and I wasn't in on the joke.

Still giggling, Pet said, "I'm so glad you were home, Robby. I'm so glad this worked out OK."

Worked out? For you, maybe. But what's going to happen to our team?

"Listen," I said. "How about if I come over?"

"Tommy might like that. But I have to go. I've got a ton of homework."

In the background Tommy said, "Passion's trigger on tiptoes."

Did I hear that right? The title of the book Marguerite gave me?

"Outback angel maiden in the palm of her hand," Pet said, and the two of them cracked up again.

What the...? Pet and Clank were mocking Marguerite's books, twisting around her lame titles.

"Where the harvest moonshine blows," I said, trying to join in. Tommy couldn't hear me, but Pet laughed. She laughed hard. And so did petty Robby Fielder, happy that this time Tommy was the one left out of the joke.

Pet said goodbye, and gave Clank the phone. I heard, "Ciao, Tommy," then a quick kissing sound. It was probably just on the cheek, but even if it was lips, so what? It was a friendly kiss, that's all. It shouldn't bother me.

It bothered me. Casually I asked, "How'd you meet Pet, anyway?"

It was pretty strange, he said. Clank had left his grandfather's bedside to go the bathroom, and on the way back he passed a waiting room with books and magazines. He went in. It was no big deal, a few shelves and chairs, crumpled copies of *People* and *Time* on the table. But then he saw a book with a half-naked woman on the cover, hugging some musclebound character in the desert while a kangaroo looked on. He had to take a look. Which is how he came to be reading *Outback Maiden* when Pet walked by. To break the ice, she pointed out the whole set of her mother's books that Marguerite had donated to the hospice. By the time he went back to his grandfather's room Tommy had laughed with Pet at Marguerite's titles, and gotten an offer of a lift home when Pet's shift was over.

"So you're cool with it?" I said. "With what Pet did with the video and all?"

He didn't answer for a while. Finally he said, "If it gets us a new coach I'd have run naked with that thing on my head."

"What if it doesn't?"

"Then I was a horse's ass for nothing." Clank hesitated. "Pet told me about this time something awful happened to her."

"That nude photo of her on the couch." I should have just let Tommy tell the story, but this was my petty way of saying, *I'm* the one who's really close to her, and knew this long before you did.

"Nude photo? Are you kidding me?"

Oh, great, way to go, Fielder. "Tommy, you have to promise not to say anything. To anyone. I only opened my mouth because I thought you knew."

He laughed. "I *did* know. But I couldn't help seeing if you'd panic."

To me Tommy had been just a backup goalie who puked before games, a quiet sophomore I'd hardly even talked to. Now

I saw he had a sense of humor—and it was the twisted kind I like. He could roll with the punches, too. I mean, how would I be taking it if my grandfather was dying, and I'd been on TV with that thing bouncing on my head?

I laughed too. "Did I? Panic, that is?"

"Not as much as I would have. Look, what I started to say—"

"Before you were so rudely interrupted."

"Before I was so rudely interrupted the *first* time, is that when you see people dying in a hospice you get some perspective. Getting embarrassed is nothing compared to that."

"I'll take your word for it."

"I'd better hang up," Tommy said. "In case my mom needs to call."

"OK, I'll see you tomorrow. Hey Tommy?"

"Yeah?"

"It was good talking to you."

"Yeah, Robby. Same here."

It *was* good talking to him. Depending on what happened next, there was even a chance of a happy ending to this mess.

Chapter 22

NEWFIELD HIGH IS SMALL, but it's not like you see every kid every day. Or maybe it's more that you don't pay attention. You notice your friends, but others aren't really on your radar screen.

That Monday, Tommy Francis was on everyone's radar screen.

The few people who hadn't heard before were clued in by the end of homeroom. I wondered if Mr. Lee would bring up the Tommy situation during the announcements, but no way. I didn't blame the guy. No matter what he said, it would have bothered somebody.

Instead, he acted like Newfield had won the state championship because the football team beat South York on Friday. That glorious victory pulled us out of the cellar of the Shoreline Conference, leaving South York the only team without a win. Kids in homeroom had tons of comments, most of them sarcastic.

"Whoopie-frigging-do."

"In the battle of the previously unvictorious, otherwise known as the Toilet Bowl."

"Hey, instead of 'We're number one' we can yell 'We're next to last!'"

The only football player there, a reserve linebacker named Eric Leonidas, looked ready to snap somebody's spine. "If you losers think you can do better, why don't you go out for the team?"

Donny McDonough pushed his greasy hair away from his eyes but it fell right back. "I'd just as soon keep all my brain cells, dude."

That cracked everyone up, since Donny's the biggest stoner in the school. Mrs. Sugg was still trying to get us under control when the bell rang for first period. "Get out of here, you barbarians," she said. "Go plague someone else."

Five seconds later the halls were swarming with students and buzzing like a beehive. For the first time ever I looked for Tommy. For about the twentieth time I looked for Pet. Zero luck either way. But that didn't mean much, since kids slowed me down bugging for details about Purgatory Practice. I barely made class before the late bell.

The whole morning was crazy like that. No sign of Pet or Tommy. I didn't even see Jim until American Studies fourth period, the only class we have together. I take lots of Advanced Placement and Honors courses while he chills in the regular classes, pulls a B+ average without straining his brain, and figures that's good enough to go to UConn on a soccer scholarship. And if UConn doesn't give him a scholarship, he'll go someplace that will. No problem; he's mellow about it. More important, Jim's *parents* are mellow about it. Once his mom told us, "It hardly matters which college you go to. There are good teachers and bad teachers at every school, and if you want to learn you'll do it no matter where. And vice versa." Sometimes that sure seems better than working your butt off the way I do, trying to impress top-tier schools. Plus, how cool would it be to play another four years with Jim?

Then I remember my brother, how proud my parents are of him and how they expect me to achieve the same standards. Suddenly, being less than the best stops looking fun and starts looking scary. I don't care how often my brain tells me I wouldn't be a loser, I'd still *feel* like one.

"Dude," Jim said, "what's going to *happen*?""

"I wish I knew," I said. "Have you seen Pet today? Or Clank?"

"Who the hell's Clank?"

"Tommy Francis. He got the name at practice Saturday."

"From running around with rags on his head?"

Vicki Geraci shot us an evil look. Jim's my best friend but he's got a big mouth sometimes. "I'll tell you later," I said. "So did you see them?"

"Nah. But I wasn't looking for *her*."

"All I know is he'd better be at practice."

Jim nodded. Reynolds's policy was clear: miss practice and you sit the next game. If Tommy didn't show up, we'd have to play a tough Riverview team tomorrow with a freshman goalkeeper. Freshmen can be good players, of course. Not to brag, but Jim and I both started varsity as freshmen. But Ravi Shankar wasn't varsity material, not yet anyway. In a year or two, yes, when he grew and got stronger.

"*Clank*?" Jim asked. "What's up with that?"

"Later," I whispered, for Miss Munro had started talking and I'm never rude to teachers as pretty as she is.

———————

"Maybe Francis got a headache from those rags bouncing off his brain!"

"I heard he was off making a commercial for Tampax!"

That was typical of the brilliant remarks flying around the halls. I'm sure most people felt sorry for Tommy and were on his side. Probably even most of the loudmouths were. But when idiots have a chance to get attention they usually take it, no matter who they hurt.

Not that Tommy was there to hear the comments. It was looking more and more like he was going to bail out on us. He must have been too embarrassed to deal with people at school. But that excuse didn't fly. Clank was letting the team down if he couldn't play tomorrow. I had let the team down when I smacked Dorsey, but at least that happened fast, before I had time to think. If anything, Tommy had too much time to think about this. But the guy had better get used to it. If he thought the jerks at Newfield High were bad, imagine the fans and players of the other teams. Those people would be merciless.

What if Tommy didn't *want* to play tomorrow? Think of all the attention he was going to get after being on the news, and the pressure, and the razzing that was sure to be part of it. Cretins who couldn't care less about soccer would show up to laugh at the kid who had worn the Bonnet. But Clank had to suck it up for the good of the team. He couldn't let us all get shafted because he couldn't take the heat, no matter how blistering.

At lunchtime I was waiting in line, breathing the ganky aroma of mystery meat and trying to sort out a thousand thoughts. Up ahead Destiny Decker and Amber Daly were whispering back and forth, agitated, like they were having an argument. Amber kept looking back. They let a few people pass and stood next to me.

"How are you doing, Robby?"

"Not bad." We weren't close friends or anything, but I knew them both. Destiny is one of the few African American kids at

Newfield, and always has lead roles in the school plays. Amber is also big in the drama club, and famous for never wearing anything but black.

Amber pointed her finger at me. Even her nail polish was black. "This Tommy Francis thing is bugging me."

"Bugging *us*," Destiny added.

"Me too," I said.

"Why? Because he was embarrassed?"

"Why else?"

Amber rolled her eyes. "Oh, my heart bleeds. The poor boy had to wear tampons one morning. Women have to wear them every month. Let him try that, *then* maybe I'll feel sorry for him."

"We're judged on our sexuality every day," Destiny said, "by the size of our breasts. How would you like *your* reproductive equipment on display?"

I had no good answer, but a couple of guys behind me had some bad ones.

"I'll show you any time you want, baby!" Dave Stanley said.

Bob King elbowed Stanley in the ribs. "Francis is hung like a mosquito so you couldn't see it anyway!"

King has the *brain* of a mosquito, but he's flaming Albert Einstein compared to Stanley. Fortunately, by the time the girls finished arguing with those two geniuses I had my lunch and could escape. Sitting with the soccer guys was an easy choice with Pet not around. Besides, we had so much to talk about after all that happened. But guess what? After about five minutes nobody had much to say. Everyone kept glancing at the cafeteria clock, watching the hands creep toward noon. That was the deadline. The school rule is if you come in after twelve you can't do extracurricular activities that day.

Both hands on the clock pointed up to the 12. The mystery meat was a lump in my mouth.

Rossi jabbed his spoon in his chocolate pudding. It stood up as straight as the hands on the clock. "We're hurtin' for certain now." Nick squished the spoon around his pudding. "*Clank*," he said scornfully. "Yeah, he's really got some brass ones."

"More like glass ones," Jim said.

"Hey," Barry Leeds said. "Check out Shankar."

Ravi was sitting with a bunch of other freshmen, laughing so hard his face was red. Two jets of milk spurted out his nose.

"Talk about brass balls," Jim said. "The little dweeb's not even scared about tomorrow."

Nick shook his head. "He's just clueless and doesn't know he'll be playing."

"Should I go break the news?" I asked.

"Hell no," Nick said. "I can't stand to see a kid crap his pants in public. Let Reynolds tell him at practice."

We were all worried about practice that day anyway. Having Ravi as first-string keeper would only add to how messed up it was. Just last week we were bummed to have Tommy in goal. Now we were bummed to lose him.

Suddenly the guys sitting across from me looked stunned. I flinched as two hands touched my shoulders. Warm breath and soft lips grazed my ear.

Pet whispered, "Tommy's grandfather died."

Next to me, Jim heard her and passed it along. No one on the team said a word after that, they just watched us and waited. But that was nothing, that was expected. Then I realized almost the whole cafeteria was the same way, even Hagan and his table of BB-brained football players and cheerleaders. Dead quiet and looking right at us.

Pet's hands still gently gripped my shoulders. The cafeteria was still. My teammates still stared at us, or so I thought. Then I saw they were all looking *behind* me.

I turned and did the same. Pet took a step back. My stomach slipped and my heart froze. Under Pet's left eye was a shiny half-moon, dark purple like a ripe eggplant.

I stood up. My legs were jelly. "What happened?"

Pet's face was like a dam breaking. She started to cry. Though I'd never done anything like it in public before, I held out my arms to her. I didn't care who was watching or what they thought. It was no time to be an embarrassed coward.

"Come here," I said.

She ran into the hall.

If I was worried about being embarrassed before, that was nothing compared to this. I stood there with my arms still stretched out, a room full of people gawking at me. It was so quiet I could hear Pet's footsteps slapping fast on the tile.

I took off after her.

"You there, wait for the bell like everyone else!" yelled Mr. Dowd the chemistry teacher, one of the lunch monitors. I thought I heard the word "detention" but that didn't matter. Only Pet counted. But what if I got in trouble and they said I couldn't play tomorrow? She turned right around a corner, out of sight.

All I knew was she had a black eye and was crying. I couldn't just sit there. I followed her around the corner, slowing down enough so I didn't wipe out into the wall.

Nothing. That hall leads down to the junior high wing, and it was deserted. I slowed to a jog, then a walk. No way she made it to the far end without me seeing her. She had stopped somewhere. There aren't any classrooms at first, just the outer walls of the gym on the left and a big custodial closet on the right. I scraped my fingernails along the top row of cinder blocks with thick, glossy paint before it changes to a cheaper thin paint halfway up. I reached a girls' bathroom.

Really, really hoping no teacher would see me, I knocked. No answer. I cracked open the door.

"Pet? Are you in there? Are you OK?"

Not that she was likely to answer, but I sure wasn't going in if anyone *else* was there. I'd never been in a girls' bathroom before, had never even thought about it. I smelled stale cigarette smoke and ducked inside. They'd probably throw me in jail for being a pervert if I got caught, but I was only in there five seconds, tops. The place was empty. I peeked out to make sure no one was coming and slipped away in a hurry.

I opened the side door to the gym. To my left was the basketball court, and straight ahead the girls' locker room. I'd searched a bathroom—was I crazy enough to check a locker room? Instead of taking that big a chance I walked into the gym, hoping to get lucky.

I was under the backboard before I had the angle to see her. Until then Pet was hidden by the big folding partition that pulls out to divide the court in two. She was sitting on the top row of bleachers, head down, arms hugging her knees. I jogged over. The bleachers were shoved in so it wasn't easy to climb up there. You had to jump and get your elbows over the edge, then haul yourself up with your arms, like getting out of a pool without a ladder, only higher and harder. Not many girls can do it. Plenty of *guys* can't do it.

I didn't do it either, at first. I stood below and looked up at her. "Are you OK?"

Pet nodded. She wasn't crying, just rocking a little and staring out at a basketball game that wasn't there.

"You don't seem OK."

She shrugged.

I felt the hard wood of the bleachers against my shoulder. For a few seconds I joined her in watching the empty court. Any minute the bell would ring and kids would be flooding everywhere.

"Pet, who did that to you?"

She managed a crooked smile. "I'm no rat," she said.

I remembered saying the same thing to her, and how she had reacted. "You can't let them get away with it," I said.

"Funny, that's what *I* used to think. Which is why I shot that video. And people have been paying the price ever since."

"That's not true. It was a brave thing to do."

"Maybe, though I doubt it. But was it the *right* thing to do?"

I pulled myself up and sat next to her. Our thighs touched, the way they had in a maple tree on a night that already seemed far away.

I took my eyes off the court and spoke straight to her. "All I know is I'm glad you did it."

Pet brightened a little, though you could tell she was skeptical. She glanced at me, then away again. It was terrible to see that angry purple splotch under her eye.

"I thought you hated rats," she said.

"I don't hate anybody. But I admire people who stand up for what they believe." The words got tight in my throat and a few tears slipped out. I wiped them away without her seeing. I think.

"People like *you*," I said.

Suddenly Pet was hugging me, her face pressed tight to my shoulder. Her whole body quivered. I held on, the world blurry from the water welled up in my eyes.

I whispered in her ear. "Pet, who hit you?"

She shook her head. It was still shaking when she said in a tiny voice, "Your coach."

"Reynolds!"

"But it was—sort of my fault."

"*Your* fault? Are you sh… spitting me?"

"I could kick myself. It was so stupid. I shouldn't have gone to his house."

"But he *hit* you? That son of a—I'm calling the cops."

"No!"

"We can't just—"

"I said no cops! Don't tell anyone!"

"The guy is scum, Pet. I'm going to make him pay."

Her moist eyes locked on me. "You're going to make him pay, huh? You know just what to do to get justice? Like when I gave a videotape to a TV station, and someone said I blew it because I embarrassed the person I was trying to help. Who told me that? I think it was someone who said he can't stand a rat."

"This is different. He hit you. He could go to jail."

"Which I don't want."

"So he should get away with it?"

Pet's voice got soft again. "He's paid a high enough price. Any more would just be revenge, and that's too ugly."

"What are you talking about? So he's embarrassed—way less than Tommy, I bet, and it's his own fault."

"You have no idea how much coaching your team meant to him."

"'Meant'? What's with the past tense?"

Pet rubbed her eyes. Fresh tears replaced the ones she wiped away.

"He resigned."

"Reynolds quit?!"

"Yesterday. He'd just got off the phone with the superintendent when I knocked on his door. Which is why I can't totally blame him for losing it. The man was stressed out bad."

"Let me get this straight. If a guy's stressed it's OK if he decks a girl?"

"That's not what I'm saying. And he didn't deck me. It wasn't like that."

"Oh yeah? What *was* it like?"

"Look, I saw the news report, and what Reynolds said. Suddenly I felt like a coward for submitting that video anonymously. So I drove over to tell him why I did it."

"Are you insane?" I said. But I was thinking, That's why I respect this girl so much. And like her even more.

"I have to live with myself, don't I? I was worried he wouldn't answer the door. I saw him peek through the curtains, then he let me in. He looked like he hadn't slept for days. 'I've already bought from a few kids,' he said, 'but I'll take a year of *TV Guide*.'

"Can you believe it—he thought I was selling magazines! When I told him the truth his eyes got all squinty. 'Go,' he said, 'you have to leave, right now.' He pushed me toward the door. But I was turning and off balance, and there was a slippery throw rug on the hardwood floor. I fell and hit the corner of a table."

"He shoved you into a *table?*"

"He was shocked. It was an accident."

"But he pushed you!"

"He started crying."

"*Reynolds?*"

"Crying and apologizing and asking me to forgive him."

"Of course. He doesn't want you to sue him."

"I was so upset, I did something cruel. I told him about Tommy's grandfather to make him feel guilty. It worked. He was in real pain. The only problem was when I saw his face I felt worse for doing it."

"He made an ice bag for my eye. He opened a photo album and showed me his two daughters and his wife who died, and said about ten times he never laid a finger on them, he had never hit a woman for anything, and then he'd apologize some more. I felt terrible."

"Then he took out another album. Nothing in it but Newfield High soccer photos. The last one was of your team. He kept saying how proud he was of you guys, and how he was going to miss you."

Pet was officially crying herself now. I was fighting not to join her.

She swallowed hard. "That's when he told me the superintendent had just called. With two choices: resign or get fired."

The bell rang. Soon the halls would be swarming, and kids would be rushing in for gym class. I kissed her, quick, and we climbed down.

"Thanks for telling me, Pet. Really. You're amazing."

She looked at the floor.

"See you in Mr. Mac's class," I said.

Pet touched my lips and turned away. A couple of rowdy freshmen ran into the gym like baboons. Pet headed for the far door, by the girls' locker room where I'd come in. Probably she wanted to duck into the quieter bathroom over there. I waited behind the bleachers as long as I dared then walked fast with my head down, trying to avoid Mr. Dowd the lunch monitor. Kids said stuff to me, asking if I found Pet and what happened to her, but I shut up and kept moving. The only one I would have talked to was Jim, to tell him about Reynolds, but I didn't see him. I made it to Mr. Mac's room without getting caught and slipped into my seat.

The bell rang. Pet was nowhere in sight. And she was never, ever late.

Chapter 23

M R. MAC STOOD UP from his desk. He crossed his arms over his chest, a pose that was definitely not normal for him. "Has anyone seen Pet Armstrong?"

Silence. Fifteen kids, and no one said a word. Which was weird, because there were lots of different personalities in the class. Most had just seen Pet in the cafeteria. But not one of them talked. Were they protecting her? The strange new girl who didn't look like them? Or maybe covering for the moron kid who ran after her.

Mr. Mac nodded and showed a tight little smile. "Don't worry, gang, I already know. News travels fast in Camp Newfield. Besides, she stopped by to see me before she went to the caf."

Skunk Darwin raised his hand. "Who popped her in the eye?"

"I believe it was an accident."

"Yeah, Skunk," said Dennis Chase. "An accident. You know, like when your parents had you."

Everybody laughed, even Mr. Mac a little. I wondered if he knew where Pet was. I had a feeling she was with Tommy. If I were a better person that wouldn't have bothered me. After all, I wasn't the one whose grandfather just died, or who got her bravery repaid with a black eye. But I'm not a better person, and it did bother me. I remembered them laughing on the phone about Marguerite's book titles, how they had seemed so close and friendly. I worried that I was losing Pet—if you could say I had ever found her in the first place.

Mr. Mac held up a hand. "OK, settle down. I don't know what deviltry you citizens were up to this weekend, but I spent Saturday night reliving old times with a friend I hadn't seen in years. To quote Loudon Wainwright—he's a singer, listen to him sometime—'we kissed the past's ass all night long.'"

A few people giggled. Most of us didn't. Mr. Mac seemed dead serious and we wondered where he was going with this. Especially me. I'd been there on Saturday night. There was no friend. Mr. Mac was crying all by himself.

"We've been discussing where stories come from, where characters come from. Well, they can come from anywhere. And one important place is the past. They'll get changed by the present, of course, but you know why? Mostly because the present has already changed *us*."

He was pacing across the front of the room. His fists were clenched. He shoved his hands in his pockets. He was talking *to* us but not *at* us, not making eye contact the way he usually did. It was like he wanted to make sure we couldn't distract him from what he needed to say.

"Look, the past is the one thing you can't change. Ever. You can try to fix it but you can't change it. And the saddest words in the whole bloody world are 'It's too late.'"

I don't think anyone was following him too great right then. I sure wasn't.

"Next month we're going to read a book by Tim O'Brien called *The Things They Carried*. It's about Vietnam but it's more than that. It's about keeping the past alive through stories. And keeping people alive, even when they're gone. Because without stories the connection is lost."

He stared out the window, hands behind his back. "How many of you own photographs?"

All of our hands went up. Ten long seconds passed.

"Why?" he asked, still looking out the window.

Finally he turned to face us. "I'll tell you why. Because those pictures tell stories, those stories are our lives and we don't want to lose the connections. Stories are a necessity, not a luxury. They're a big part of being human. Even if they sometimes hurt."

I thought of Pet, that awful party photo of her, the video she took of Purgatory Practice, the albums Reynolds showed her of his life. Those pictures were part of my story too—even if they sometimes hurt.

"If I don't teach you a single other thing, please learn this—nothing really matters but your relationships with people. And that includes yourself. Those are our stories, our connections. If you put money, or pride, or a career or anything else first, you won't be happy."

"What about God?" Christine Doyle said accusingly.

Mr. Mac didn't hesitate. "That's one more relationship." He sat on his desk. "I'm going to level with you. My friend on Saturday night wasn't just a friend. It was my ex-wife. We remembered a lot of stories, some of which I wish I could rewrite, but they're in the past and it's too late for changes. Because unlike our written stories, life is always a first draft."

I wiped my palms on my pants. It was kind of creepy, but kind of cool too that Mr. Mac's visitor had only been in his head.

But that didn't mean she wasn't real. It's like reading, when people come to life in our minds because our eyes see little ink marks that we call words. It's almost magic, when you think about it, but totally real at the same time.

"OK, let's try an exercise. Think of a pleasant experience you've had (rated no worse than PG-13, don't get any ideas), then add a conflict that didn't really happen. Add more than one if you can. Because fiction needs...?"

"Conflict!" we all said, like Pavlov's puppies.

"Bingo. No trouble, no interest. We might want to *live* without problems, but we don't want to read about it."

Most everything that had happened to me lately had some trouble attached to it, even the good stuff. I remembered a double I hit last baseball season to win a game. What if the ball had gone a foot to the right? Maybe the third baseman makes the catch, or even a double play. What if the ball had kicked off a pebble and bounced up into the guy's face? That reminded me of Pet's black eye, which got me thinking about her, and five minutes later I'd hardly written a word when the door creaked and slowly opened.

Principal Lee practically tiptoed in, as if somehow we wouldn't notice him if he kept quiet. He whispered to Mr. Mac, who tapped his pencil on the desk as he listened. I wondered if I was in trouble for skipping out on lunch. That could cost me a detention, or even mess me up for playing tomorrow. Maybe I shouldn't have taken off after Pet. But what choice did I have?

"Robby?" Mr. Lee crooked his finger at me. I stood up, my heart slamming harder than before I take a penalty kick. Way harder. On the field at least I'm in charge; it's up to me what happens next, because if I kick the ball right no keeper in the world can stop the shot. But now someone else was in control.

Mr. Lee walked fast. I stayed a step behind him; somehow it felt safer where he couldn't see me. He stopped at Miss Amenta's room. "Wait here," he said. "I'll be right out."

Man, did I have an urge to run down the hall, out the door and just keep going. I stood with my hands crammed in my back pockets, shifting my weight from one foot to the other. The door opened and Nick Rossi came out.

"I believe you two have been introduced," Mr. Lee said. He gestured for us to go first, so Nick and I could only trade a quick glance before we started walking.

Why did Mr. Lee come to get us instead of using the intercom or sending a secretary? This had to be important. It couldn't be over me and Pet. Nick had no part in that.

"Hold up," Mr. Lee said, and went into Mr. Lombardi's room. I didn't need Sherlock Holmes to know why. Jim had him for English that period. Lee wanted all three captains—I was first only because Mr. Mac's room was the farthest away from the office.

"Is she OK?" Nick said. "What happened to her eye?"

What a difference. A few days ago he can't stand Pet, now he asks how she's doing. And he seems to actually care.

I didn't know what to say. Would Pet want me to cover for Reynolds or tell the truth? All my old ideas about being honest or a rat were mixed-up.

"I think she's OK," I said. "Considering."

The door opened and Jim stepped out like a prisoner on Death Row. Jim almost never gets scared, or at least almost never shows it. But one look at him now and my confidence sprang a leak.

In the principal's office Mr. Lee sat at his desk. He nodded at three chairs lined up in front of him.

"Park your carcasses."

We did.

"Would somebody mind telling me what's going on with this soccer team?"

No one said anything. I remembered about body language, though, and didn't cross my legs or fold my arms. I looked him in the eye.

"I'm going to give it to you guys straight. This school does not need publicity like we got over the weekend. Coach Reynolds has been successful for many years, and has a lot of support in this community. But other people are calling for his head. Bottom line, it's time to move in another direction, and I wanted the captains to know first. Preston Bass will be your coach for the rest of the season."

Nick and Jim grinned like we'd just won the state championship. I would've too, if only I didn't feel sorry for Reynolds at the same time. And I knew how conflicted Pet would be. So I didn't have a big grin—but I sure had a little smile.

Mr. Lee stood up. "That's it, back to class. Mrs. Caldwell will give you passes."

We started to leave. "Boys?"

Oh no, I thought, here it comes.

"Be ready this afternoon. God knows what kind of circus we might have on our hands."

I alternated feeling crappy for Coach and happy that he was history. No, that's a lie—I felt both things at the exact same time. Like I felt bad for Pet, but mad that she blew off class—and me—and was probably with Tommy right then. Gimme a break, I told myself, he's just her friend, that's all. But this little voice in my head kept whispering that maybe I was the one who was only a friend.

Mrs. Rieth's class crept like a snail, as usual. I could see the soccer field outside her window, all green and waiting, and as she droned on I watched Mr. Raebeck the custodian put fresh chalk on the lines. It was rude to stare out the window so I didn't, not really, though Mrs. Rieth couldn't have cared less as long as you kept quiet. She just wanted to get through the year and retire to Florida.

I checked the clock for about the fiftieth time. Finally, class was almost over. I took a last look at the field before the bell rang. A Channel Two truck pulled up. Is this what Lee meant by a circus? Well, the joke's on them. Clank's not even here. There's nothing to take pictures of but our game, and you don't care diddly about that.

We captains had spread the word, so by the time we hit the locker room the whole team knew about Reynolds. Preston was in the coaches' office, looking pretty nervous to tell you the truth. He kept running his hand over the back of his head. Which is when I noticed his ponytail was history.

"Check it out," I said. "Preston got a chop job."

"What's up with that?" Nick said.

"Less hair for us to turn gray," I said.

Preston came out a few minutes later. "Meeting in the Team Room. You know the drill."

Actually, we didn't. We knew the drill with Coach Reynolds, but now we were Preston's team.

Everybody squeezed into the Team Room. I smelled Icy Hot that guys had rubbed on sore muscles. Preston stood in front of the chalkboard. He scanned the room, taking the time to look at each one of us. Finally he nodded, like he was satisfied with what he saw.

"In case you're wondering, I didn't cut my hair because I was sick of it. I cut it to show a new beginning. It'll grow back, and this team will keep on growing, too. But something can't grow out of nothing. So listen up—we're going to win this game for Coach Reynolds. His way wasn't always my way, but no one has done more for this program than he did. Every single one of you is a better player because of him. Don't forget that."

He paused to let it sink in. "Does anyone here not know what we need to do to beat Riverview?"

No one answered.

"Good. So I won't insult your intelligence repeating what you already know. Instead I want each of you to dig deep inside. Find your center, get calm and think about what you have to do. What you're *going* to do. *Visualize.* See things before they happen. Then perform when the time comes. Especially you, Tommy. This is your last game before Jim comes back. Make it count."

What? Suddenly hopeful, every guy on the team looked around. No Clank.

Preston's face looked like mine when I'm doing chemistry problems. "What's going on? Where's Tommy?"

I met Nick's eyes; he gave me a little nod.

"His grandfather died," I said. "Tommy didn't come to school."

Preston must have been blown away, but he didn't show it. In fact, the confusion on his face a minute ago was gone, replaced by confidence. "All right, let's win this one for Coach Reynolds *and* Tommy."

He pointed at Shankar, slouched in a corner. "This is your day to shine, Ravi. OK, guys, find your centers and visualize."

We tried, we really did. But it's tough to find your center while listening to a kid barf his guts out, because Ravi hauled butt to the bathroom soon after he heard the news. That answered our question in the cafeteria, when he was laughing with those other freshmen. The kid didn't have ice water in his veins, he was just too clueless to realize he might be starting in goal this afternoon. Now he knew, and up came lunch. Great, I thought, just great. Riverview was going to eat him alive.

Preston realized the meditation wasn't working. "Let's hit the field. Two easy laps, then do your stretches."

We headed out, not too psyched. Ravi might be a disaster. Suddenly there was a huge bang against the lockers, like Reynolds used to do. I nearly jumped out of my cleats.

Preston grinned at us. "Just once, gentlemen, for old times' sake." The grin disappeared. "Now go out, show some pride and do what you know how to do."

"What about Ravi?" I said. We heard retching, and the toilet flushed again.

"Just get yourselves ready to play. He'll be all right."

"Yeah," Nick said, "if they don't get any shots on goal."

Preston stared at him hard. Not angry, just hard. "Well, you defenders know what you have to do then."

A tense couple seconds went by. Then Nick said, "No problem, coach," and took off, setting the pace. I joined him at the front and we started the chant, barking out "Newfield!" as we ran. It's a four-step rhythm: "*New*-field!" step-step, "*New*-field!" step-step. Sure it's dorky but too bad, it gets you psyched and makes you feel like a team, all together. And the closer we got to the field, the more it looked like we'd *have* to get psyched and be a team to make it through this game.

Remember I said we never got big crowds for our games, even though we were winning, while the football team could be losers of the universe and people would still go? Well, it was half an hour before game time and the two sets of bleachers were already jammed, with dozens of other people standing around. I saw tons of faces—kids, adults, girls, boys—who'd never been at our games before. I looked behind me. Plenty more were streaming around the far side of the school. They must have had to park by the football field, because the lot near our field was packed—including trucks from three TV stations.

Don't get me wrong. It was great to see a real crowd, and hear loud cheering when we took the field. But there was something creepy about it, too. Most of those people weren't there because they followed our team or cared about soccer. It took strange stuff on TV to bring them out. And I had a scary feeling that seeing more strange stuff now was all they cared about.

We quit the "Newfield!" chant as we started our laps. Nick and I led the way, a little faster than usual. A crowd gets you pumped up, gets you psyched, which is good unless you lose control. Or instead of getting psyched up you get psyched out.

"Ain't it great how everyone loves us?" I said.

Nick smirked. "Practice your autograph." He picked up the pace a little more. "With Shankar in goal we're in crap up to our eyeballs."

"Hey, like you said, just stop 'em from taking any shots."

He turned his head and spat. "That's what I like about you, Fielder. If reality gets in the way you kick it in the nuts and keep on going."

We did our cals and stretches and Ricky Prentice was just rolling out the balls when Riverview showed up. Normally I ignore the other team, or try to, but not much was normal about today. With the lot overflowing, their bus couldn't pull up anywhere near as close as usual. They had to walk across ten yards of asphalt to reach the grass. And I'll tell you what—those guys looked pretty freaked out. No way they expected TV cameras filming them as they got off the bus. I doubt they expected boos, either, but that's what they got from lots of the rowdy kids—and some adults, too—who were probably at their first soccer game ever. Boos are maybe common at a pro game or somewhere like England with hooligan fans, but in high school it's more or less bogus. Boo a jerk like Dorsey if you want, for cheap shots or dirty play, but not a whole team for just running onto the field.

I kept an eye on the far-off locker room door, hoping for a sign of Ravi. Until Preston came out Nick and I had to take charge, and now we didn't even have a goalie to practice shots on net. And the crowd kept growing.

"Robby Fielder!"

I turned around. Burlin Barr was striding toward me, a microphone in one hand and a camerman trailing right behind. He smiled like we'd been friends for years, and stuck the mike in my face.

"Where's your goalie, pal? He and Reynolds having a heart-to-heart talk in the locker room? How's team morale after this weekend?"

Three things were obvious. One, Barr wanted to talk to Tommy, not me. Two, he didn't know Clank wouldn't be here. Three, he hadn't heard about Reynolds resigning. I saw other news people rushing over. Where was Preston to deal with this?

"Are you guys are supposed to be on the field?" Nick said. We didn't know for sure—we'd never had to deal with reporters before. At least not this kind of reporter, asking questions instead of just watching the game and writing about what happened.

Barr ignored Nick. Reporters were talking to our players at random: "Which one is Tommy Francis?" "Where is he, then?" Soon they all knew Clank was a no-show, and they weren't happy. They were only interested in the tampon-boy, not our team. No Tommy and they might as well pack up their gear and go find a real story.

Ricky Prentice came up to me. "Robby, I'll get in goal so the guys can warm up."

He tried to be casual but I could tell this meant a lot to him. I wanted to say yes as much as he wanted to hear it. But there was a reason Ricky had to stop playing; multiple sclerosis is no joke.

"I don't know, RP. What if you get hurt?"

He nodded toward the reporters. "Good. Maybe I'll get on TV."

This was turning into a zoo. The crowd kept growing, including a bunch of teachers who'd never come to our games before.

It might be a mistake, but hey, what was one more? "Go for it," I said. "But be friggin' careful."

Suddenly the crowd started going nuts, totally bonkers, clapping, hooting, whistling, yelling like maniacs. Every guy on both teams stopped and looked around. I caught Nick's eye and it was obvious we had the same thought: OK, what *now*?

Then I saw about the last thing I expected: Tommy Francis, in his long-sleeve yellow goalie shirt, running toward the field. No, not running, *sprinting*, as fast as in Purgatory Practice with the Tiara bouncing on his head. But why? It's not like he could play.

As Clank got closer some people in the stands stood up to cheer. Within seconds, every single person in the bleachers had joined them. By the time Tommy hit the field he was getting a standing ovation, from everyone in the seats and from the much bigger group already standing because the bleachers couldn't hold them. And I mean everyone. I didn't recognize a lot of those faces. Plenty must have been from Riverview, or wherever.

Were they applauding Tommy and his courage, or were they just happy the show they'd come to see had finally got on stage? All I knew was that our whole team, me included, started clapping too. So did some of the Riverview players, till their coach made them stop. The cameramen were shooting like crazy. Tommy ran up to me as reporters swarmed around.

"Preston's on his way. Ravi's got the dry heaves."

"Sorry about your grandfather," I told him.

"I can't believe you made it," Nick said.

Clank shook his head. "It's what he wanted." Ignoring reporters' questions he took off toward our goal. "Let's go!" he said, waving us over.

Nick stood with one foot on a soccer ball. "But he can't play, right? He wasn't in school."

"Man, I don't know *what's* going on." I started dribbling a ball, making cuts. "But we gotta get warmed up in a hurry."

Which is what we were doing when Preston jogged out a minute later, followed by Ravi. I knew he'd be running no matter how ganked he felt. Reynolds might be gone, but a Newfield soccer player never walks to the field.

Preston hustled over and told the reporters to stop pestering Tommy. So they turned to him instead.

"How can Francis play if he missed school?"

"It's an administrative decision," Preston said. "Tommy's grandfather died, for God's sake. That's a pretty good excuse."

"The kid must be heartbroken. He comes right out and plays soccer!"

"Look, the man held on these past two weeks mostly because his grandson was starting for the varsity. He made Tommy promise he wouldn't miss a game because of him."

The reporters pressed closer.

"What's it like replacing a legend?"

"Coach, did you shoot that video on Saturday?"

Preston waved off the questions as he walked toward the bench. "Later. We've got a game to play."

"And I've got a deadline," Barr said. "Don't you want your side of the story on the six o'clock news?"

Preston stopped and looked him in the face. "What part of 'We've got a game to play' don't you understand?"

Barr smiled, but it wasn't friendly. "You're going to regret that, mister. This was your big chance to get started on the right foot."

"Maybe. But I kick damn well with my left foot, too."

The newspaper reporters laughed and scribbled Preston's quote in their notebooks. I got the impression they weren't great friends with the TV guys.

Nick and I went to take our traditional pair of practice penalty kicks. But we only hit one each before the whistle blew. Both shots found the back of the net, though, low and hard.

"Money," I said.

"Come on, Francis," Nick said. "I want to hear 'em clanking when you dive for those balls."

Tommy tried to smile, but it didn't happen. He and Nick started over to our bench. Before I joined them I threw another look at the crowd. It was huge, at least by our standards. Jim was over there, looking so psyched to play that he couldn't sit down. I saw Mr. Powell, as usual, and Jim's mom, and Mr. Mac—oh man, there's Marguerite! That bald-headed bear next to her must be Pet's stepfather.

"*Vamos*, Roberto! Quick goal, what do you say!"

Unbelievable. It was the first game Mom had made all season. For a second I was bummed that it took a scandal to get her to show up. Maybe she was hoping to sell a house to Burlin Barr. But what the hey, she was there and I was glad. She waved but no way would I wave back. A nerd waving to his mother? I held up my cast and made a fist, hoping that at least had a *chance* of looking cool.

"Captains!" the ref called.

Nick headed out. Preston shoved Tommy after him.

I met them at midfield. "What's up?"

"Clank's a captain," Nick said. "Preston said to pretend he's Jim today."

We shook hands with the Riverview captains. "Yo," said Tim Truxes, their best player, "that sucks what happened to you, dude."

Tommy shrugged. "There's worse things."

Nick and I knew what he was thinking of.

Truxes grinned. "But we're still going to beat your butt."

We lost the coin toss. I scanned the crowd again on our way back to the bench. Mr. Lee came out the back door and held it open. Tommy's mom followed. Then Pet.

Suddenly I was no more nervous than before, but my heart started beating faster. I bent over into the huddle. We all stretched forward to pile our hands on top of each other.

"No speeches," Preston said. "Just one team with every guy doing what he has to do. Ready?"

"One, two three, NEWFIELD!"

I don't know if it was the big crowd, our new coach, dedicating the game to Reynolds or what, but we came to play. If you've ever been on a team you know what I mean. You always try your best, but sometimes the pieces just really fall into place (just like sometimes they really fall apart). We were running hard and winning every loose ball. Our passes were crisp and controlled. Guys were playing smart. Our defense was so tight that Tommy was hardly tested, and their one tough shot he dove and deflected over the crossbar. I saw Mrs. Francis going nutso, jumping up and down, and Pet right with her. Remember Sam Castro, our Third Selectman who supported Reynolds and said our team was a bunch of wimps? He went as berserk as anyone else, whooping and stomping his feet on the bleachers.

All in all—man, was it fun. At the half we were pounding a good team, 2–0, and I had both goals, including a left-foot rocket from fifteen yards that was the prettiest shot of my life.

"Gorgeous shot, Robby," Preston said during halftime. "One for the highlight reels."

Nick took a big gulp of water, and spat most of it out. "Yeah. Too bad the TV cameras were gone."

"Who cares?" I said. It *would* have been cool to see a replay, though. But the TV people had left soon after the game started. They had their story already, and it didn't depend on who won. They could call in for the final score if they wanted it.

I lay back on the thick grass, and felt the big old world underneath me. Puffy clouds drifted across the sky like pillows. I closed my eyes, relaxed for the first time in quite a while. We'd made it through. Jim was coming back. Our season was saved. And Pet was watching our game, not crying someplace…with Tommy.

I leaned up on my elbows. Clank was slumped on our bench with his head down. I went over and sat next to him. "Great half," I said.

He nodded without raising his head.

"It's amazing what you're doing, playing like this after what happened."

Across the field, Tommy's mother and Pet were waving. I waved back. Clank was still having a staring contest with the ground.

"Your mom and Pet are waving to you."

Instead of at them he looked at me for a second, then back down. "She likes you, Robby. She really likes you. With me she only wants to be friends."

I felt terrible that what was good for me was bad for him. So what did I do? I said something totally lame.

"That's life, I guess."

Tommy sat on his hands. "So's death," he said. "Doesn't mean I have to like it."

As we warmed up for the second half I noticed how much the crowd had withered away. It was still our biggest of the season, but barely a third the size as at the start of the game. Some people had left when the TV cameras did, and lots more took off at halftime. They'd come to see the Bonnet Boy, not a soccer game.

Mom was gone, too. Probably a client called and she was off showing a house. Oh well, I thought, at least she saw me score those goals. I hoped so, anyway. For all I knew, she might have left before the first one.

I'll be honest. I wanted a hat trick—three goals in one game—and I wanted Pet to see me do it. Despite what she said in the hall that time about not liking jocks, I figured she might be impressed. Anyway, if I scored again it just about guaranteed we'd win. So what happens? Five minutes into the half, Tommy gives up a goal on a floater that Jim would have saved with his eyes closed. Suddenly the score was 2–1. You could feel Riverview's confidence rise out of the toilet. Just like that, they thought they had a chance again. And just like that, a lot of the cheering died down.

We didn't fall apart or anything. Nick muttered, "Even friggin' Shankar would have stopped that horseshit shot," but we all knew the goal was a lucky fluke that wouldn't happen again.

Except it did.

This one wasn't Tommy's fault, not really. It was a beautiful header off a corner kick. But I'd seen Jim run out and leap high to grab or punch away plenty of balls like that before the guy could get to it. The key was to take charge and not hesitate. Which is what I told myself I had to do now.

So the slaughter became a dogfight. We had more chances to score, and Nick was playing absolutely animal defense to protect Tommy. But we couldn't quite put the ball in the net. I hit the left post with one shot, and bounced another a couple inches wide right. Barry Leeds headed one off the crossbar. We had some wild scrambles in front of their goal where they just cleared the ball at the last second, or their keeper fell on it like a soldier on a grenade. It was only a matter of time till we scored, but time was running out. I wasn't psyched for overtime, because anything can happen then. I didn't want luck to be part of this.

Then Truxes took me down.

He tried a sliding tackle as I was lifting my foot to shoot, and cut my leg out from under me. I fell hard on my side. It wasn't a dirty play, like something Dorsey would have done. Truxes went for the ball. But he got me instead. My spikes slipped in the turf—I was lucky they didn't catch or my knee would have been spaghetti. My ankle twisted, the kind of sprain you have to keep running on and not let stiffen up. And as I lay there in the torn-up grass, the shrill blast of the ref's whistle pushed the hurt away.

Penalty kick! Yes!

"Sorry, dude, my bad." Truxes reached down to help me up. "You OK?"

"Yeah."

Truxes smiled like an evil choir boy. "You're gonna choke and blow this kick, though, aren't you?"

I didn't answer. I couldn't let him play with my head. My left ankle was throbbing like a heartbeat, but it was nothing I couldn't handle.

Nick ran up. "You all right, Robby? You cool to kick?"

I nodded. "No problem."

It was déjà vu all over again. Bad memories of my last penalty kick flooded back. Maybe I should let Nick take it. But my ankle's not too bad, I can do this. Hat trick city, baby.

The ref handed me the ball. I bent down to set it on the penalty kick stripe, a little off-center to get the goalie guessing, mess with his mind a little.

But what if you mi—

Don't even think it. Pet's going to see you nail this shot to ice the game and everything will be fine.

Or is she?

Unbelievable. As I backed away from the ball, getting ready to kick, Pet walked behind the goal. Not like last time, standing there and cheering for me. Now she was heading away from the school, up the slope toward the woods on the hill. She turned around and walked backward to watch me, but she didn't say a word. And she kept moving away.

What was she doing? My concentration went down the tubes. That was my fault, not hers, but it was a fact. When she started walking there was no way she knew a penalty kick was about to happen. Where was she going?

My head was not right. I had to concentrate on this shot, not on some girl drifting away from me. To stall for time I picked up the ball, pretended to adjust its position and returned it to the exact same spot.

Tell Nick to kick it, I thought. For the good of the team. You know you should.

But people will think I'm a pussy.

Oh yeah? Well, only a coward *cares* what they think.

The ref blew his whistle. Still torn by what I should do, I knew it was too late. Maybe the crowd was going wild, maybe the place was cemetery quiet. I have no idea. I was in a zone all alone. My world had shrunk to a leather ball sitting dead still on a three-foot stripe of chalk. I ran forward, still not even sure where I was aiming. Four words—KEEP YOUR HEAD DOWN!—pushed aside thoughts of Pet and pain as I drove my right foot through the ball.

A bullet. Lower left. Goalie sprawled with his face in the grass, no prayer.

I saw Pet jumping up and down like a cheerleader before my teammates mobbed me, pounding on my back. I heard the crowd now, going nuts for the hat-trick hero. And not a single one of them knew the truth.

I'd only done it because I was too afraid to let them think I was scared.

Minutes later the game ended. The win was sweet, real sweet. And I'd never scored three goals in a game before.

"Robby? Randy Turcotte, Hartford *Courant*. How much of a distraction was the Tommy Francis situation today?"

I'd seen Turcotte's picture a hundred times in the *Courant*, but he was taller than I'd expected, and wore thick hornrim glasses that weren't in the photo.

"Not *too* big, I guess. We won, didn't we?"

Turcotte smiled. "Mind if we move out there? It's so noisy by this bench I can't hear myself think. Not that I do much thinking in my line of work."

He grinned, and I did too. I knew he was only there because of Tommy, but at least he *was* there, and at least he had stayed for the whole game. We always complain how soccer gets ignored, so I'd have to be an idiot not to talk to him.

We moved out near the center of the field. I tried to come up with comments that halfway made sense and weren't total clichés. Over his shoulder, I scanned the corner behind the field where Pet had been.

"What's so interesting?" Turcotte asked.

"Nothing. Just kind of looking for somebody."

He turned around. "Up there?"

You know in the comics, how a light bulb goes on over somebody's head when they realize something? Well, it was like a searchlight turned on over Turcotte.

"Well, bugger a beehive," he said. "That's the angle they took the tampon video from!"

Suddenly my interview fell off his radar screen. "Thanks, Robby, but it's time for a little investigative journalism."

He stuck his pad in his pocket, lit a cigarette and started walking, fast. I followed for a few steps, then stopped. Better to stay out of it. He'd either find them or he wouldn't. They'd either talk to him or they wouldn't.

Because through the leaves I'd seen the flash of white hair. And next to it, the reflection off a camera lens beneath a camouflage army helmet, which used to be in the soccer coach's office and now sat on Ed Reynolds's head.

Chapter 24

OUR LOCKER ROOM WAS rocking after the game. We had survived Purgatory Practice, gotten a cool new coach and a tough win in front of the biggest crowd we'd ever played for. Even Tommy was laughing and celebrating. Guys congratulated him like crazy, and I was glad to be one of them. He deserved to enjoy this. Soon enough he'd remember about his grandfather, and Pet, and riding the bench again because Jim was coming back.

A towel snapped against my butt, not hard enough to sting. I turned around. Nick Rossi stood there naked holding his lucky NASCAR towel, grass stains mixed with blood on his knee.

"I knew you'd nail that PK, bro," he said.

"You would have too."

"Well, no shit." He grinned. "Fielder, I used to think you were a dick. Either I was wrong or you've changed, because you're not *really* a dick."

What could I do but grin back? "Coming from you, Nick, that's a real compliment."

He tipped an imaginary cap and gimped toward the showers. I wasn't the only one who would have kicked that penalty with a hurting leg. Maybe I was selfish and cowardly to take it, but had made the right move anyway. The shot went in, after all. I didn't choke—and the shot went in.

Chris peeked around the corner of the lockers. "Sorry, Studly, but I have to rush. We're going to see my grandmother in the hospital."

"Not like Clank's...?"

He shook his head. "Sure hope not. But she broke her hip."

So instead of hanging loose at the celebration we were the first to leave. As we passed the school trophy case I wondered if my name would soon be in there on more than the Joel Bukiewicz Hustle Award. If not, I'd feel like they needed to engrave it in huge letters on the first annual Loser Award.

Chris's green Taurus was in the second row of the student parking lot. Usually the lot was almost empty after a game, but with the big crowd that day and the fact that we were leaving so early, some cars were still there, and some kids hanging around.

"Way to be, Fielder!" someone yelled. "You kicked ass!"

Unbelievable. It was Billy Hagan, perched on the hood of his BMW with one arm around Sarah Malinowski and his other fist pumping in the air. He actually sounded serious, not like he was ragging on me. I smiled and held up my own fist. "Thanks!" I yelled back. I wasn't sure what any of this meant, but it certainly felt better than what was there before.

Then I noticed a silver BMW convertible, and my heart hopped. What had happened in the trees with Pet and Reynolds and the reporter? Should I have followed Turcotte up there?

"Earth to Studly," Chris said. "Come on, dude, I gotta roll."

Pet walked around the corner of the building, fast, her head down.

I let go of the door handle. "Thanks anyway. I have to talk to someone."

Chris followed my eyes. He shot me a look like he'd trade places in half a second. "Go for it, Studly. Don't do anything I wouldn't do."

I don't know if Chris has ever gone on a date. Ever.

"I hope your grandma's OK," I said as I slung my pack over my shoulder and left him.

Sarah and Hagan were watching me and I didn't care. I was going to meet my girlfriend, and the world was welcome to know. Beyond Pet I saw the maple tree we'd climbed that first night together. Soon its leaves would turn red and gold, then float to the ground—and no one could hide in its bare branches until spring.

I reached Pet's car before she did. What? Where's the MY PET license plate? Does another kid have a silver Cabrio—

"I traded them in for normal ones. My dad's idea of cute was too mortifying."

Pet stood a few strides away, a half smile on her face that made her black eye seem not quite real. I mean I saw the bruise, it was there, but it so didn't belong on her that my brain couldn't totally accept it.

"Are you all right?"

"Yeah, I guess."

"What happened up in the woods?"

Chris drove by with a quick blast of his horn. He pointed at us, trying to look cool and succeeding in looking like a dork. Pet and I waved.

"Can we go somewhere?" she asked.

"Where?"

"You decide. I don't want to think anymore today."

"Boston?" I said. "Manhattan? How about Foxwoods? I feel lucky."

She tossed me her keys. "You're the driver." She took off her backpack and got in the passenger side.

So just like that first night I found myself behind the wheel of her car. On the radio Mick Jagger was wailing that wild horses couldn't drag him away. I kind of knew how he felt. By the cemetery with the glowing tombstone we had to wait for a red light. Pet looked out her open window and I did too, at the rows of graves and fresh-trimmed grass. So neat and tidy from here. Only people who go inside ever see—or feel—how some words have worn off forever, and some stones over the hill are toppled by tree roots. We turned left on the Boston Post Road, toward the town green and the old stone building that used to be the library and is now the historical society. I had no plan. Pet's fingers tapped on the backpack in her lap. She reached up and tenderly touched her black eye. We drove around the triangular green and ended up back where we'd started. I heard a whistle screech and I followed it, like some sort of sign: around the town hall and firehouse, past the playground and basketball courts, to the soccer field where I'd found Pet that night, practicing imaginary penalty kicks in the dark. There was a game going on, kids around eight, most with no clue how to play positions and just chasing the ball like wild things. Ever put iron filings on a paper, then drag a magnet underneath? It looked like that, only colorful and with parents cheering.

I parked between two monster SUVs. We could only see ahead and behind, not to either side of those hulking metal dinosaurs.

"Another game," I said.

Pet nodded. "Places look different in the light, don't they?"

I checked the rearview mirror. The tennis courts were as empty as the beach in December, and almost as sad.

"So what happened with Turcotte and Reynolds?" I asked.

"How did you know Reynolds was there?"

A little blonde munchkin squibbed in a goal and her teammates mobbed her.

"My hand might be broken but my eyes are still 20–15."

Pet opened her door. "Come on," she said. She grabbed her pack and walked away without locking the door.

What? I caught up to her, feeling like that first night after the football game. When was she going to trust me?

"Come on where?"

She reached for my hand. "Come on. Don't you trust me?"

Hand-in-hand and without a word we walked two blocks to the water, down a quiet street with some really nice houses. I'd only been there a couple of times before. The beach was private, the kind of place where someone might kick you out for not belonging.

At the dead end of the street was a post with a small but conspicuous sign. RESIDENTS AND GUESTS ONLY. It had a few BB dents and rust spots but otherwise was in good shape.

"We're guests," Pet said. "Invited by the ancient beach god of righteousness."

I smiled. "Hey, we're residents too. It doesn't say of where." I squeezed her hand and led the way down a short path to the sand. At this time of year chances were we wouldn't meet anybody.

We didn't. We walked on the lonely beach by ourselves, smelling the fresh salt air, feeling the sea breeze cool off the

Sound. We still held hands, walking so close that our hips kept touching, little waves lapping inches from our feet. There was no gravestone between us now.

And Pet told the story of Ed Reynolds in the woods.

She had noticed the same glint I did later, which was why she passed behind the goal during my penalty kick. She wasn't sure what was there in the woods, but she had to investigate. If someone else had been coming toward him, Reynolds probably would have taken off. But Pet was different. He had hurt her; he owed her. Besides, after what had happened at his house and the personal stuff he told her, there might not have been anyone in the world he felt closer to right then.

I nudged her shoulder. "So did Turcotte get his interview?"

Pet nodded. "Right there in the woods. And I told him I took the Purgatory Practice video."

"Good," I said, "that's good." Who knew what people's reactions would be, but it was time for the truth. We came to a wooden jetty and leaned against it. Pet took off her pack.

Time for the truth. "When you went by the goal I couldn't help it, I lost my concentration again. I remembered how I missed that last PK."

Pet scuffed the sand with her toe. She stared out over the gray water toward Long Island.

"So I'm the black cat?" she asked.

"The what?" I edged closer to her on the rough boards. It seemed like wood always brought us together: a tree limb, gym bleachers, this jetty smelling of creosote and salt water.

"A person who brings bad luck. My stepdad owns some trotting horses. That's what his trainer called me the first time I went to the track, and his ponies lost."

"Do they usually win?"

Pet smiled. I couldn't see the black eye on the other side of her face. "Now that you mention it, almost never."

"Well, *we* do. You're no black cat. And I made the shot."

It was half tide. Barnacles and mussels clung to the rocks, and dark green seaweed billowed in the ripples. So much life right there, in another world under the waves.

Suddenly something hit me. "Wait a minute. Don't tell me Reynolds did an interview wearing that army helmet!"

Pet stood up and stretched, her arms reaching for the first star in the sky. "I warned him about that. He told me the helmet was a symbol of courage and pride."

"But people will think he's a loon!"

"Well, I did mention that some people might get the wrong idea. So he reluctantly took it off before Turcotte could see. Then this weird light came into his eyes. 'Here,' he said, 'it's yours. I want you to have it.'"

"Are you serious? What did you do?"

Pet unzipped her pack. "I did what any civilized person would do. I said 'thank you.'"

She pulled out the helmet and handed it to me. It looked like a camouflaged turtle shell and was heavier than I'd expected. The leather band inside was cracked and sweat-stained. I wondered about its history, about who had worn it and what had happened to him. I knew that helmet meant a lot to Reynolds, so it meant even more that he gave it to Pet.

"Put it on," she said.

I did. Gently, I put it on her. It was too big, dropping over her ears and almost covering her eyes. It looked all wrong, yet somehow beautiful, like a wish that all helmets could be worn by girls at the beach instead of being needed for war.

"Look," I said. A huge, glowing moon was rising in the darkening sky. Standing at the water's edge I put my arm around her shoulders, and felt her arm slip around my waist. Suddenly she threw back her head, and had to reach with her free hand to keep the helmet from falling.

"Aaaoooooo!" she howled. "Aaaoooooo!"

She held me tighter. "Come on, Robby, let yourself go. Don't be afraid, be a coyote."

I could feel the life surging through her to me. I howled as loud as I could, not caring who saw or heard. A second later she joined me. We were two wild creatures howling at the moon.

Together.

Chapter 25

So THERE YOU GO. That's the story. I left out a lot, but I guess writers always do. In case you're interested, I'll fill in some details.

Randy Turcotte's interview scooped everyone in the next day's paper. Coach Reynolds apologized for the Tampon Tiara— but mostly for the way people took it and what happened to him. Two months later he sold his house and moved to Florida, ending the rumor that he would become coach of the Newfield High girl's soccer team. Now *that* would have been interesting.

Because of the way things worked out, with us winning the game and Reynolds practically becoming her friend, Pet didn't catch the flak you might expect. She was a hero to way more of the town than she was a villain, especially later when she lost only one match all season at #1 singles for the tennis team. People laugh and tell me my girlfriend is a better athlete than I am, and all I answer is that they're probably right. Pet has changed her hair color half a dozen times but her skin stays totally white. She slathers on the SPF 45 sunblock and wears a cap when she plays tennis, or spends any time in the sun, because her favorite aunt died of skin cancer.

Jim came back for our next game and Tommy rode the pine for the rest of the season. He's got a girlfriend now, a sophomore who writes for the school paper, but I bet he wishes he was with Pet. I feel bad for him, but you know how that goes—I'd rather feel bad for him than for myself.

Speaking of feeling bad, we lost 1–0 in the state tournament semifinals to Atherton, the team that became state champs. Ours was a totally close game and Atherton dominated the final 3–0, so I figure we were the second-best team in our division. And that's only because Nick Rossi broke his ankle early in the game. With him playing defense no way they would have scored. Next year our goal is to win it all. Period.

One thing I don't feel bad about—much—is that Nick won our Most Valuable Player award. He deserved it, though Jim and I did too. Preston told me that he chose Nick because he was a senior, and Jim and I would have our turn next year. Co-MVPs? That would be cool.

In December a package came in the mail, postmarked Orlando. Inside was a cheap videotape with no label. Of course I was curious and stuck it in the VCR. Onto the screen popped the biggest crowd ever at a Newfield High soccer game, and me lining up a penalty kick—with Pet walking toward the camera in the foreground. My throat went dry. It was the video Reynolds shot of my hat-trick game. I shook the padded envelope and out fluttered a bent Christmas card. PEACE ON EARTH, it said. And written inside, "Show this to college recruiters and you're a lock. They'll see your potential. Good luck. Coach." There was no return address for me to even thank him.

You know what? For the first time, that word "potential" didn't bother me. I even almost enjoyed it. Yeah, I've got a lot to live up to, and my parents' and other people's expectations can be a real pain. But that's a whole lot better than being written off, and no one having expectations for you. My brother carved out high standards for me to follow, but he didn't try to. He was just himself. Now I'm going to just be my self. But it's going to be the best self I can be.

All in all, we were pretty lucky. We could have blown it in so many ways. I've seen how easy it is to be stupid, and what stupid does. How ugly it is.

Summer's almost over. Our senior year starts next week. We're already sweating bullets at two-a-day soccer practices, with Preston running us as hard as Reynolds did—minus the screaming. Yesterday I went with Pet to the town beach. The sun was setting as we stood barefoot on the wet sand, holding hands. I flicked a clump of seaweed with my toe and thought of the first time I saw her at that assembly.

I couldn't resist. "So, Pet, how many magazines are you going to sell this year? It's your last chance for first place."

She stuck her tongue out at me, then smiled. "Yours too," she said. Pet squeezed my hand tighter and we started walking, cool water lapping at our feet as the tide came in.

About the author

Tom Hazuka played varsity soccer in high school and college and still follows the game. He spent his junior year of college in Switzerland, and after graduation, over two years in Chile with the Peace Corps. Currently he teaches fiction writing at Central Connecticut State University. He has published two adult novels and many award-winning short stories, as well as a book on the NCAA Final Four, travel articles and poetry. LAST CHANCE FOR FIRST is his first crossover novel—for adults and young adults—and returns to his love for soccer. If you'd like to write to him, his email address is hazukaj@ccsu.edu.